Dear Reader,

Home, family, community and love. These are the values we cherish most in our lives—the ideals that ground us, comfort us, move us. They certainly provide the perfect inspiration around which to build a romance collection that will touch the heart.

And so we are thrilled to have the opportunity to introduce you to the Harlequin Heartwarming collection. Each of these special stories is a wholesome, heartfelt romance imbued with the traditional values so important to you. They are books you can share proudly with friends and family. And the authors featured in this collection are some of the most talented storytellers writing today, including favorites such as Laura Abbot, Roz Denny Fox, Jillian Hart and Irene Hannon. We've selected these stories especially for you based on their overriding qualities of emotion and tenderness, and they center around your favorite themes—children, weddings, second chances, the reunion of families, the quest to find a true home and, of course, sweet romance.

So curl up in your favorite chair, relax and prepare for a heartwarming reading experience!

Sincerely,

The Editors

LYNN PATRICK

is the pseudonym for the writing team of Linda Sweeney and Patricia Pinianski. *Shall We Dance?* was inspired by "some of the most romantic mediums we've ever seen"– the dances of Fred Astaire and Ginger Rogers. "They told an entire story in a single dance, and we always secretly wished they were together in real life, as well."

HARLEQUIN HEARTWARMING

Lynn Patrick

Shall We Dance?

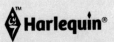

TORONTO NEW YORK LONDON
AMSTERDAM PARIS SYDNEY HAMBURG
STOCKHOLM ATHENS TOKYO MILAN MADRID
PRAGUE WARSAW BUDAPEST AUCKLAND

Recycling programs
for this product may
not exist in your area.

ISBN-13: 978-0-373-36433-6

SHALL WE DANCE?

Copyright © 2011 by Patricia Pinianski and Linda Sweeney

Originally published as CHEEK TO CHEEK © 1991 by Patricia Pinianski
and Linda Sweeney

This edition published by arrangement with Harlequin Books S.A.

For questions and comments about the quality of this book
please contact us at Customer_eCare@Harlequin.ca

® and TM are trademarks of the publisher. Trademarks indicated with
® are registered in the United States Patent and Trademark Office, the
Canadian Trade Marks Office and in other countries.

www.Harlequin.com

Printed in U.S.A.

Shall We Dance?

To Fred and Ginger,
for all the wonderful hours
of entertainment you gave us

PROLOGUE

Hollywood, 1953

"FEELING BLUE, KIDDO?"

"Hmm?" Snapping out of her pensive mood at the sound of Lucille Talbot's gravelly voice, Anita Brooks whirled around to face her dressing room door.

Lucille cracked the door open farther and stuck in her sharp-featured face. "Can I come in?"

"Sure."

"Anything wrong?" Lucille asked again. "Seems like you could use a little cheering up before you go back on the set." Warm and supportive as usual, the woman who provided comic relief for the Brooks/Garfield movies gave Anita a one-armed hug, careful not to muss the multiple spangled ruffles that trimmed the straps and low-cut bodice of the white satin evening gown. "Tell Auntie Lucille all your troubles."

Anita forced herself to smile reassuringly

at the woman she considered a good friend. Lucille was her professional mentor, always giving her advice on how to milk a laugh or a tear from a scene. And the older woman was unfailingly sensitive to Anita's personal problems, as well. But this time was different, Anita thought, as she tried to bluff her way out of explaining.

"There's nothing wrong, Lucille. I'm always nervous before I have to dance in front of the camera."

"After three weeks of constant rehearsal?" Lucille rolled her eyes. "Honey, you must have those steps memorized. It's a wonder you don't hoof it through your dreams."

"I do dance in my dreams," Anita admitted, laughing.

"With Price Garfield, of course."

Anita glanced down, unwilling to let Lucille see the emotion in her eyes. "I'd better check my makeup and hair."

She turned toward the large curving mirror that hung above the dressing table. A vision in silvery white with the lacquered strawberry blond waves, heavily mascaraed lashes and red rouged lips of a 1930s starlet stared back at her. Even though she'd seen herself in professional makeup many times before, Anita was still surprised at how much older she appeared—no one would guess she was only eighteen. She licked a finger and smoothed down the only errant hair she could find.

"Your hairdo looks fine, so leave it alone. The makeup and hairdressing guys don't like it when we tamper with their work." Lucille glanced over Anita's shoulder and made a rueful face. "Not that they can do that much for *me*."

"You look lovely," Anita insisted, admiring her friend's long, graceful neck and beautiful dark eyes.

"Let's get back to the subject of Price. You're in love with him, aren't you?"

Faced with a direct question, she couldn't quite deny it. "I...I think so."

"And he loves you, too, right?"

"Maybe." Anita sighed, feeling very uncomfortable, and not only because she was uncertain of Price.

"The man *has* to be in love with you. His whole expression changes when you dance. He actually looks like a romantic hero."

Anita nodded. "He's certainly different on and off the dance floor."

As well as on and off the movie set. But she

had learned to appreciate the quieter, more serious side of Price, too.

Both women jumped at the sound of a loud knock at the door. One of the director's assistants shouted, "Ready on the set!"

"Oops, got to go," Anita murmured. *Thank goodness.* She picked up the edge of her long fluted skirt and hurried outside, heading for the expanse of polished dark floor already lit by bright lights.

"Break a leg," she heard Lucille call after her as the other woman also ran to take her place.

But Anita's attention had already shifted to the tuxedoed man who awaited her at the edge of the set. Price Garfield was leaning against one of the painted white railings of the set's Art Deco nightclub. He appeared relaxed and nonchalant in spite of the surrounding film crew, cameras, lights and "audience" of extras and other actors who were seated at tables set on built-up tiers that curved around the dance floor. But Price's cool manner was only a facade. He straightened, his intense green gaze meeting hers. She felt his suppressed tension when he took hold of her hand.

"Anita," he murmured, the intensity of his tone thrilling her as always.

The director stepped forward and interrupted the private moment, "Take your positions."

And assume your character, Anita thought, not finding it at all difficult to imagine herself the reluctant but lovestruck heroine of *White Tie and Tails,* an homage to the 1930s musical. More lights came up, their brilliance hot against her skin and nearly blinding. She blinked, willing herself to ignore them and concentrate. She was playing a woman who was already engaged to another man but was drawn to Price's character, anyway.

And so the music began.

Anita forgot about the cameras entirely as Price sang the lyrics of "Dance of Love," an ardent invitation: "Come here, darling, let me hold you in my arms…." When the music paused and she turned away, he grasped her wrist and pulled her back, continuing to sing, "Life was meant to be a dance of love."

Heated by his yearning touch, Anita almost acquiesced right then, but she remained reluctant, as the part demanded. He stepped closer, his eyes searching, his feet already moving slowly into the rhythm of a sophisticated mating dance. When she tried a cursory escape, Price swung her into his arms, imprisoning her with a secure grasp and moving her across the floor with sensuous, flowing steps.

"Don't you love me?" asked the music.

Don't you love me? asked Price with eloquent gestures.

As if to give her time to think about an answer, he released her for a moment. They danced a few steps side by side, then reunited, dipping and whirling, Anita's skirt flowing gracefully around them.

The music built. Their movements became more intricate, more quickly executed. Price spun around, daringly wrapping himself in Anita's embrace. Then he grasped her waist and lifted her above him. Their eyes locked. He let her down slowly, holding her body against him as the music continued to climb.

Yes, I love you, Price, Anita admitted for the second time that day, telling him with her eyes alone.

Jubilant, he swung her down in a swirl of skirts and she melted into his arms. Finally they danced cheek to cheek, for the characters loved each other and would eventually whirl off the screen to live happily ever after.

If only life were as simple.

The music peaked and Anita clung to Price,

every expression, every nuance revealing her feelings for him. Her love for the real man gave credence to her character and wings to her feet. She would never dance so well with another. Only with him.

Only with Price Garfield...

CHAPTER ONE

New York, Present Day

GABRIELLE BROOKS LACROIX reached the half-open doorway in her mother's second-floor apartment just in time to catch the final clinch of the "Dance of Love" scene in *White Tie and Tails.* As she watched her mother's youthful monochrome image lovingly embrace that of Price Garfield, Anita herself looked on raptly from the peach-colored couch in front of the television.

"Life was meant to be a dance of love…."

Gabby instantly recognized the theme song from the famous nostalgia musical set in the thirties. After teaching three classes in a row, she'd left her first-floor Broadway Bound Dance School to relax in her own apartment upstairs. Even though she was pooped, Gabby couldn't ignore the fact that her mother was viewing her old movies again.

Opening the door wide, she asked loudly, "Feeling nostalgic today?"

Anita started and glanced over her shoulder. "Oh…hello, sweetheart." She immediately clicked the remote control, shutting off both the television and the DVD player. Then she smoothed back her white hair, as if she were trying to wipe away her guilty expression. "I didn't notice you standing there."

"I wasn't. I just heard the music and decided to see what you were up to."

Gabby wouldn't really care about her mother watching the old movies if Anita could do so unemotionally. Maybe, by now, that was possible. It had been quite a while since Anita had dug one of them out.

Her mother looked over Gabby's new lavender leotard and matching wrap skirt. "You look good in that color. You ought to wear it more often." She motioned to the overstuffed chair across from her. "Sit down and tell me how your classes are going."

Not particularly in the mood to discuss her work, Gabby skirted the couch to plop down in the chair. "The classes are fine. What have *you* been doing this afternoon?" she asked pointedly. Since Anita only coached a few special students herself, the older woman had plenty of time to indulge in past triumphs and troubles.

"Oh, a little of this and that," Anita hedged before changing the subject. "Did Heather get that part she tried out for?"

"Nope."

"Too bad."

Gabby sighed. "None of our students has gotten a job lately."

"Kirk's still dancing in that off-off-Broadway horror musical."

"If you can call doing the limbo as a zombie dancing."

"Ah, well, that's not the worst job in the world," Anita insisted. "Broadway candidates have to pay their dues."

In hopes of getting somewhere, Gabby thought, though many never did, including herself. She'd been fed up with the constant rat race by the time she'd retired last year. At thirty-three she'd been a little long in the tooth for Broadway chorus lines, anyway. She stretched out her legs, glancing down at her tights and kidskin dance slippers, eternal reminders of what might have been.

"If you want to go somewhere, I can get Jane to take my tap class this evening," Gabby offered, thinking she could use some extra time away from the school.

"I don't want to go anywhere. Can't we just

sit here and share some small talk?" Anita asked sweetly. "I'm always interested in the business."

Certainly not because of the income, Gabby knew. When her father died of a heart attack two years before, he'd left his wife with enough investments to retire on and still continue to live comfortably in the Greenwich Village building they'd bought years ago.

"The school's in the black and everyone's doing a fine job," Gabby said. Her mother had given over the management of the business to her youngest child when Gabby had agreed to work with her. "I'm satisfied." She glanced at the television, thinking about the topic the older woman had cleverly avoided discussing. "How come you're watching your old movies, anyway? You know how they get to you."

Anita smiled reassuringly at the child she'd always been closest to. "You don't have to worry. I wasn't sitting here mooning over the past."

"Are you sure?"

"Absolutely."

Gabby remained suspicious. At seventy-five her mother was in excellent physical and mental health but still capable of becoming distressed over Brooks/Garfield movies. The first time Gabby had caught her mother viewing her personal copy of *White Tie and Tails*—with a VCR in pre-DVD days—Anita had been weeping openly. Ten-year-old, empathetic Gabby had been very upset and had needed to be comforted and urged to keep the secret from her absent father.

"I just wish you'd quit carrying a torch for that jerk Price Garfield, Mom."

Gabby was still resentful of the man who'd ruined her mother's life in more ways than one. Undoubtedly aware that he'd been second best, that his wife would never love him as much as he loved her, Robert Lacroix had immersed himself in his surgery practice ever since Gabby could remember. He'd been an uninvolved, distant father.

"I know Price for what he is," Anita said, sounding exceptionally calm.

Gabby was surprised. Her mother's faded blue eyes seemed brighter, as if, for once, she was more excited than sad after viewing the old film.

"Besides, Price wasn't dancing alone in those movies. I also enjoy watching myself," Anita went on. "After all, I don't have any film clips from my Broadway musicals." She laughed shortly. "Not that the critics would think that was footage worth saving."

"The Broadway critics were blind." Gabby was certain her mother's career had floundered merely because of bad luck precipitated by the split with Price Garfield. Anita had been the victim of lackluster scripts, forgettable songs and poor timing. "You were always a wonderful performer. You just didn't click with the right material." Something that had also happened to her the few times she'd won small roles, she reflected.

Anita rose to give Gabby a hug. "Have I told you lately you're a beautiful, wonderful daughter?"

"Not for a while."

"Well, you are. And you're a fabulous dancer to boot. Never forget that." Anita patted her daughter on the back before moving away. "A professional needs a healthy ego."

"Thanks, Mom. My ego can always use some strokes."

Gabby almost said she only wished she were still in the professional category, but thought better of it. Having feigned to be happy in retirement, to consider the school a new, invigorating challenge, she would only upset her mother if she admitted otherwise.

"Actually, I had a more practical reason for looking at *White Tie and Tails* this afternoon," Anita admitted as she headed for the bedroom. "Come on, I want to check on something."

Curious, Gabby followed, her footsteps muffled by the apartment's cream-colored, wall-to-wall carpeting. The peach shades dominating the living room carried through to the bedroom, as well, though the bedspread and the drapes were a pale Pacific aqua. A portrait of her mother—commissioned by her father just after they were married—hung over the bedroom fireplace, reminding Gabby of how much she looked like Anita.

"Here we are." Her mother threw open the lid of a small trunk that had been dragged outside the closet. Leaning over, she riffled through wads of tissue paper to withdraw a slippery satin gown. The smell of mothballs permeated the air. "Remember my costume from the 'Dance of Love' scene?"

"Of course I do."

The dress was her mother's favorite piece of memorabilia, one Gabby hadn't seen in years. Anita had kept her stash of old costumes, props and scripts hidden from her family, but Gabby had managed to find them. Another secret she'd had to keep from her father, she thought sadly as her mother stroked the material. Now yellowed with age, the once-white garment was a beautiful re-creation of the thirties bias-cut.

"It's still gorgeous," Gabby murmured, fingering one of the skirt's wide godets. "The Metropolitan Museum's costume department would love to get their hands on this, especially since the Brooks/Garfield movies are considered classics of nostalgia."

"Well, I'm not giving it to them." Anita held the gown at arm's length, lining it up against Gabby as she narrowed her eyes. "Hmm, you're a little taller than I, and you have wider shoulders, but this dress might fit, anyway…"

"You want me to try it on?"

"Don't you think that would be fun? We've got the same coloring, same eyes, a similar shade of hair." Anita paused. "At least I *used* to be a strawberry blonde." She sighed. "Time flies. Come on—let's see what you look like in this."

Unable to figure out why her mother was insisting, Gabby took the dress from her. "I suppose I can try the dress on, if that would make you happy."

"Making *you* happy is what I'm most concerned about." When Gabby raised her brows, Anita went on, "I don't want to do this just to get even, you understand. I'm hoping you can make a name for yourself."

Gabby didn't understand at all. She frowned. "What on earth are you talking about?"

"How would you like to go to L.A. to perform?"

"Perform in what?" Despite the crazy circumstances, Gabby's heart gave an excited lurch at the very thought of dancing professionally again.

"You've been offered a job appearing at the grand opening of a plush new Hollywood nostalgia club that will showcase re-creations of famous numbers from musicals of the '30s, '40s and '50s."

"By whom? And why would someone have contacted you instead of me?"

"Because Lucille Talbot was the person making the offer. She called me today and told me all about her idea."

"Lucille?" Gabby hardly knew the woman,

though Anita and the former comic actress had corresponded from time to time.

"She owns a percentage of the place. It's going to be called Cheek to Cheek." Obviously excited, her mother beamed. "Cheek to Cheek." A thirties classic and an apt name for a nostalgia club.

"Is this offer for real?" Pulse thrumming, Gabby clutched the dress tighter, wondering if she were dreaming. "Why didn't you tell me right away?"

"I wanted to surprise you." Anita made an expansive gesture. "They're paying for our plane fares as well as for the performance itself. Not that the opportunity isn't far more important than the money."

"You're going, too?"

Her mother nodded. "As a consultant. I told Lucille we'd need a week or two to make arrangements for the dance school."

"Oh!" Unable to contain her excitement, Gabby dropped the dress on the bed and hugged her mother. "This is wonderful news."

"Isn't it? And you're going to be great. I can just see you whirling across the floor in front of the crowd. They'll have an orchestra, you know, and be playing tunes like 'Dance of Love.' I told you I had a practical reason for watching that movie." Anita glanced at the satin gown. "I was hoping we could use this costume—for nostalgia's sake—but I guess it's too discolored and fragile. Oh, well, a good seamstress can whip up a copy."

"So I'll be doing ballroom dancing?"

"That and a little tap. You know, the sort of numbers you'd find in a classic musical." Appearing a little uneasy, Anita suddenly sobered. "Umm…you won't mind appearing as Gabrielle *Brooks,* will you? Please don't feel threatened," she continued quickly. "For once, my name can be of help to you."

"I'm not threatened."

Gabby smiled at her mother warmly. Sure of herself as a performer even though she had never made it big, she also had a solid sense of personal identity. Though she'd never used it professionally before, Gabby had always liked having Brooks as part of her legal name, something Anita hadn't given to her three older children. The name had been part of the special bond she and her mother shared.

"And once the media sees the extent of your talent, you'll stand on your own," Anita was saying. "All the papers will have reporters there, you know, not to mention several television news crews. The club's supposed to be a beautifully renovated place, all Art Deco."

"Sounds great."

And full of possibility. Gabby's spirit hadn't risen so high in years. Her mind, however, dealt with the practicalities. She felt the length of her ponytail, thinking she should get her long hair cut. She also wondered how many dances she...*they'd* be performing. But first things first. "I'm going to need a dance partner," she told her mother.

"That's been taken care of," Anita said, quickly stooping to rummage in the trunk again...as if she were hiding.

"How so?"

"I have a couple of more dresses in here," Anita said without looking up. "They're not in much better condition, but we should show them to the seamstress. They flow beautifully when you dance."

Gabby frowned as her mother chattered on. "Wait a minute. Who's taken care of finding me this dance partner?" A mismatched partner could mean a disaster.

Anita straightened. "Lucille said everything's been arranged."

Something about the older woman's expression made Gabby suspicious. Anita might be an actress, but she couldn't fool the child closest to her. Gabby had always been able to sense her mother's moods at a gut level. "What are you hiding? Come on, Mom, out with it."

Anita took a deep breath and sat down on the chair in front of her dressing table. "I knew it would be impossible to string you along." She looked even more guilty than when Gabby had caught her watching the videotape earlier. "All right, your partner is going to be Kit Garfield."

"Garfield?" The infamous name seemed to bounce off the walls.

"Kit is Price's son, his only child."

So the attraction of the performance was to be a reuniting of Brooks and Garfield. Gabby's high hopes plummeted. "I don't want to dance with a Garfield."

Anita nodded. "I understand how you feel."

"I *won't* dance with a Garfield." Price had ruined her mother's life, and Gabby had resented him since she was ten.

"Uh-huh."

Her dreams turned to ashes, Gabby asked, "How could you even suggest it? Call Lucille Talbot right now and tell her she's going to have to get someone else. Tell her…"

Anita held up a silencing hand. "That was my first reaction when she broached the subject today. But my second reaction was a bit less emotional. I made myself listen to what she had to say. She mentioned the opportunities—all the media coverage, West Coast theater, films. And the opening night proceeds will go to charity, funding a group home for indigent show business seniors. Not all of my old friends were lucky enough to find security in their golden years, you know."

Gabby knew how strongly her mother felt about the way Hollywood treated aging film stars. And considering her own experiences with that problem on Broadway, she could understand. Still, a retirement home wasn't the issue here.

"I thought you despised Price Garfield." But even as she spoke, Gabby realized her mother's feelings for the man were far more complex than that.

"I have no use for the man. But listen." Anita rose to face her daughter. "You have to be clever to survive sometimes. Why not take advantage of this situation? Price is a legend. His name will draw all the most important people to this opening."

"He used you."

"So let's use him back."

Gabby was amazed her mother was being so cool. In the past Anita wouldn't have been able to remain unemotional where Price was concerned. "You don't think this will make you look like you're eating crow?"

"I can stand a little crow after all these years. Think about dancing in front of that audience."

Gabby had to admit her mother was making sense—in a perverse sort of way. "I guess I've danced with partners I didn't like from time to time."

"And you can do it again."

"Maybe we should both sleep on this to-night," Gabby said, still unsure. Trying to find a personal reason to back out and thereby save her mother grief, she asked, "Is Kit Gar-field a professional dancer? I don't want to get on the dance floor with some amateur who happens to have a famous name."

"Lucille claims he used to be professional, though he never became an actor in the movies like his father. He used to dance with a partner in clubs." When Gabby didn't im-mediately agree to work with the man, Anita said, "We can call Lucille back with our final answer tomorrow."

Protective of her mother as always, Gabby was concerned about how Anita would handle the situation. "But what if Price shows up? That's likely, you know, especially if his son is going to be a featured performer. What if you meet him face-to-face? Even though he retired decades ago, he probably still lives in the L.A. area."

"I can walk the other way." Anita set her jaw. "And I can hold my tongue and collect his debt. Please do this, Gabby. A Garfield owes a Brooks a career."

Tempted beyond good sense, Gabby paused. "If you put it that way…"

"Then you'll go?"

"You really want me to?" How sweet it would feel to be in the spotlight, to work an audience again, even if a Garfield were involved.

"I haven't wanted anything so much in years," Anita stated adamantly.

"All right. I'll do it."

The two women hugged, Gabby pushing away her lingering doubts. Already concentrating on the idea of a Brooks/Garfield type of performance, she gathered up the dress to take it upstairs and try it on. Perhaps the general design would look good as it was. She could tell if any changes were necessary. She also thought of the perfect mental practice for the upcoming event.

Her mother would have a good laugh when Gabby asked to borrow her Brooks/Garfield DVDs!

ANITA HAD MORE DIFFICULTY than usual falling asleep that night and finally got up to make herself a cup of warm milk. Not that she was worrying about what she'd told her daughter. She'd meant every word about getting revenge on Price.

Even so, Gabby's remark about encountering her former partner had gotten her on edge. Sitting in her bedroom and sipping the milk, she closed her eyes and imagined the situation. Would Price even recognize her now, with white hair and wrinkles? Would she recognize him? Of course she would. Who could ever forget eyes that had once glowed with such love? Arms that had cradled her for kisses as well as for some of the most romantic dances that had ever been choreographed?

Anita sighed, got up and wandered over to a window. She pulled back the drapes. Outside, the city was alive with lights. New

York had its own undeniable charm, even if it wasn't a place she'd ever imagined living.

A Californian born and bred, she'd had her hopes pinned on Hollywood, had dreamed of being a movie star since childhood. Always a ham, she had adored all the hoopla and the fans and the public appearances. She'd thrived on making people happy…and feeling their love in return. She'd been thrilled to place her concrete footprints in front of what had then been Grauman's Chinese Theater.

Price Garfield was different. He'd come to Hollywood after World War II merely to find work as a choreographer and had been reluctant to take the acting role he was offered. He'd loved to dance but had always told Anita that his highest goals were more personal than fame could ever allow. Creative work was important, true, but Price had told her that a large family and a love that would last a lifetime were more so.

How ironic, Anita thought, that neither her own wishes nor Price's had ever come true. Her career had gone steadily downhill after she'd fled to New York in 1955. And Price's five broken marriages hadn't reflected his hopes for a lifelong romance…or a large family, since he'd only produced one son.

Had he been as disillusioned as she?

Anita was less bitter than Gabby seemed to be on her behalf. Not having wanted to obtain a glittery career at the expense of love, she'd always been thankful for her blessings. She'd had a kind and generous husband—whom she probably didn't deserve—and four beautiful children. She'd also had the school and the thrill of teaching dancers who were as full of dreams as she had been in her youth.

Dreams.

Once again she closed her eyes and tried to picture Price Garfield as he was now. Would the sight of him create the same electricity within her? Surely not. She was being a sentimental old fool.

Anita sighed, left the window and headed back for her bed. Maybe she would run into Price in California. Maybe she'd tell him off. Maybe she'd walk away. Maybe she'd punch him. Or maybe they'd actually be able to exchange a few civil words.

Whatever happened would be stimulating. Anita had been in a state of suspended animation since her husband's fatal heart attack. Lucille's insistence that she accompany Gabby had resurrected old dreams and old emotions, making her feel truly alive for the first time in years.

Anita wouldn't have spent half the time trying to convince her daughter to take the job if she herself weren't going to be smack-dab in the middle of the action.

CHAPTER TWO

LUCILLE TALBOT LIVED in a twenties-style Beverly Hills mansion. Catching sight of the amazing structure through the trees—part German castle, part rambling Spanish hacienda—Kit Garfield smiled and slowed his BMW before turning it onto the hilly side street that would take him to the entrance.

The flamboyant style of architecture had long been out of mode, but Kit thought Lucille's "Dream Palace" far more interesting than the conservative L.A.-area mansions built in later decades—like the graystone Italianate Price Garfield owned. Not that he'd ever spent much time in his father's home. Price and Lana Worth, Kit's actress mother, had been involved in divorce proceedings by the time he'd started grade school, and since then he and his father had maintained a distant and somewhat uneasy relationship.

Kit turned the car sharply when he reached Lucille's driveway. Considerably shorter than it had been when the estate had encompassed dozens of surrounding acres, the curving drive wove through a stand of trees and past a small overgrown flower garden before looping in front of the house.

Four women in colorful leotards were doing aerobics on the lawn. The curvaceous blonde in command halted the exercise and approached as Kit got out of the car. Up close the woman looked older than she'd seemed from a distance—at least a well-preserved sixty.

"Hi, I'm here to see Lucille."

"You must be Christopher Garfield." The blonde grinned and held out her hand.

"Call me Kit."

"All right, Kit it is. You know, you resemble your mother," she went on. "I once made a movie with her." When she realized that didn't ring a bell with him, she introduced herself. "Jayne Hunter. I'm living here now. Say hello to Lana, will you? I watch her on *Hawk's Roost* every week."

"Sure, I'll tell her I ran into you." Now he remembered Jayne. So the glamour queen of yesteryear had become one of Lucille's impoverished boarders. Jayne hadn't been as lucky as his mother, who'd maintained a sufficiently high profile to be cast in a new television show. "It's nice to meet you...you look great," he told her honestly.

"Guess I'm in pretty good shape for an old broad. Comes from teaching exercise classes." She nodded toward the other women, then gestured toward the house. "Go on in—it's not locked. Lucille's expecting you."

Jayne returned to her aerobics class, and Kit strode up the crumbling concrete steps to the mansion's massive entrance. He stared at the red paint peeling off the door before letting himself in. The place was falling apart. Perhaps the reason his godmother wanted to see him was to take that long-term, low-cost "loan" he'd been offering to give her for years. He didn't really expect the money to be paid back, which was undoubtedly the reason Lucille had refused his help time and again. She must be in some financial bind if she was ready to sacrifice her stubborn pride.

Ambling across the marble floor of the two-story hallway, he called, "Hey, anybody home?" He stopped at the foot of the open staircase.

"Hey, who wants to know?" rasped a familiar grating voice.

Kit headed for the living room that opened off to one side of the grand foyer. "Don't get up," he told the slight, silver-haired figure who was already rising from one of the serape-covered couches.

"Of course I'm gonna get up." Lucille stepped closer to embrace him. "I might be moving slower than I used to, but I'm not crippled." When she released Kit, she was smiling. "And I'm not gonna miss out on a big hug from my favorite...my *only* godson. I don't get to see you very often. Must've been four or five months since you were here last."

And that was his fault, Kit knew. "I spend too many hours in the office."

"The Garfield Corporation can get along without you once in a while. It's gotten along without Price all these years."

"My father never had any real interest in his investment company." Which was why Kit did—although he had no intention of discussing his relationship with his father. "I'm glad you called. This will give us a chance to just sit around and chat."

He really cared about Lucille and knew that the woman wasn't going to be around forever. Despite the camouflage of her flowing printed caftan, he noticed the slight curvature of her once-erect spine. Like other elderly people, she'd become a little shorter and frailer with the passing years.

When she sat on the couch, he slid into the nearest high-backed, leather-covered chair. Overhead, staring down from the wall, was an ancient mangy bison head, one of the many relics Lucille kept in remembrance of her late husband. Jim Dix had been a star of Westerns and the original owner of the mansion. Nearly twenty-five years older than his wife, Jim had died when Kit was young. Kit's memories were of a big, jovial man who always gave him butterscotch candies and taught him to ride a pony.

"Want some tea or coffee?" Lucille asked.

"Coffee sounds good."

She rang a small brass bell that was sitting on the side table. Like many of the mansion's older conveniences, the servants' buzzer was obviously broken.

"Elsie, bring us some coffee, will you?" she shouted loudly. The eighty-three-year-old maid had been her bosom companion for half her life. She turned back to Kit. "It'll take her a while to get here, so sit back and relax. You look like you could use some perking up. You must get bored with all that business stuff." She gave him a penetrating look, dark eyes opaque above her long, thin nose. "You've always been the more artistic type."

He had the distinct notion she was fishing for something. "I find ways to keep myself challenged."

Lucille snorted. "Challenged, sure, but happy? What happened to the little boy who loved to sing and dance?"

Kit laughed. "He grew up."

And though he was sometimes nostalgic for the old days, he'd learned that his parents' occupations often weren't as glamorous as they appeared—as Lucille well knew.

"But you were some dancer," she went on, "especially in your twenties."

"I had a good time," he agreed, giving her a suspicious look.

"You were wonderful. You never should have given up performing in nightclubs to run the Price Garfield Dance Studios."

"Performing was fun, but not something I wanted to do all my life," he hedged.

Especially not after the news leaked out that "Kit Worth" was really Kit Garfield, Price's son. *Price's son.* That was exactly why he'd used his mother's name onstage—so no one would make the connection.

"Why are you bringing this up again,

anyway?" Kit asked, anxious to get to the heart of the matter. "That chapter of my life is dead and buried."

"But not too deeply, I hope." She ignored his questioning look. "I have a real big favor to ask."

What could he say to the woman who'd been more like a warm and loving grand-mother than a godparent? Childless herself, Lucille rather than his father had spent weeks and months taking care of him when Lana had been away on location shoots.

"Name it," Kit said. "Are you willing to accept that loan to fix this place up?" He hoped it was money she wanted. "I can make out a check…"

She held up a hand to silence him. "It's not money."

Great. Kit tried not to frown, but he had a feeling he wasn't going to like what she was about to propose. As a matter of fact, he was certain of it.

"It's kind of complicated," she went on. "See, I'm the new owner of a nostalgia club."

Now they were getting somewhere. "What did you do—fix up the old stables or garage?"

"Don't be ridiculous. I couldn't get that kind of a permit from those old fuddy-duddies who run Beverly Hills. We bought a run-down nightclub in Hollywood and renovated it in thirties Art Deco, in honor of the golden age of the Hollywood musical. We're calling it Cheek to Cheek."

"We?" he echoed.

"Well, I'm part of a core group of investors."

How could Lucille afford any kind of investment? Kit wondered. He was certain she used every cent of her now-modest income—and any rent she got from the various retirees she took in—to pay rising taxes and living expenses. She probably hadn't paid Elsie wages for years.

"An old friend's backing me," she explained. "It's a real chance for me to get back on my feet. The club's classy, Kit. We're having a week-long gala opening to start the place out." She took a deep breath. "And now we get back to that favor."

"Uh-huh." Figuring she was going to ask him to get involved somehow, he tapped his long fingers on the worn arm of the chair.

"I want you to dance for me."

The fingers froze and his brows raised. "You want me to what?" This was even worse than he'd expected.

"Dance. You know—move your feet around," she joked, sounding a bit uncomfortable. "Only for a few weeks," she went on quickly. "That wouldn't be impossible, would it? I've never asked a favor like this before."

Maybe not, but she sure was twisting his arm now. But why? "Why me?"

"I need a name act that will draw a big audience." She made a sweeping gesture that encompassed the room. "Opening night will be a big, splashy benefit to make this old place into a show business retirement home. And every month a percentage of the club's profits will be set aside to help run it."

Kit was still focusing on the name business. He had a sinking feeling Lucille didn't want Kit Worth to appear. "I wouldn't be a big draw and I don't have an act," he stalled.

"But you could put one together pretty fast. I've already talked to Anita Brooks, and her daughter is an experienced professional. Just think what people will pay to see Brooks and Garfield dance again."

"Anita Brooks?" He couldn't believe it. Clutching the arm of the chair, he leaned forward. "You're being outrageous!"

"Outrageous?" Lucille grinned crookedly and adjusted the neckline of her caftan.

"Thanks, kiddo. I'm amazed I dreamed up such a great idea myself."

"You know I would do anything for you—"

"Great, then it's settled!" Avoiding his gaze, she muttered, "Where is that coffee, anyway?" She grabbed the bell and rang it again. "Elsie!"

Kit knew she was trying to bluff, but he couldn't let her get away with it. "As I was saying, you know I would do anything for you…but you can't expect this."

Lucille gave him her full attention once again. Her lips were curved in a brave, too-bright smile. "Why not? It'll be weeks before the club opens. You'll have time to get yourself back into shape and to rehearse."

"I know I can still dance—I'm not concerned about that." He leaned back in the chair and loosened his tie. He had a sinking feeling she wasn't going to let him go so easily.

"Then the idea of a partner must be making you nervous," Lucille said, gazing at him steadily. "Don't worry—Gabrielle has appeared on Broadway."

"I'm not worried about my supposed partner, either." Though he had little use for anyone who was related to the overly ambitious hoofer who'd probably ruined his father's life, not to mention his mother's or his own. He decided to spit it out. "There's no way I'm going to get on a dance floor and perform as some imitation Price Garfield."

Lucille didn't blink an eye. "Ah, come on. You've gotta have more faith in your own talent. You've already developed your own personal style. No one would confuse you with your father. Thanks to Lana, you're better-looking than Price—"

"I don't want to be compared to Price Garfield at all," he broke in. He'd never wanted to compete against his father. Besides, who could stand up to a legend?

"I guess it can be tough to be a famous star's kid," Lucille said, "but I thought you had enough moxie to rise above that."

Did she think she could get him to agree by baiting him? "I don't want to do it," he told her firmly.

"But will you agree, anyway?" she wheedled. "Just think about all those aging show business people who are starving on social security and have nowhere to live."

"Only because they haven't run into you yet."

At last count there were at least six boarders living in Lucille's house, including an arthritic stuntman and a comedian who hadn't learned a new joke in years.

"I can't take care of these people by myself forever. I'm getting pretty old myself. If Cheek to Cheek is successful, I'll be able to set up this place as a nonprofit institution while making a nice income on the side for myself. I'm fronting the club."

Knowing that Lucille needed the money and that her pride would keep her from taking what she thought of as a handout, Kit felt his determination waver. "You'll make an income for sure?"

"I'll be salaried, which would really help me out a lot." She gazed at him soulfully. "Please, Kit."

He sighed. He was thirty-eight, a highly successful corporate executive. How could this frail old woman reduce him to feeling like a kid eager to please?

"Just this one favor." Her lower lip actually quivered.

Kit groaned. He supposed it was time he quit worrying about competing with his old man.

"Please do it for *me*."

That wistful note got to him, right smack

in the heart. Knowing when he was defeated, he muttered, "All right, all right, I'll do it."

"Thank you!" She rose to hug him. "You won't regret this, kiddo. You're going to knock 'em dead."

He tried to grin. Was it possible after so many years of being out of the spotlight? His godmother had more confidence than he.

"We oughta make a toast or something," Lucille went on, drawing back to beam at him. "How about some champagne? I think there's an old bottle around here somewhere."

He got up from the chair, sliding a supportive arm around her fragile shoulders. "Actually, I'm still waiting for that coffee."

"Oh, right." Lucille looked around. "Where on earth is Elsie? Drat that silly old twit. She must've forgotten to put on her hearing aid again…or maybe she fell asleep. Come on. Let's go out to the kitchen and help ourselves."

Lucille enthused about his coming performance all the way down the shadowy halls of the mansion. Kit asked about the nostalgia club and the way it was going to be run. He also questioned her about his new dance partner, though Lucille claimed to know little more than her age, marital status and the titles of some of the productions she'd danced in.

A chorus girl rather than a star, Anita's daughter hadn't been that successful, Kit realized. Was she as ambitious as her mother? Did she expect a career boost from teaming up with him? Not if he could help it. That kind of stuff wouldn't wash with him. He wasn't as gullible as his father had been.

Furthermore, Gabrielle Brooks Lacroix had better know her stuff, or she was going to be one unhappy hoofer.

"HE AGREED TO DO IT."

"Good." Price Garfield relaxed his tense grip on the telephone receiver. He'd had faith in Lucille.

"I'm not doing this just for the money, you know," Lucille assured him.

"Of course not, but you're going to need some more up-front money to buy new duds that'll impress the customers. They've got to believe you're the owner." Price alone made up the remainder of the supposed investment group. "Buy whatever you need and charge everything to the club." Then he anxiously asked, "You ordered those airline tickets, didn't you?"

"Anita and her daughter should be receiving them any day. Everything's cooking. You're going to get another chance."

"I hope so." He'd been dreaming about seeing Anita again for more than a year, ever since he'd heard she'd been widowed. That desire had added impetus to his and Lucille's scheme.

"You hope so? Better be more positive. Surely you've learned something after half a century." A longtime friend who'd become his closest confidante over the past few years, Lucille was the only person who had the nerve to talk to him like that.

"I've learned a lot." About loneliness, estrangement, his own stupidity and pride. "But Anita will have something to say about things, too."

"You mean you still doubt she loves you? The feelings you two had for each other aren't the type that evaporate overnight, you old fool."

But then Lucille was an incurable romantic who slept with her late husband's photo under her pillow. Price knew that she believed when she died, Jim Dix would return for her, galloping over the heavenly horizon on a big white horse to carry her away.

"Get in there and do your stuff!" Lucille ordered. "I'll be rooting for you."

"Thanks." Considering his age, this would be his *last* chance with Anita.

"You also might think about having a heart-to-heart with your boy one of these days."

"Kit? Why? We get along." At least now that the younger Garfield had reached adulthood and had ostensibly recovered from his resentment over the divorce.

"Yeah, maybe, but your relationship sucks," Lucille said in the no-nonsense way Price had come to respect over the years. "You shoulda been the one who asked him to perform, not me."

He sighed. "True." Though he didn't know how to span the distance between himself and his son.

"He's the only kid you've got."

He'd once dreamed of having more. But maybe he would have been just as inept at parenting several as he had been with one. "I'll be seeing more of him as we work on the show."

"Going to give him some tips on choreography? Uh-oh. I'd be careful about that. He's very proud."

A trait father and son shared. Price just

hoped that Kit wouldn't let his pride get out of hand. "And you be careful that you don't let him know where the money's coming from, okay?"

"My lips are sealed. Anita won't know a thing, either."

Anita. After finishing the telephone conversation with Lucille, Price thought about the woman he'd lost so long ago. Would Anita be able to forgive him, or would she still be angry? Had he any hope of rekindling their love?

Restless, he paced around the house for a while, then decided to take a drive. By himself. He told the chauffeur he wouldn't be needing his services that night. And since the early autumn air was warm, he lowered the top of the Mercedes convertible after he backed it out of the garage. Then he sped along the roads that wound through the hills above L.A., letting the breeze blow through what was left of his hair, almost able to imagine he was young again, strong and in complete control.

What an illusion. There was no way he could forget a life spent making every mistake in the book when it came to love and marriage. Not that there hadn't always been

good reasons for each of his four divorces—
lack of communication, ego conflicts, career
conflicts. And not that there hadn't seemed
to be good reasons for each marriage in the
first place. He'd thrown himself into every
relationship with passion and commitment
and the hope that it would work out.

None of them had, not even the last. Devot-
ing himself to his fifth and, he determined,
his *final* wife, he'd been stunned when Rachel
had been diagnosed with cancer. He'd nursed
her through a long illness only to lose her.
Perhaps, having walked away from the first
and greatest love of his life, he'd doomed
himself.

If only he could lift the curse.

On Mulholland Drive he pulled off onto
an overlook with a stunning view. Struck by
the vast, sequined panoply of lights spread
out in the valley below, he realized the sight
at this particular spot was familiar. It should
be; he'd once vowed never to forget….

Hollywood, 1953

"WE'RE ON TOP of the world!" Anita cried,
rising from the seat of the parked convertible to get a better view of the city. Holding

on to the windshield, she demanded, "Isn't it grand?"

"Fantastic," he agreed, knowing she was referring to the gala premiere they'd attended that evening as much as the sight of Los Angeles. Their newest film was going to be a big success.

"We've done it, Price. We're stars." And she looked the part—exquisite and glamorous in a fur stole and strapless gown. "We're famous."

He fingered the steering wheel. "Yeah, I guess so."

She gazed down at him curiously. "How come you're not more enthusiastic? That crowd tonight loved us."

"They love the characters we play."

"But there's a part of *you* in every one of your characters."

"A small part." He wasn't half as clever and carefree as the roles he played. "I just wish people would allow the rest of me some privacy. I'm getting tired of signing autographs and being hounded to dance with every woman I meet."

That's why he disliked the big parties and public outings they were expected to attend.

But Anita seemed to thrive on them, responding warmly to everyone.

"I can't sit and finish a meal or even talk to anyone for more than five minutes," he complained.

"Aw, poor Price."

She laughed, the sound high and clear in the empty darkness of the night. Theirs was the only automobile in sight. At least he'd managed to get her alone for a while.

"Why wouldn't women want to dance with you?" Anita asked, sliding back down to stroke his arm. "You're a honey of a leading man. Those women think that if they're in your arms, you'll make them feel as beautiful and romantic as the movies they watch. They're all in love with you."

Price had to smile. "I still find that hard to believe."

"Why? I fall in love with you, too...every time we dance."

"Only when we dance?"

He turned toward her and grasped one of her gloved hands, feeling the warmth of the vibrant flesh through the material. Hadn't she realized by now that *she* was the one who put cupid's wings to his heels?

She drew a deep breath and gazed at him

steadily. "If you're asking me for a declaration, you'll have to make one first."

His heart beat faster. "I love you, Anita." Something he'd known for a long time. He slipped his arm around her shoulders and drew her close. "I love you even more than words can say."

Shuddering when he lowered his mouth to kiss her, she responded passionately, winding her arms around his neck. She tasted of lip rouge and champagne and smelled of roses. They were crushing the corsage she wore, but Price didn't care. The world itself could have stopped turning that very moment and he wouldn't have known the difference.

"So tell me." He drew back slightly to stare into her eyes.

"You already know."

"Say it." So the words would echo down through the eternity he wanted to spend with her.

She actually seemed shy when she murmured, "I love you, okay?"

"It's more than okay." And far more thrilling than any movie career or applauding crowd. "We belong together, Anita."

"Together," she whispered, kissing him again.

He closed his eyes but not before he'd promised himself to memorize every nuance of their surroundings—the stars above, the dark hills, the blazing lights in the valley. He would store the memory and keep it forever in his heart....

CHAPTER THREE

THE LARGE BUILDING housing Cheek to Cheek was faced in white stucco and trimmed in gray-painted wood. According to Lucille, neon signs identifying the nightclub would go up in a couple of days. Having just arrived for her first planning meeting with Kit Garfield, Gabby gave the place a cursory inspection as she and Anita alighted from a taxi. Her nerves frazzled from the time they'd spent in the hotel lobby waiting for the vehicle, Gabby paid the driver what she thought was an exorbitant fare and glanced at her watch.

"I'm a half hour late. I wish you had told me we might have a problem getting a taxi," she complained.

"It's been more than fifty years since I've lived in California," Anita said as they hurried inside and mounted the steps leading up to the nightclub's main floor. "How would I know?"

"And everything is miles and miles apart. We're going to have to rent a car."

"We can take care of that later," Anita assured her in her most soothing mother's tone. "You should concentrate on your meeting for now."

"Right."

Gabby took a deep breath. She'd been both nervous and excited since getting off the plane the day before. Thinking about the great chance she'd been offered—as well as how devastated she'd be if things didn't work out—she'd hardly been able to sleep the night before.

"My, this looks wonderful," Anita mused. "Just like one of my old movie sets."

Gabby glanced around the cavernous room, her eyes lingering on the expanse of black dance floor spreading out before a crescent-shaped stage with a curved staircase. The rest of the place was painted white or pale gray, the moldings and lines pure Art Deco.

"Go on. Don't let me keep you," Anita whispered. "I'll stay out of sight and wander around back here." She pushed her daughter forward.

Gabby gazed toward the empty stage and dance floor again, the meeting place she and Kit had agreed upon. Where was he? Surely he hadn't been so annoyed with her for being a little late that he'd left. Clutching the large manila envelope that contained notes and photographs for the upcoming production, she crossed the room, her feet crunching on cardboard and loose plaster. Finishing touches were still being added, though no workmen were in sight at the moment.

"Gabrielle Brooks Lacroix?"

Gabby halted as a man slid out from behind some half-built panels near the stage. A tentative smile hovering about her lips, she gazed at him curiously. Dressed in a black turtleneck and jeans, he was tall and dark and moved with a dancer's lean grace.

"Kit Garfield?"

"Who else would be waiting for you for—" he glanced at his watch "—thirty-four minutes?"

Her smile died at his tone. Besides, *he* wasn't smiling, not even politely. Having convinced herself to be positive about the situation and to act in a professional and friendly manner toward Kit Garfield no matter what, she felt her doubts return. Explaining the taxi problem would sound like an excuse. Instead, she suggested, "Now that I'm here, shall we get right down to work?"

"Fine." He gestured toward the short flight of steps leading up to the stage. "Have a seat."

Although she was dressed in a wrap dress, Gabby was undaunted by the debris that littered the area. Brushing the sawdust and plaster off the top step, she sat down and placed the manila envelope on her lap. Kit was carrying a similar parcel under one arm. He leaned casually against the four-foot-high stage and looked her over.

Unblinking, she stared right back and tried to discern a resemblance to Price in the younger man's features. But only the lines of Kit's high forehead and elegant, aquiline nose reminded her of his legendary father. The strong cheekbones, thick dark hair, square jaw and wide, sensual mouth must have come from his mother's side of the family.

Particularly appreciating the luminous green of his eyes, she said, "You're very good-looking."

He seemed startled. "Thanks," he responded stiffly. "How nice that I meet with your approval."

"I always consider the physical presence as well as the skills of a dance partner," she told him honestly, pleased to have ruffled his calm surface. At least the laugh lines around those remarkable eyes hinted that he could be warmer on other occasions. "We'll look good together—I'm light, you're dark." He sported the ubiquitous California tan. "We should emphasize our contrasts with costuming, use a lot of black with pastels or cream or white."

"I've already considered the costuming."

That made two of them. "My mother kept some of the original dresses from the Brooks/Garfield movies," Gabby told him, nervously fingering the envelope. "We had patterns made from them."

He nodded. "I'll have to approve the designs, as well...if we use them. No one's made any final decision about vintage costumes."

Gabby hated having to be on guard, but she was getting the feeling that Kit Garfield resented her...and would also resent any suggestions she might make. He seemed to think he was in charge.

"We've got less than two weeks to pull everything together. Using the patterns would be sensible. Besides, why shouldn't we use my mother's dresses in a nostalgia club?" she asked pointedly.

"We can have original costumes with a vintage flavor."

Gabby raised her brows. "For an act labeled 'Brooks/Garfield'?"

"Do you want to dance as a clone of your mother?" Kit asked, sounding slightly appalled.

"It wouldn't bother me."

"Well, I'm not appearing as Price Garfield."

Hmm, that statement certainly made him sound insecure—quite a contrast from his assertive behavior. Trying to reassure him, Gabby said, "I don't think anyone would confuse you with your father, even if you wore the same tuxedo." Which wouldn't fit, anyway, Gabby thought, considering Kit's size. Price had always been whippet-thin.

Kit tapped his fingers on the edge of the stage. "Enough about the costumes. We can talk about them later. First we have to set up a rehearsal schedule—"

"And decide on how many and what numbers we're going to perform," she finished, opening the manila envelope.

She'd brought a few musical arrangements— a combination of Brooks/Garfield tunes and other songs from musicals. She intended to be a full partner, not a freeloader.

"We'll only have time to choreograph and

rehearse three or four numbers at most," she continued. And if they weren't well matched as partners, they'd be lucky to polish one or two dances.

"How versed are you in ballroom dancing, Gabrielle?" he asked, throwing her off base.

"It's Gabby." She glanced up from the material she'd dumped in her lap. "And I studied ballroom along with modern dance, some ballet and tap. I appeared in several Broadway musicals—"

"*Dime Store Boogie, Red Roses* and *Pretty Marietta,* among others," he cut in.

"I guess you've done your homework. Then you must also know that *Marietta* was a remake of a twenties production that included a tango and other partnered dances. I was a featured player."

"Ten years ago," he added. "And I never saw it, so I don't know how well you dance."

Despite her good intentions, Gabby frowned at him. "I'm not going to audition here, if that's what you're driving at. I've already been hired." Next thing she knew he'd be asking to see her legs.

"No one mentioned auditioning. I have a right to ask questions of a new partner."

"That goes both ways. What about you?"

she asked, neatly turning the focus of the discussion onto *him.* "How much dancing have you done through the years? Did you take courses through your father's dance studios?"

He raised one brow. "*I* run the Price Garfield Dance Studios, not my father."

"Oh, really?" His air was seemingly confident, yet Gabby thought she detected that insecurity again. "Being a businessman doesn't mean you can dance, though."

"I started as a dance instructor, then went into ballroom competition. I've covered pretty much the same territory through classes as you."

"Hmm." She gazed at him thoughtfully. "You've also performed professionally?"

"I did the nightclub circuit for a while," he admitted, his tone guarded.

"Then I would assume you had some skill… just as you should assume I know what I'm about," she continued, wishing he'd loosen up. "And for your information, I still keep up. I retired from the stage last year, but I teach five days a week."

"Uh-huh. You're thirty-three."

"Right. Too old for the chorus line," she said swiftly before he could stoop to mention it. And too old for another lucky break if this one failed, though she'd die rather than let him know how vulnerable she felt.

"I'm sure you weren't happy about having to retire." He straightened, tucking the envelope under his other arm.

"Broadway was a rat race. Teaching can be just as fulfilling." She only wished that were true for her.

"But stardom must have been your goal… if you're anything like your mother."

Overly sensitive when it came to Anita, Gabby felt herself tense. "What do you mean by that crack?"

"Show business success was more important than anything *or anyone* to Anita Brooks, wasn't it?"

"Of course my mother wanted to be successful." And she would have been if Kit's father hadn't driven her out of Hollywood. Gabby couldn't forget the sadness her mother had attempted to hide through the years. Kit was stomping on shaky territory and was making her angry. She rose to her feet and stepped down to face him. In her high-heeled boots she was only a couple of inches shorter than him, and she wasn't in the least intimidated.

"Who doesn't want to be successful in their

chosen field?" she asked. "Wasn't success what you were after when you appeared in nightclubs?"

"I was dancing mainly for fun."

She crossed her arms, holding the papers against her chest. "Performing is a pretty demanding way to have fun. Not that it can't give a person the highest form of pleasure." She wondered how he'd like being baited. "But what really happened? Why did you stop? Surely you didn't get booed off the stage."

He didn't blink an eye. "Certainly not. I simply became more involved in the other subsidiaries of the Garfield Corporation."

"But don't you miss dancing? How long has it been?"

Two tiny lines formed between his eyes. "I've never given up dancing. I take dates out to dance clubs whenever I get the chance."

"So you're still single." She couldn't resist getting back at him for his implied criticism of her mother. "At thirty-five? Thirty-six? If you have the same goals as your father, you'd better think about getting married pretty soon."

For a moment he seemed struck speechless, then his eyes blazed. "I'm thirty-eight, and my plans for marriage are none of your business." He scowled and leaned toward her. "You know, this has gone far enough. You have no right to bad-mouth my father's personal life."

She made no move to step back. "Was that what I was doing? Simply by mentioning his multiple marriages? Well, you have no right to make remarks about my mother's career."

"I don't recall saying anything nasty about your mother."

"You mean you were too clever to say exactly what you meant. Believe me, I got the dig."

"You're being paranoid."

"I'm being honest. Now how about you? Let's put our cards on the table here."

Kit straightened and glared at Gabby, who glared right back at him. He had to admire the woman's guts. She was as courageous and intelligent as she was beautiful, a combination he hadn't expected.

"I don't have any cards, if you're referring to ulterior motives." His poor opinion of Anita Brooks had nothing to do with Gabby herself. "I can see we're going to have to avoid talking about our parents."

"That would be a good idea," she agreed, "unless we're discussing their dancing styles."

"I don't want to go around and around every time we get together."

"I don't want to argue, either. A change in your attitude would help."

"*My* attitude? You're blaming me?"

"You started this," she insisted. "You already had a big chip on your shoulder when I walked in the door. You couldn't even smile, for Pete's sake."

"Maybe I'm a serious person." He hadn't really meant to be openly prickly, but his resentment toward the whole situation must have crept through.

"Ha! I think it's more likely that you don't want to work with me."

Bingo. "That I admit is true."

She tossed the papers she'd been holding onto the steps and placed her hands on her hips. "Well, I don't particularly want to work with you either, buddy, but I'm trying to be gracious about it."

"And just why should you have anything against working with me? My father was the one who helped your mother realize her ambitions." And as far as Kit had figured, Gabby ought to be happy for the publicity that could renew her own stage career.

"Are you kidding?" she asked, her expression disbelieving. "Surely you're aware that your father drove my mother away."

Anita Brooks had been angry? The news was a revelation, which Kit digested quickly. "I suppose I've only heard my father's side of the story."

"Your *father's* side? What has he got to complain about?"

She was being honest, Kit could tell. So Anita Brooks thought she'd suffered at the hands of Price. This was the first he'd heard about it. Struck by the irony of the circumstances, he grinned.

"Now you're smiling!" Gabby cried. "What's so funny?"

"This bizarre situation…you and I…our parents." He shook his head. "It's just too much."

"I'd call it ridiculous."

"Look, let's make a peace pact, all right? I've already suggested we don't talk about Anita or Price. Obviously we'd be opening a can of worms."

She nodded and relaxed her stance slightly.

"Surely you can force yourself to try to get

along with me for a few weeks," Kit continued, sobering.

"Of course. I'm a professional. I'd already decided I could do so before I came to California."

Kit suddenly noticed there were tiny freckles sprinkled across Gabby's nose and that her eyes were a clear aqua-blue. As if she felt uncomfortable under his close inspection, she stepped back and smoothed the taupe skirt of her dress. The color brought out the reddish highlights in her pale hair. Medium-length and wavy, it curved around her oval face and softened her small, stubborn chin.

"Then it's peace, not war." He would be tempted to reach out and touch the tiny cleft in that chin of hers if the action weren't so totally inappropriate.

"Peace." Her lips curved into a smile, making her even lovelier.

He ignored his growing attraction to her and gestured toward the stage. "Okay, take a seat again."

Gabby stared at him angrily.

"Please," he added. "We'll make out that rehearsal schedule we should have been talking about in the first place." He sat a step below her and opened his envelope. "We have to get down to business if we're ever going to put an act together."

They worked amicably after that, though Kit could see they weren't always going to agree in the future. Gabby wanted old-school costumes and dance tunes; he preferred updated versions. He liked to work within a precise format; she wasn't keen on using dance diagrams to block out every step before getting on the dance floor.

For the moment, however, they both kept themselves in check. He figured the partnership was going to be workable, especially since it would be time-limited. Maybe the trap he'd fallen into wasn't going to be so bad after all.

"Like to try a whirl around the floor?" he asked after they'd agreed on a couple of dance numbers and set up a working schedule for the week. Might as well get the feel of her from the very start. "The sound system's working."

Kit chose swing music. Gabby immediately began moving around the dance floor, improvising steps, her eyes half closed while her willowy dancer's body swayed gracefully to the rhythm. He joined her and grasped her hand. She looked up, smiling as she swung into a side-by-side tap sequence with him. She was lovely, indeed.

And her dancing was wonderful, too. He spun her out and back into the circle of his arms. They moved so perfectly together whether they were face-to-face or cheek to cheek, she followed his lead without missing a beat, something that was very unusual for a brand-new partner.

Kit felt the underlying tension he'd experienced since first talking to Lucille drain away with each turn across the floor. With Gabby, forgetting the logistics of every dance movement and losing himself in the romantic artistry of the performance would be easy. When they did several cross-steps and faced the seating area, he could imagine working the crowd. He'd pick out faces, colors, anchor himself to reality in the heat of the spotlight, enjoy the thrill of making people sit up and take notice.

Enjoy the thrill?

Kit smiled and met Gabby's eyes. He'd forgotten how stimulating performing could be. Perhaps working with Gabrielle Brooks Lacroix was going to be better than "not so bad." Perhaps their performance would be memorable.

THOUGH ANITA HAD INTENDED to explore the entire building, she stopped short when she spotted Kit Garfield. Unable to resist, she took refuge behind one of the thick columns that bordered the nightclub's central area—that way, while able to see him, she could remain hidden in the shadows of the outer hallway. She searched for any discernible resemblance to his father—that would almost be the same as seeing him again—but Kit looked nothing like Price.

At least that was Anita's disappointed opinion after watching Gabby and Kit interact for a few minutes. Her daughter's expression didn't seem happy. Worried, Anita wished she could hear their conversation. Their unamplified voices barely carried across the huge room.

Oh, dear, she was acting like a mother hen!

Reprimanding herself, Anita moved away past boxes stacked in the hall. She reached the lounge area, entered the ladies' room and checked her makeup and hair. As if there were anyone around to impress….

The mirror curving the length of one wall was etched with geometric designs and lit by marquee lights. Velvet-covered seats were tucked under a marble counter. How posh.

Cheek to Cheek was going to be a very impressive night spot.

Suddenly Anita heard the strains of swing music and was drawn back to the central part of the club. There, sweeping around the dusty black dance floor, she saw Gabby and Kit caught up in the music, perfectly attuned to each other. Anita halted near some crates, impressed with the beauty of the dance, then struck by Kit's fluid movements. The set of his shoulders, the turn of his heel, the relaxed look of his stance—all bespoke Price Garfield.

Anita took a deep, shaky breath. Kit *was* Price's true flesh and blood, after all. Her eyes filled, and she rummaged for a tissue in her purse, then blew her nose quietly. What a crazy, sentimental old fool she was. She could almost imagine she was watching Price himself.

"Anita?"

And now she was even imagining Price's voice.

Soft footfalls in the hallway finally made her realize someone was behind her. She turned.

"Anita?"

She stared.

Price—or a thin, aging manifestation of the man she'd always loved—was standing several feet from her, his expression intense, his eyes flickering with a multitude of emotions. She'd expected to see him…but not now…not like this. She wasn't prepared!

Her mouth dropped open and she backed against a crate. She placed a hand over her heart, which she feared was going to stop. "Go away! I can't stand it…."

His eyes widened and his expression closed as he backed away and disappeared, wraith-like, into the shadows.

Anita stood stock-still a few seconds longer, then slowly slumped to the crate.

"Ahh…" she moaned loudly.

Her heart began palpitating, and she heard the sound of running footsteps before deliberately closing her eyes.

"I STILL THINK we should call a doctor," Gabby said, continuing to worry about her mother even after they'd returned to their hotel room. She bent over the bed where she'd forced Anita to lie down and placed a cool washcloth across the older woman's forehead. "You could be seriously ill."

"I don't need a doctor. I'm not sick." Anita

tried to rise, but Gabby pushed her back. "Come now, I didn't faint. I just closed my eyes for a moment while I caught my breath."

Caught her breath, indeed! Kit would have taken them to a hospital if Anita hadn't adamantly refused to go.

"But what in the world happened?" Gabby demanded to know. "Your pulse was racing. This could be indicative of something more serious, Mom. Maybe it's your heart."

Anita laughed softly. "It's my heart, all right." At Gabby's alarmed expression she hastened to explain. "Don't worry. My health's fine. My emotions are all mixed up. I came face-to-face with Price while you and Kit were dancing."

"Price?" Gabby hadn't seen anyone else around.

"I didn't want to say anything in front of Kit...I mean, the man *is* his father...."

Her imagination running wild, Gabby asked, "What did Price say to you?"

Anita patted her hand reassuringly. "Nothing, sweetheart, honest. He just spoke my name and backed away...and then I had some trouble breathing, that's all. Isn't it ridiculous? I never thought I'd become some wilting lily the first time I encountered him." She laughed again.

But Gabby wasn't amused. "I was afraid something like this would happen. We're going back to New York."

"Going back? Why?"

"We've barely been here twenty-four hours, yet you've already run into Price Garfield and he's upset you. You can't take this kind of strain." When it came to her mother's health, Gabby was ready to put everything else second—even a second chance at a career.

"Oh, bosh." Sitting up, Anita threw aside the washcloth and assumed a steely-eyed expression. "We are *not* going back to New York. I was merely shocked when I saw Price today. This won't happen again."

Hands on her hips, Gabby loomed threateningly over the bed. "And what *will* happen when you see him again? How will you feel when you're constantly being reminded of your old movies, your dances? That's what this trip is all about."

"I'm not going to have heart failure, which seems to be what you're worried about," Anita said irritably. "I'm made of sterner stuff. I want to get up."

Sighing, recognizing the stubborn tone,

Gabby stepped back while her mother got to her feet. If the older woman looked even the slightest bit peaked throughout the coming evening, she was going to call the airlines… if not an ambulance.

Anita ran her fingers through her mussed hair and picked up the purse she'd thrown aside. "So what's Kit like?" she asked, obviously wanting to change the subject. "He's an excellent dancer. He moves like his father."

"Kit's very good," Gabby agreed. Thinking of the tension between them, she chose not to mention the tiff concerning their parents. "I can't tell you much about his personality, though. We're trying to keep things impersonal."

"Perhaps he's always a bit aloof with people he doesn't know," Anita murmured speculatively. "And then when he gets involved with something or someone he cares about, he can be emotionally intense…."

"Possibly." Gabby had the feeling her mother was thinking of the elder Garfield. "All I care about is that Kit is talented and willing to work out a dance routine."

"He appears capable of that, doesn't he?"

"So far so good."

Gabby took off her dress and slipped into a

kimono. Rather than jumping into the shower immediately, she lay down on her own bed. She wanted to watch her mother closely for any symptoms of weakness.

"Kit's very organized," Gabby went on. "He's already making out charts and diagrams for dance routines before we've even practiced them."

"Hmm. Perfectionistic enough to make diagrams? Sounds like he inherited more than talent from Price."

Gabby wasn't particularly thrilled with the news. Recalling an anecdote her mother used to tell about rehearsals, she decided she'd walk right out if Kit Garfield ever made her dance so long and hard that her feet bled.

The telephone rang, interrupting her thoughts.

"I'll get it," Anita told her daughter, reaching for the receiver. "Hello?" Her face lit up with a big smile. "Lucille! You're downstairs? Wonderful. Come right up. Gabby is anxious to meet you."

"Oh, boy, and I'm not ready."

Gabby rushed into the bathroom and straight to the shower. She was just drying off when she heard her mother open the room door. Anita and Lucille shared a tearful reunion while Gabby ran a comb through her wet hair. Leaving the bathroom, she smiled as she approached the silver-haired, elderly lady next to her mother.

"Well, well, well." Lucille looked Gabby over with discerning dark eyes and reached out to give her a big hug. "You're gorgeous, toots. Such long legs. But maybe I've shrunk a coupla more inches today."

"I can't believe you're still putting yourself down," Anita said.

Lucille chuckled. "Hey, it's part of my comedy routine…which I'll be doing for the club, you know, when I act as MC."

Anita beamed. "I think it's all wonderful."

"It's gonna be a trip, as the young people say." Lucille paused. "Oops, I mean as the young *used* to say in…when was it? The sixties? I've seen a few generations come and go in my time."

Everyone laughed.

"But speaking of coming and going, I have another proposition for you," Lucille went on. "How about if I take you both out to dinner and then to my house? Instead of bunking in this hotel, how about staying with me?"

"Oh, we couldn't," Anita objected.

"We shouldn't," Gabby agreed.

"Of course you should. I've got a big place in Beverly Hills with ten times more ambience than this joint. And you can have your own suite." Obviously assuming Anita might have reservations, Lucille attempted to stem her next objection. "Price won't be hanging around," she assured her. "We're friends, but he doesn't drop by unless I invite him. Now tell me you'll agree—we've got years of gossip to catch up on."

"Well..." Anita wavered and exchanged a glance with Gabby that said she wasn't going to mention the chance encounter with Price that afternoon.

"And I want to get to know this one better, too," Lucille continued, grinning at Gabby. "You and your brother and sisters were supposed to be my godchildren. And what happened? Your mother moved outta state."

Gabby smiled. Lucille was as warm and charming as Anita had always claimed. "I never had a godmother."

"You can have one now." Lucille slapped her on the back as if sealing an agreement. "And so we're all going to my house, right? Soon as we get some grub."

Gabby gazed at Anita, who shrugged and said, "Why not? I'm sure it will be homier."

That settled it. Gabby dressed while her mother packed their things. Having heard stories about Lucille through the years, she was certain the stay at the elderly lady's home was going to be interesting. Lucille and Anita were still chattering away when Gabby put the finishing touches to her makeup.

She picked up a light jacket and her purse. "Ready?"

"Sure." Lucille grinned. "I've got a limo downstairs waiting for us. If you want, after dinner, I can have the driver take us around and show you a few sights."

"That would be nice," Gabby agreed. The guidebook she'd read said they weren't far from some famous landmarks. "If it's not too much trouble," she added hurriedly.

"Hey, I'd go to any length of trouble for a new godchild."

"Do you have others?" Gabby asked.

"Just one. With no kids of my own, I kinda enjoyed having Kit to make over once in a while."

Kit Garfield. Of course. Gabby only hoped agreeing to stay at Lucille's wasn't going to mean closer contact with her new dance partner. The scant inches between them on the dance floor was going to be plenty close enough.

CHAPTER FOUR

AFTER A TOUR OF THE TOWN that left them completely exhausted, Gabby and Anita decided to delay the move to Lucille's until the following afternoon, when the comic actress provided colorful commentary to more impromptu sight-seeing. Passing Pantages, which Lucille insisted was one of the most splendid Art Deco theaters in the world, Gabby was reminded of Kit and their act. She was anxious to start working on the choreography, but, tied up by an important meeting, he wouldn't be able to get away from the Garfield Corporation until the next day.

"Everything looks so different from New York," Gabby said as the limousine headed west on Sunset Boulevard. "Almost as if L.A. were a foreign country."

Lucille chuckled. "It's foreign, all right. The old stars of the golden age of Hollywood made this part of Southern California into a regular magical kingdom—and I'm not talking about Disneyland. Course now the tinsel's a little tarnished here and there."

"And everything's so much more crowded than I remember it," Anita said, her expression mildly distressed as she gazed out at the traffic.

"But still fascinating," Gabby hastened to add.

She knew her mother had fond memories of her birthplace—one of the reasons Anita had been anxious to return. Having often wondered why her mother had never so much as vacationed in California after moving to New York, she was now sure it had to do with Anita's fear of running into Price Garfield.

The driver turned the limo north and, on a whim of Lucille's, swept up and down the side streets of Beverly Hills. Lucille pointed out houses that had once belonged to famous stars, like the one built by Charlie Chaplin.

"People called his estate Break-away House," Lucille told her. "To save money on construction that old cheapskate Charlie had his studio carpenters do the work. Ornamental trim was always falling off walls. At one party a doorknob came off in my hand."

Gabby laughed, but when they pulled up to Lucille's deteriorating mansion, she wasn't so sure the place would be in much better condition. Her mother had warned her the elderly actress had been in financial straits for years. Indeed, what must have been one of the finest estates in Beverly Hills in the twenties looked as if it had been sadly neglected for at least a decade. It would take a small fortune to restore the mansion and grounds to their former glory. Still, Gabby couldn't help but be fascinated by the sheer size and the architecture of Lucille's mansion.

"Your home certainly has atmosphere."

"Yeah, that's one thing we're loaded with, toots. My dear departed Jim dubbed his estate the Silver Stallion after his favorite horse." Chuckling, she added, "Now it's nothing but a white elephant. But we're gonna change that soon when the club is a big hit...which it will be with you and Kit headlining the entertainment."

Feeling a mantle of responsibility settle over her shoulders, Gabby nevertheless tried to tell herself that Cheek to Cheek would succeed or fail on all of its merits, not solely on whether or not she and Kit made a successful team. Surely Lucille's hopes couldn't be pinned on them. Her mother's old friend had never even seen them dance together.

With the help of the driver the women unloaded the luggage from the trunk. Inside, an elderly black woman met them in the foyer. Gabby assumed she was a boarder until Lucille introduced Elsie as the mansion's maid and her lifelong companion.

"I'll show you folks to your suite." Elsie slid one bag over a plump shoulder and started to pick up another.

Gabby immediately took the larger suitcase from her hand. "You don't have to carry those. We're not guests. We can manage."

Dark eyes peered at her through a pair of the thickest glasses Gabby had ever seen.

"And I can still manage my job," Elsie replied smartly.

"Elsie, you know what I told you about overdoing it," Lucille scolded. "Harold can bring up the larger cases as soon as he parks the limo."

Though she didn't insist on carrying the heavier suitcase, Elsie kept hold of the shoulder bag and slowly led them up the stairs to a third-floor suite that consisted of a living room, bathroom and two bedrooms, all of which were decorated in a white, cream and gold color scheme. Gabby thought the quarters must have been quite elegant when new, but now the furnishings—couches, carpets and curtains—were worn and a bit thread-bare.

"Whew, those stairs are something," Lucille said, puffing as she entered the suite. "That's why no one's been living up here. The elevator's been out of operation three or four years now."

"More like seven," Elsie muttered as she set down the shoulder bag near a large bay window. "I don't know what this place is coming to. I surely don't."

"It's coming to nothing but good," Lucille stated. "Once the club is a big success, everything that's broken can be fixed and everything that's worn can be replaced. It'll be like the old days."

Gabby thought that a bit of an overstatement, but she didn't say so. It would probably take years of investing Lucille's share of the profits to restore the entire forty-room mansion, but she didn't want to put a damper on the elderly woman's enthusiasm.

"You two take it easy until dinner, which won't be until six-thirty or so," their hostess said, following Elsie toward the hall. "Kick off your shoes, take a long soak. Mae West used to love that bathtub. We decorated this entire suite to her taste so she'd feel at home, you know."

When Lucille left, Gabby was happy to do as her hostess suggested. The spacious bath was of white Italian marble, the tub almost big enough for a swim, she thought, taking advantage of the small luxury while her mother napped.

So when they headed for dinner a couple of hours later, Gabby was rested, relaxed and ready to meet Lucille's boarders.

Two men stood talking in the open parlor off the dining room. Gabby recognized Neil Delaney, a second banana in the light comedies of the fifties and sixties, and Yancy Knight, who'd been a movie heavy until a decade before when he'd suddenly dropped out of sight.

"Be still my heart," Neil declared as they entered the parlor. The white-haired man strode forward and held out a hand to each woman. Dressed in comfortable trousers and an open-throated shirt, he looked to be an attractive seventy. He gave Anita a flirtatious smile. "I think I'm in love."

Anita laughed. "Some things about Hollywood never change."

"They mighta got rid of the cowboys," Lucille said as she joined them through a second doorway, "but they left the bull behind."

"And this guy actually imagines he has a way with women," Yancy rasped, his distinctive, knife-edged voice as hard as the rest of him.

Although he was only a few years younger than Neil, Yancy still had the well-toned, muscular body of a man half his age. Not to mention the hair, Gabby thought, trying not to stare at the obviously fake coal-black color that matched his dramatic black knit shirt and slacks.

"If the truth be known, Yancy's the real ladies' man around here," Lucille stated with a chuckle. "So watch out for him."

The man's rugged face softened with his smile. "Lucille, that's positively the nicest thing you've said about me in years."

Although their hostess had told Gabby and Anita all about her little group of retirees on the ride home, she introduced the two men and spoke enthusiastically about their backgrounds. Jayne Hunter joined them just as the doorbell rang.

"Ah, our guest has arrived. Whaddya say we stop yappin' and get some grub?" Lucille turned to Gabby. "Say, toots, would you mind answering the door? If we wait for Elsie to do it, dinner'll get cold."

"Sure. You go ahead and sit."

Neil and Yancy escorted the three older women into the dining room while Gabby headed for the door, wondering who she would find on the other side. Another of Lucille's famous old cronies? She froze for a second. Surely Lucille wouldn't have invited Price Garfield....

Before she could move to find out, the door opened and Kit walked in.

"I didn't expect to see you until tomorrow," she said, trying to convince herself she was glad to see him only because the unexpected guest turned out to be the younger rather than the senior Garfield. Unfortunately she couldn't help admiring Kit, who looked as comfortable—and handsome—in business attire as he had in jeans.

"Lucille ordered me to show."

With a sheepish smile Kit shrugged his shoulders, which were encased in a perfectly tailored silk-blend gray suit jacket. Gabby suddenly felt underdressed in her white capris and purple cotton pullover.

"I wouldn't have thought you were a man who takes orders."

"Depends on who gives them…." The skin around his green eyes crinkled as his smile broadened. "And whether or not I want to do what's demanded of me. Then again, I just can't say no to some people."

His affection for Lucille was so obvious that Gabby smiled in return. "Well, you arrived in the nick of time. The others are already at the table."

Kit followed closely as she crossed the foyer and parlor and entered the spacious dining room. Overhead, a wagon-wheel chandelier softly illuminated the room. The rough-hewn wooden table was long enough to accommodate double the number of people who gathered there. Elsie picked up a turquoise stoneware bowl from the intricately carved wooden sideboard and set it on the table in front of Anita.

"Dinner is family-style," Elsie told her.

Placing a polite hand on Gabby's arm, Kit escorted her to her seat. Too aware of his closeness, of his warmth, of his after-shave, she was relieved when he helped her with her chair, then moved away. Kit kissed Lucille's cheek before taking his seat on the other side of the table.

"Glad you could make it, kiddo. I wanted to

celebrate new beginnings with the two young people who're making it all possible."

Once more Gabby felt the burden of responsibility press down on her. She exchanged a significant look with Kit. It seemed that he, too, was somewhat uncomfortable with his godmother's expectations. Still, they both lifted their glasses in a toast with the others.

"May your partnership be more successful than mine ever was," Harvey Morris grumbled.

Gabby knew the balding little man dressed in a dapper if threadbare suit was a comedian who had broken up with his partner in the sixties. Lucille told them Harvey's career had hit the skids soon afterward. These days, if he was lucky, he emceed shows at local clubs for a little extra money.

"To success," Gabby said, smiling at Harvey and taking a sip of the California blush.

Two of their dinner companions shared the toast but not the wine. Risa Shaw, in her mid-eighties, had been one of the most respected dramatic actresses in Hollywood for decades. Now the Academy Award winner was thin and brittle and one side of her face drooped slightly. Two strokes, Lucille had said. And

Chester Novak, a former stuntman whose hands were deformed by crippling rheumatoid arthritis, looked as if he might not be able to lift his glass.

"It will be wonderful to see this mansion restored to its former glory," Risa said, her Boston accent as distinctive as ever.

Lucille took a platter of turkey from Elsie. "So much is riding on the success of the club," she admitted, taking a slice. "This place won't ever be another Motion Picture Country House, but at least a coupla dozen show biz retirees will be able to call it home."

"What's the Motion Picture Country House?" Gabby asked as Lucille passed the platter to her.

"A luxury retirement home. Johnny Weissmuller stayed there in the early '80s," Lucille added with a grin. "Until he started roaming the halls at all hours of the day and night, yelling like Tarzan."

Everyone smiled at the story, which was at once funny and sad.

"The buildings and grounds are often used as a backdrop for some television series," Yancy rasped, heaping his plate with salad. "Residents are sometimes employed as extras."

"Maybe they'll want to use this place once it's fixed up," Neil said hopefully. "We might even be able to get work again."

"Just be glad you're among friends." Chester fidgeted awkwardly with his fork as if he were trying to find a comfortable way to hold it. "We're all blessed to have a place to live where people care about each other. Last week a guy I used to work with died alone and in poverty over in Watts."

Harvey muttered something under his breath and adjusted his horn-rimmed glasses. Gabby wondered why Chester's news agitated the comedian so much.

"Hollywood has little use for the aging," Risa said, carefully tucking a napkin over the bosom of her old-fashioned flowered dress. "Unless someone has been a big star for many years and has never lost her audience."

Gabby knew Risa must be thinking of herself as well as the others. Lucille had confided that Risa had stopped getting roles long before her first stroke, and that Chester had been forced into retirement two years before, even though, at fifty-five he still could have been useful training new stunt people or creating new gags.

That she was in the presence of these

people who had been at the top of their professions in their prime and now were literally forgotten made Gabby angry. Society's values left a lot to be desired when it came to respect for the experience that came with age, and nowhere was that more apparent than in show business. Her dinner companions were examples of how fleeting fame and how fickle audiences could be. She hoped that no matter what came out of the club engagement she would keep her perspective.

"Maybe things are changing a little," Jayne said. "I didn't want to say anything until I was certain…but my agent heard about a new series that's being cast. The producers want a 'Jayne Hunter' type, and I plan on offering them the original! I have an appointment with the producers next week. My agent says the part's in the bag."

Yancy set down his fork and frowned, making his already homely face formidable. "Then you'll be leaving. We'll miss you."

"Leaving?" Jayne echoed. "Are you kidding? I have no intention of moving out. This is where I belong—with my friends. Besides, I like having a Beverly Hills address." Smiling, she looked down the table at Lucille. "But maybe I can move into one of the empty third-floor suites and renovate it. And I'll have the elevator fixed and I'll be able to contribute more to the expenses."

"You pay your fair share," Lucille stated.

"Well, if you let me have more space, my share will have to be more generous, as well," Jayne insisted.

Conversation continued in a more positive vein, thanks to Jayne's news, and dinner ended on a happy note. The boarders left the table one by one until only Kit, Anita and Gabby were left with their hostess.

Lucille's expression was worried as Chester slowly made his way out of the room.

"He's in such misery," she said, keeping her voice low. "His arthritis is getting worse, and his disability money barely keeps him going. If only the big swimming pool was usable, he could get the kind of exercise that would help him. And one doctor told him a special medication with gold in it might help, but so far Medicaid hasn't approved the prescription because of the expense. The club just *has* to be a success so I can help him."

Kit frowned. "Lucille, until that happens, maybe I could contribute—"

Lucille interrupted. "Aw, kiddo, that's a real

generous offer, but Chester's too proud to take money from you."

Gabby was staring at Kit, impressed and touched that he was willing to help the former stuntman whom he didn't seem to know all that well.

"What makes you think Chester will let *you* help him if he would refuse to take money from me?" Kit asked his godmother.

"Because we're more than friends in this home," Lucille explained. "We're family. And when this family gets on its feet, we're gonna get Chester his medication and hire a nurse-nutritionist and a part-time physical therapist. We're gonna get all these old bodies into working condition yet."

"That's it. Concentrate on the positive," Anita said as she rose from the table. "Now, why don't you show us those old scrapbooks you were telling us about last night?"

Lucille chuckled. "We'd bore these two kids to death. Kit, why don't you show Gabby around while Anita and I do a little reminiscing."

"How about it?" Kit asked. "We could take a short walk down to the old stables."

"Sounds great."

Twenty-four hours ago Gabby had been

wary of getting too close to Christopher Garfield, but now she felt her best interests would be served by spending a little social time with Price's son. Maybe getting to know the real man better would ease the tension that was sure to arise out of their working together so intensely for the next few weeks.

Stripping off his jacket and tie and leaving them in the large family room, Kit opened one of several sets of double doors that led onto the patio. He held out an arm, indicating she should go first. Gabby exited and took in the hilly panorama spread out before them. Her gaze skimmed the empty, cracked pool and the awningless cabanas—relics like the house, only less useful.

She looked up at Kit. "This estate must have been magnificent when it was built."

"I wasn't around then," he said dryly, "but I've seen those scrapbooks of Lucille's." His voice turned wistful. "And I remember what this place was still like when I was a kid."

Though the early-evening breeze was cool, Kit undid the top two buttons of his shirt and rolled up the sleeves. He started down the broken concrete footpath that wound around the grounds. Keeping up with him, Gabby enjoyed their companionable silence as they passed a weathered gazebo that sat on a knoll overlooking neighboring mansions. Ahead, tucked among the trees and camouflaged by the overgrown grass and scrub on the hillside, were several tiny boarded-up guest cottages and a small free-form swimming pool.

"The grounds are more extensive than I realized," Gabby said.

"But not as enormous as they once were. Lucille's late husband, Jim, bought almost thirty acres before Beverly Hills was even a gleam in some developer's eye. He was much older than Lucille and back then, this whole area was nothing but bean and barley fields, orange groves and cattle ranches. His was one of the first of the famous 'dream palaces' ever built."

"Was Lucille's husband a native Californian?"

Kit shook his head. "Nope. Born in Arizona…on horseback, to hear him tell it. When they first married, he and Lucille kept a half-dozen quarterhorses on this property. Things changed when Jim Dix movies stopped making money."

"Then he became a stuntman."

"Not exactly. He stayed behind the scenes, masterminding stunts for other stars' movies.

He had to sell all but these three acres of land, though he managed to buy a modest ranch in the San Fernando Valley. It would have killed Jim to get rid of his beloved horses. He never even had the heart to tear down the stables here. Of course, they've been in the process of falling down for decades."

"Like all the other buildings on the estate." Gabby looked at what was left of the shabby L-shaped stable and oval corral ahead—truly an eyesore. "Lucille must have had a tough time after her husband died."

"She hadn't been able to get work for years by then, and that didn't change. Unfortunately neither did Lucille." Kit shook his head but didn't really sound disapproving when he said, "She should take my father's advice and sell this place, then buy a cheaper house and live off the money. Even empty lots in Beverly Hills are worth millions. But she won't hear of it—the Silver Stallion is a shrine to her late husband."

"And the expenses have broken her."

"They've broken her bank account, but not Lucille herself. She has too much moxie to let life beat her down," he said, using one of his godmother's colorful expressions.

Gabby noticed that Kit sounded proud of

Lucille. The woman hadn't chosen the easy path, but one that had a great deal of integrity. How many people took on responsibility for others the way Lucille had? Gabby looked at Kit covertly and thought the elderly woman must have instilled at least some of her values in her godson, or he wouldn't have made the generous offer to pay for Chester's medicine.

Her mood as soft as the summer evening, she wanted to reach out and touch Kit's face, wipe away the worry and leave a smile in its place. She tried to assure him instead. "Well, now Lucille has another chance at success."

"Through Cheek to Cheek," he said. "I really hope all her dreams come true—the club being a success, her being able to turn this estate into an official not-for-profit group home as she wants. Who knows what kind of mess those people would be thrown into if something happened to Lucille."

Touched by his very real concern for the elderly woman and her retirees, Gabby said, "I'm beginning to feel personally responsible myself."

"I know what you mean. I just can't fail that lady. Talk about proud—I've been trying to 'lend' Lucille money for years, but the stubborn woman won't take a cent from me. She wants to make the money on her own."

Kit put a hand on Gabby's arm to turn her to the right where the path circled around the back of the guest cottages they'd passed. Feeling extraordinarily close to Kit, she savored the light touch.

"We all have our pride, don't we?" Gabby said. "You can't blame Lucille for wanting the sense of accomplishment that comes with a job well done."

"I guess you're right. A lot of older people must miss feeling useful."

Gabby nodded. "Even though Mom is semiretired, she always has to have her fingers on the pulse of the dance school. Lucille has that very same attitude about Cheek to Cheek."

"What about you? What's important to you?"

The personal question startled her and instantly put distance between them once again. Older people weren't the only ones who had pride. And Gabby's had been stomped on quite enough. If she told him the truth and then failed...

"It's a little chilly," she said, avoiding Kit's

eyes. "I think we should head back for the house."

Without waiting Gabby raced up the footpath, away from the man who made her question her own ability to succeed.

ANITA STOOD on the balcony overlooking the property. They'd barely gotten into the scrapbooks when Lucille had to take an important telephone call. The interruption had been a relief, although Anita would never admit that to her old friend. While she'd had fun looking back on the past, the pictures and souvenirs from her movies with Price brought back too many wrenching memories.

Below, movement caught her eye. It was Gabby striding up the walk as if the hounds of hell were after her and Kit catching up. They stopped for a second. Gabby raised her head, her back straight with what? Defiance? What in the world could her daughter be angry about? Anita wondered. Then, when Kit spoke to Gabby and put a hand on her shoulder, she seemed to relax.

Anita's heart drummed unevenly. Not only did she sense something special pass between the two, she could almost imagine she was looking at herself with Price.

How many times had she and Price visited this estate together?

Too many to remember.

Anita started to turn away, then changed her mind. She had to start remembering…and dealing with her feelings. She had to face the past, or she would forever be running away from ghosts. She had to face Price the way Gabby was facing Kit. Below, her daughter and Kit were walking—and talking—together. Whereas before Gabby had seemed closed and angry, now she was animated.

And Anita's sense of déjà vu was overpowering. She couldn't shake the feeling that something special might easily happen between the two young people….

"Hey, Anita, I'm off the phone," Lucille called. "Ready to get back to those scrapbooks."

Anita's mind was made up. "I'm coming, Lucille. And I'm more than ready," she added, ignoring the thrill of fear that shot up her spine.

CHAPTER FIVE

SWEPT AWAY BY THE MUSIC, Gabby arched as Kit lifted and turned her, then swung her effortlessly around his hardwood living room floor. Two rotations. He slowed; she touched one foot to the ground, then the other. Kit stopped suddenly and held her fast as momentum propelled her forward.

"Great," he said, his hands warm where they securely encircled her waist. "Let your head drift toward my shoulder next time. I want to make sure the audience thinks you're totally under my spell."

"No problem."

Pretending to be under Kit's spell wasn't difficult. When they danced together, reality had a way of disappearing, leaving in its place a magical dimension where anything was possible. They complemented each other so well that Gabby was beginning to think she and Kit were destined to be partners. She almost felt bereft when he released her.

They were working on the choreography of

"Mesmerizing You" from the movie *Happy-Go-Lucky*. Kit was the famous magician, she his new assistant, a rich girl who, on a lark, was pretending to be from the working class so that she could experience life first-hand. The dance would be both romantic and sensual—the magician putting his assistant under his spell only to fall under hers by the end of the number.

Kit reset the CD they'd been using for the session. "Let's try that part again without the music. Only this time, when I let you down, I want to go directly into the horizontal lift."

"We can try it," she said doubtfully.

Kit led Gabby into the movement once more, but when she put both feet down, she couldn't keep her balance as Kit then tried to shift her back into his arm. Almost falling, she grabbed his shoulders.

"Whoa." Gabby pulled herself upright, for a moment wondering if she was breathless from the near miss or from the close contact. She quickly removed her hands. "This isn't going to work."

"So I see. We'll have to add an intermediary step or two."

"How about a whole bunch? We don't have to do one lift after the other so quickly."

"But that's how I envisioned it. Intense."

His eyes were intense. So green. So alive. So *mesmerizing* that she almost let him have his way. But she thought of how well the original worked.

"Lyrical might be smoother," she said. "Let the tension build."

"Who's choreographing this number?"

A spurt of annoyance overpowered the attraction, and Gabby took a step back. "In case you forgot, we both are."

Kit's jaw clenched, but he didn't argue with that. "Do you have anything more special to add than 'a whole bunch'?" he asked.

"Not offhand, but I will…" Gabby quickly moved to the dining room table where he'd left his dance diagrams and she her large rehearsal bag. Digging into its depths, she pulled out a DVD and offered it to him. "After we watch this."

She had been amazed that they'd been able to agree on the numbers they would perform without argument, and she expected Kit to balk at this suggestion. He didn't prove her wrong.

"I don't need to watch the movie version of *Happy-Go-Lucky* to stage this number."

"I'm not suggesting we have to duplicate

the way our parents danced to it, but a little inspiration couldn't hurt."

Kit remained adamant. "I don't need choreography lessons from my father."

Realizing how sensitive he was on the subject—he obviously had some kind of competition thing going with Price—Gabby figured she'd better try to soothe his ruffled feathers or they'd never get anywhere.

"I'm not denigrating your ideas, Kit. Given enough time, I'm sure you could outdo Price," she told him, even though she didn't really believe in that sort of competition. Everyone had merits of his or her own. "But you know we don't have that luxury. I thought watching our parents' movies might help us move along a bit faster. Your all-day meeting yesterday took up valuable time, and—"

"The meeting couldn't be helped," he said tersely. "I have obligations in the real world that I can't ignore."

"I'm not criticizing. I'm just trying to point out how limited our time is. We need to have this number choreographed at least roughly before the day is up."

"True. I guess watching the film wouldn't hurt," Kit said grudgingly. "As long as we agree that we only use the original for reference, not as a bible."

"Agreed." Gabby hadn't expected convincing him would be this easy. She smiled and handed him the DVD.

Taking it from her, Kit approached the single windowless wall in the room. The heavy pale wood unit that filled the large space held the audio-visual equipment. While Kit turned on the DVD player, Gabby wandered to the nearby sliding glass doors, which he'd left open to the ocean breezes. The roar of the surf beckoned, and she stepped out onto the wooden deck that was a good twenty feet above the sand beach.

Kit's house was on stilts, one of hundreds lining the sweep of Malibu's oceanfront property, a locale more concentrated with celebrities than anywhere else in the L.A. area, if not in the world. The advantage of living here was the breathtaking view. The disadvantage was nature's price for such glory—tides and storms and landslides.

A few swimmers and surfers enjoyed the perfect summer day, Gabby noted, part of her envying them. The beach was hardly crowded, however. Kit's place was part of a celebrity compound called Malibu North

Cove. Privacy was the biggest benefit of living in an ultraexclusive enclave of beach houses guarded by gates, barrier reefs and a large security force.

"Do you ever have thrill-seekers get by the guards?" Gabby asked. She'd felt as if she were crossing the border to a foreign country when she'd checked in. She wouldn't have been surprised if the guard had asked her for a passport.

"Rarely. More often than not movie lovers haunt the shopping center on the public side of the Cove gates. They get their thrills by catching stars shopping at places like the market or the pharmacy or the bank…just as if they were 'real' people."

"The price of fame comes high, I guess."

A price Gabby wouldn't mind paying, given the opportunity. She remembered how she'd bristled the day before when Kit had asked what was important to her. That he'd been inordinately sensitive when she'd shut him out came as a pleasant surprise. When he caught up to her on the path, he'd apologized for putting his foot into his mouth and sworn he hadn't been trying to bait her. Gabby hadn't been able to resist his charming—and unnecessary—apology.

And, for a brief moment, something special had passed between them....

"Ready?"

Kit's voice snapped Gabby out of her reverie. She turned and admired his trim, fit body clad in a green T-shirt and white cotton pants. He wasn't a man who was hard to look at, that was for sure.

"Ready."

Kit began repositioning a buff-colored love seat in front of the television, where a freeze-frame of Anita and Price awaited them. She hurried to help as she had earlier when they'd cleared the living room area to make an impromptu dance floor. She wouldn't give Kit the opportunity to say she wasn't pulling her share of the weight—not that he had said anything negative until they'd gotten to the DVD issue.

She plumped up a brightly patterned pillow and threw it onto the love seat. Then she sat, kicking off her dance heels and tucking her legs under her while Kit headed for the dining room.

"Going to get the popcorn?" Gabby teased.

At the dining room table he picked up a notepad and some pencils. "Nope. Popcorn's fattening, and terrible on a dancer's figure."

"Only if it's loaded with butter," she returned, eyeing his organizational tools with distaste.

"I thought you were in a hurry to get this dance choreographed," Kit said, plopping down next to her. Using the remote control, he started the DVD.

Gabby watched their parents as if she hadn't viewed this disc over and over in the past week. She was aware of Kit scribbling notes to himself, making quick little dance diagrams. Annoyed when he stopped and hit Rewind to play a sequence over, she wanted to tell him to forget the notes, to watch for enjoyment. Afraid that he'd tell her to forget the old choreography altogether, she kept silent until they'd watched "Mesmerizing You" several times and Kit had filled page after page with scribbles.

Knowing she was taking a chance on ruining their friendly rapport, Gabby suggested, "Before we follow those copious notes you made, why don't we play the movie from the top and mimic the steps. That way we can get a real feel for the music. We can improvise as we go along," she added quickly.

She figured Kit was about to disagree when his brow furrowed. Then he seemed to change his mind. "It won't hurt to give your way a try first."

Gabby smiled as she stood and waited for him. Kit reset the DVD to the beginning of the dance sequence and threw the remote onto the love seat.

For the next few minutes they mimicked the screen characters as the magician first took "control" of his assistant without touching her—he hypnotized her with his hands. They moved through swirls, leaps and floating lifts with hardly a pause. Gabby suspected Kit knew his father's choreography better than he'd let on. He added some new twists to the original, however, and increased the intensity of movement.

Her hand in his, Gabby swirled around Kit as if in a dream. Then he partnered her from behind, his body swaying with hers. His warm breath ruffled her hair. Emotion shot through her at the delicate contact. She tried to convince herself that she was totally in character, no more, but her response was very real.

Kit took her wrist and turned her, then with his free hand extended, palm toward her face, dramatically commanded her to stop just as

Price did to Anita on-screen. He passed the hand in front of her as if issuing a command.

"Let yourself sway and fall limp," he told her, "as if I'm overpowering you."

"Make sure you catch me," she muttered breathlessly.

Gabby went limp as requested and fell backward into Kit's embrace. Then he drew closer, his face mere inches from hers. Her breath caught in her throat. He was so close, his expression so intense, that she was convinced he was feeling the same attraction she was. Was he about to kiss her?

She was holding her breath expectantly when Kit let her up, leaving Gabby unreasonably disappointed. She'd felt real attraction, while he'd merely been acting. Embarrassed, she hoped he wouldn't notice.

"Let's do the lift we were working on," he said, sliding his arm around her, lifting and turning her in a double circle. "Feet down…"

Instead of following the movement with the second lift, Kit drew her across the floor. They drifted together, her dance skirt swaying around her legs. They separated briefly while still holding hands. Then Kit snapped her inward so that she spun toward him.

"Now," he said.

He gathered her in his arms horizontally and carried her across the floor while whirling in a circle. Finally he set her on her feet. Gabby allowed her body to flow naturally out of the turn to glide backward as he still held her. He dipped forward and she arched toward him, ending the piece in the classic Hollywood kiss position.

As the last strains of music built to a climax, Gabby impulsively reached up, wrapped her arms around Kit's neck, then gradually, languorously, pulled her body up until her face met his.

The kiss was an exploration of what might be, she thought before they both became caught up in the moment. His lips searching, Kit drew her closer. She felt the power of his lithe body and forgot about the dance, about the audience they would have at a real performance. She was lost in the wonder of Kit's embrace.

Suddenly Kit seemed startled. He straightened and let her go. Gabby tottered and caught herself. Reality rushed back with a bang, making her flush. The music had ended and Price and Anita were arguing on-screen. She and Kit stared silently at each other for a moment. Before she could even guess what he was thinking, he broke the tenuous connection.

"I need to get this down in my dance diagrams." His back to her, Kit was already heading for his pad on the love seat. "Then we can try it again and refine the patterns. Perhaps we should drop the kiss, have the lights fade out and leave what happens to the audience's imagination."

Gabby stared at his straight back throughout his little speech. Hands on her hips, she shook her head. "You're incredibly uptight about this, aren't you?" He whipped around and seemed about to deny it. "It was only a kiss, for Pete's sake! And a staged one at that," she added, though the kiss had felt real enough to her.

Kit smothered a smile and glanced back down at his pad. In a professional tone he said, "All right. If your considered opinion is that the number will benefit by ending it with a kiss, we'll leave it in."

"Forget it!"

Gabby knew she sounded peevish, but she couldn't help herself. She was flushed and breathing with difficulty, but if he dared accuse her of being affected by the kiss, she'd swear the exertion had done her in.

She was thankful when Kit let this one pass.

"Let's rehearse to the music alone," he suggested. "We can break the number into segments, make changes and get the ideas on paper."

Gabby sighed. It was only fair to try it his way now.

Kit was a perfectionist when it came to getting the choreography exactly right. They went over and over the same steps and lifts, Kit making subtle changes each time they went through the routine. Gabby supposed she should be adding her ideas, but the truth was, she couldn't improve on his now that they'd come to a compromise inspired by the video. He was good; she had to give him that.

They stopped briefly for lunch, then began again. By the time the afternoon sun slanted into the room, filling it with brilliant light, Gabby was exhausted. But Kit made her go over and over each movement until her every body position was exactly right. His perfectionism reminded her of her mother's stories about Price. She was ready to drop and still they hadn't gotten all the way through the music.

"Do you think we can call a halt?" she finally asked, wanting nothing more than to take off her dance heels and prop her feet up.

Kit seemed lost in his notes, but he'd heard her. "Not yet. As you reminded me before, with my schedule, we have to make the most of every moment."

"What's so time-consuming that you can't take what amounts to a vacation from the dance studio business?" Gabby asked, thinking the question reasonable.

Kit apparently didn't.

"The corporation is a lot bigger than the dance studios," he explained tersely as if he, too, were tired. "We own a dance-wear company, a recording studio and a major club. While each division is run by a vice president, there are always problems that I need to take care of."

"Surely you can count on one of your assistants for a few days." Gabby couldn't envision Kit hiring anyone who wasn't efficient.

"I still have to check in at the office every morning and take some meetings as I did yesterday," he insisted.

"What about Price—"

"What about him?" Kit's voice rose, startling her. "My father certainly never wanted to be bothered with the corporation or with anything else that wasn't directly related to his own dancing and choreography."

His words made Gabby think Kit believed Price didn't care about him, either. His tone made her wonder if he wasn't using corporation business to outshine his father in an area that didn't interest Price. Even though she empathized, she was ready to revolt.

"Look, I think we're both tired and should call it quits for the day," she insisted.

"But I'm willing to continue until we get this dance right."

"Well, I'm not. My feet are already tender," she said, limping to the love seat. Now she was beginning to sound testy. "Don't think you can make me keep working until my feet bleed like Price did to my mother."

Kit seemed taken aback. "Why didn't you say your feet were in such bad shape? Sit down and slip off those shoes."

That was one order Gabby was willing to take. She kicked off the heels and sprawled across the love seat, her legs up on an arm- rest. "That's better," she murmured.

Before she knew what he was up to, Kit had one of her feet in his hands. He was checking it over. "A few red areas, but no blisters." He began rubbing the foot gently.

Gabby sighed, "Oh, that's heaven," and felt as if she were being mesmerized by his touch.

She closed her eyes for a few minutes and felt herself relaxing totally as Kit worked on first one foot, then the other. The toes, the ball, the arch, the heel. When she peeked up at him, she noticed a subtle difference in Kit's stance—he was tense, like a bow strung too tightly, as if massaging her foot was some-how too personal. The notion made her smile, but she bit the inside of her lip to quell the response. After all, he couldn't even handle a little stage kiss.

He must want to stick to his preconceived notions of her, and she would be smart to do likewise, Gabby decided. Remaining imper-sonal with each other would be the wisest course....

Gabby pulled her foot free and sat up. "Thanks. You made a new woman of me—almost."

She was surprised when he said, "Maybe a walk along the beach will complete the trans-formation."

Thinking that a walk along the beach sounded too romantic to be impersonal, Gabby knew she should refuse and take her leave. Getting involved with a Garfield would be a dumb move on her part.

Her eyes met Kit's, and she found herself saying, "Yeah, maybe it will."

KIT WAITED IMPATIENTLY for Gabby to change out of the dance clothes that made her look like a dancing angel. She could probably wear rags and still look like that, he decided, thinking of her grace and style. He didn't know what impulse had prompted him to suggest the walk along the beach. Probably a dumb move on his part. He didn't need a Brooks to foul up his life the way Anita had ruined his father's.

But when Gabby entered the living area wearing her turquoise sundress and carrying matching sandals, his good sense vanished. He wanted to be with her.

"All set?" he asked.

Gabby nodded as she swung past him. "I thought I'd go barefoot. The sand and water will be a finishing touch to that wonderful massage."

Dropping her sandals onto the deck, she descended the stairs before him and rushed across the sand to the ocean's edge, where a small wave was rolling in. The breeze played with her long cotton skirts so that they billowed around her bare legs. She laughed delightedly as water drowned her feet and ankles and splashed upward to leave sparkling drops on her arms.

"This feels wo-o-onderful," she said, spinning around.

Kit smiled at her enthusiasm. She was a charmer, all right. So free and open, whether with opinions or enjoyment. He managed to catch up with her while staying out of the water's reach, trying to keep his deck shoes dry.

"Tell me the bleeding feet story," he said.

She looked up at him, her pale brows lifted in surprise. "Stories, plural. Every time they made a movie, Price forced my mother to rehearse hour after hour until her feet got blisters that opened and bled. She said that one time she had to use so many bandages afterward that she couldn't get into her street shoes."

"That sounds like my father the perfectionist, all right. So what other stories did your mother tell you?"

"Let's see. She used to play practical jokes on your father, like the time she had a mouthful of gum and blew a bubble right when he was supposed to kiss her. Mom said that no matter how hard she tried, though, she never quite managed to lighten Price up. I think my favorite is the one about her costume made with feathers."

"But he's allergic to feathers."

"I know. Mom hid the costume so that he couldn't get rid of it, as he was threatening to do. Then, after they had a row over something, she wore the dress and made sure feathers flew everywhere until he had a sneezing fit." Gabby laughed. "Didn't your father ever talk about any of this?"

"Maybe...but not to me. He and I rarely shared intimacies."

"Something else we have in common."

"You certainly seem close to your mother. Weren't you close to your father, too?"

She shook her head and turned away from him toward the ocean. Because she wanted to watch the gulls as they wheeled and dived for supper? Or so he couldn't see her expression?

"My father was a very successful and busy doctor," she said, stopping.

The sun haloed her loose hair, giving it a rich golden sheen that fascinated Kit. He wanted to touch it, but the rigid set of Gabby's shoulders stayed his hand. She drew a line in the sand with her toes, but a wave soon erased it.

She turned back to face him. "He was too busy to indulge his youngest child, I guess."

"I don't see a parent's being close to his child as indulgent."

She sighed. "Those are my words, not his. We never really discussed what was wrong. And now it's too late. Dad died a few years ago."

Gabby sounded so sad and angry and cheated that Kit wanted to take her into his arms and comfort her. Instead, he shoved his hands into his pockets and concentrated on moving out of the way of a larger wave.

"At least you had your mother," he finally said.

"True. We're best friends. I have to admit that I felt a certain amount of hostility toward you when we first met because of the special relationship I have with Mom." She appeared a little guilty. "I couldn't help it. I was being protective, equating you with your father and expecting the worst."

"Please, I'm nothing like him." Kit thought her look said that he was fooling himself, but if so, she didn't put the thought into words.

"Was the closeness with your mother the reason you wanted to go into show business?"

She shrugged and began walking again. "I never analyzed it before. I just always knew what I wanted. Ever since I can remember I used to put on 'shows' for my family and people in the neighborhood."

"By yourself?"

"No. I was always able to talk other kids into helping. Friends from dance or voice classes, mostly. My older brother and two sisters were never interested in the same things I was. Maybe that's why I've never been close to them."

"If I'd been lucky enough to have a sister or brother, I would have been sure we stayed close," he said.

"If you're so sure you could do that with siblings, why not with your father?"

Because Kit didn't have an answer—at least not a valid one—he changed the subject. "Maybe we should turn around and go back. Get back to work."

"I thought we were through for the day."

"Dancing, yes. But we should decide whether or not we need props or special lighting. And we can listen to the music of the other two pieces we decided on."

"And watch the originals?" she asked.

"We could do that," he said grudgingly.

Kit wasn't thrilled about doing that, but he knew Gabby had her heart set on it. And he had to admit her suggestion hadn't been a bad idea. Their "Mesmerizing You" would be similar to their parents', yet have a stamp of individuality that satisfied him.

Feeling close to Gabby—whether from dancing or their personal revelations or both—he didn't want to see the day end.

"And afterward I don't want you driving off into the sunset," he told her. "Not when we could share it over dinner. How about it? Will you stay? We could even take a swim if you like."

"I don't have a suit."

"You don't need one," he said, quickly adding, "I have a couple of extras for guests. One is bound to fit you."

"I guess I could stay. I just hope Mom won't be disappointed."

"She'll have enough company at Lucille's."

"True. It's just that she might have been counting on me to go somewhere with her."

"You can call to make sure it's not a problem."

Kit hadn't realized how dependent Anita

was on Gabby. Then again, they were on a vacation of sorts, albeit a working one. He was a little envious of their special closeness. He and his mother got along well, but she'd always been working, often on location.

He put all negative thoughts away, however, as he and Gabby headed back toward his house and to what he told himself was the start of a professional friendship.

DELIGHTED THAT GABBY had something fun to do with someone her own age, Anita was looking forward to spending an evening with her own contemporary. She was dining out with Lucille. She was standing in the hall of the mansion, waiting for her old friend when Harvey Morris came down the stairs, smoothing the sides of a bad toupé. He was dressed in an aged brown suit with checked vest and matching bow tie.

"Are you going out with Lucille and me for dinner?" she asked the comedian.

"Uh, no. Why?"

"Well, you're all spiffed up. So where are you off to?"

He checked his watch nervously. "I'm going to find a friend, that's all."

"Can we give you a lift?"

Harvey became downright agitated as he backed away from Anita. "No, I'll get along just fine in my old junker. I don't need someone else's limo to impress anyone."

Anita thought the comment puzzling, but before she could ask him to explain, Lucille started down the stairs and Harvey ducked out the front door. Frowning, Anita stared after him.

"Something wrong?" Lucille asked, adjusting her mink stole over her gray lace cocktail dress.

Anita shrugged. "Harvey's acting awfully peculiar."

"I think something's been buggin' him, but he mostly keeps to himself. Oh, well, I suppose we'll get the scoop soon enough."

"I suppose."

"C'mon. Let's roll." Lucille tucked her hand behind Anita's arm and headed for the door. "I'm so hungry I could eat a rattler. Raw."

They were in the limo and well on their way before Anita thought to ask where they were going.

"Chasen's. I thought you'd get a kick out of going back to the place."

Anita didn't say anything. She remembered

it all too well. Price Garfield had often been her escort.

A fit of nerves made Anita's stomach clench. How ridiculous. She had to stop reacting every time something reminded her of her former partner. She'd already determined to deal with the past. But that reminder didn't make her any less nervous as, a quarter of an hour later, they entered the restaurant with its pine-paneled walls and were seated at one of the large red leather banquettes. The waiter took their drink order and left them with menus.

"Rumor has the ghosts of W. C. Fields, John Barrymore and Errol Flynn haunting this place in search of the glory of Hollywood's good old days," Lucille said. "Look. There's a live one—Debbie Reynolds. Chasen's chili is her favorite." Lucille laughed and lowered her voice. "She had buckets of the stuff shipped overseas when she was filming *The Singing Nun.*"

Anita was looking at her menu. "That must have cost her a small fortune. The chili has got to be the most expensive in the world."

"Maybe, but it's worth every penny. Matter of fact, that's what I'm gonna have." Lucille grabbed her purse and started to slide out of the booth. "You take your time figuring out what you want to order. I gotta powder my nose."

"Wait. I'll go with you."

"Nah, I don't need a chaperone. I'll be right back."

"If you're sure…"

Anita felt strange, no doubt because she was in an old haunt, alone with her memories. She wasn't aware that someone was staring at her until a single rose crossed her menu. Eyes wide, she looked up over the top of the banquette and took a deep breath. Her past had come to face her whether or not she was ready for the experience.

"Hello, Anita," said Price. "Aren't you going to invite me to join you?" When she didn't answer, he slid in beside her and casually asked, "So, how have you been?"

CHAPTER SIX

"WHAT DO YOU MEAN?" Anita asked as her shocked expression faded. She picked up the rose and set it away from her. "How was life for the past fifty-five years?"

"Has it really been that long?" Price asked innocently, knowing full well exactly how many years, months, weeks and days had passed without her. "You've kept count. That must mean you still care."

"Care? You're having delusions."

"I care about *you*." He couldn't believe how beautiful Anita was—just as he remembered her. "I always have cared and I always will."

"Hah!"

He stared into her angry aqua eyes, their sparkling color complemented by her light blue flowing dress. "We both made mistakes, Anita."

"You're the one who made the mistakes."

"What do you call your going off and leaving California and the career that was so all-fired important to you?"

"What do you call marrying the first starlet to come along?"

"That was a big boo-boo," he admitted. "Four out of my five marriages were mistakes of varying degrees."

"You really loved one of your wives, then?"

Price smiled to himself. She actually sounded a little jealous.

"A man can't pine away for one woman forever...though I seem to have done a pretty good job of it. What about you?" He leaned over the table and tried to take her hand, which she jerked out of his grasp. "Did you love your husband?"

"Of course I loved Robert, or I wouldn't have married him!" she said indignantly.

Still, something in Anita's eyes gave her away. "So you *never* thought of me?"

"Oh, I thought of you, all right—whenever I saw a promo for one of our old movies on television."

As feisty as ever. And as evasive. Price sensed she wasn't telling the entire truth. But he would get it out of her if it was the last thing he did. From the corner of his eye Price saw a waiter approach with two drinks on his tray.

Waving the waiter away, Price told her, "I thought of you all the time."

"Between marriages?"

And during. "There wouldn't have been other marriages if you hadn't been so stubborn," he told her, irritated that she was making him feel guilty that he hadn't been able to forget her. "You should have married me when I asked you."

"You mean when you demanded I do so. You were smothering me, Price. Your trying to get me to the altar every other moment was a prime example of the way you were trying to take over my life!"

Old wounds didn't always heal with time. Price felt his dander rise at the all-too-familiar accusation. "So instead of sticking in there with the man you professed to love and teaching me better, you walked out of mine!"

"Well, well, the two of you are going at it just like in the good old days," Lucille said, dropping her clutch purse onto the table. "Tsk, tsk, tsk."

Price groaned and leaned back against the red leather cushion. Couldn't Lucille have stayed lost just a little while longer?

Her expression suspicious, Anita looked from Price to her friend. "You don't seem surprised to see Price. Could it be you knew he was going to be here?"

"Now don't go blaming Lucille," Price told her. "I found out where the two of you were having dinner and decided to drop by to say hello."

That was at least partly true. Setting up this meeting had been his idea, although Lucille had been happy to go along with the plan.

"You found out how?" Anita challenged him.

"Whoa!" Lucille put out a hand and sat on Anita's other side. "Listen, you two, knock off the arguments and try to be civil to one another. Try to be friends…for your kids' sakes."

The last thing Price wanted to be was Anita's friend, but if she agreed, it would be a start. At least he would have a chance with her.

He held out his hand for a shake. "Friends?"

"I'd sooner grab hold of a viper," Anita said with a sniff.

"How about if we agree not to disagree, then?" Price said.

"We won't be seeing each other enough to worry about it."

Sighing, Price rose. His dejected air wasn't

an act. "If that's the way you want it, Anita.
I thought…well, never mind." He turned to
go.

"Wait."

Smothering a smile, he turned back to her.
"Yes?"

Small nose in the air, Anita held out her
hand. "Friends. For our children's sakes."

"Great," he said, the smile now irrepress-
ible.

"I'm sure I'll be seeing you at the opening
of Cheek to Cheek."

"You'll be seeing me, all right," Price
promised while thinking that if he had anything to say in the matter, it would be before
the opening. He strode off, his step jaunty.

Her emotions in a turmoil, Anita watched
him leave with a sense of loss. The room suddenly seemed empty without him.

"You okay, toots? Maybe you wanna go
home, huh?"

Lucille's gravelly voice snapped her back
to her reason for being there.

"Home?" Anita echoed. "Whatever for?
We're out for a night on the town. Right?"

Lucille winked. "You betcha."

The waiter returned with their drinks and
took their orders. Throughout dinner Lucille

kept her entertained with stories about Hollywood personalities. Wisely she left the topic of Price Garfield alone. After dessert she suggested they go to a night spot for a drink, but Anita begged off when she noticed that her friend was tired. Lucille had more than a decade on her.

When she left the table, Anita took the rose. And during the drive home, the conversation with Price replayed itself in her head, especially the part about Robert. She'd been truthful when she'd told Price she had loved her husband, though perhaps she hadn't loved Robert enough. For years she'd waited for Price to realize his mistake, divorce the starlet and come after her. Then she'd hardened her heart toward him and started dating other men seriously. Robert Lacroix had been easy to love. Who was to say that all relationships and the emotions that went with them should be equal in intensity?

Ironically, a few months after her marriage, Price had obtained his first divorce....

Faced with a love that had been locked away but never really put to rest, she'd wept. She had also renewed her determination to be the best wife Robert could hope for. She did love him and the four children they were blessed with. She had been happy most of the time, only getting maudlin when she was alone and foolish enough to watch one of her old movies.

Somehow, though, Robert had looked into her very heart and recognized the truth. Anita knew that was the reason he'd eventually insisted she get rid of all her Hollywood memorabilia. She'd refused and they'd never spoken of the problem again, but their relationship had changed subtly.

Her reverie was brought to an end when they arrived at the Beverly Hills mansion. Anita made her excuses and went up to the third-floor suite. The first thing that caught her eye when she entered the sitting room was the scrapbook Lucille had left on the coffee table. With a sigh of resignation she sat down and traded the rose for the scrapbook. She flipped the pages until she found what she was looking for.

The picture was black and white, but Anita remembered the exact shade of her peach dress studded with sequins. She touched a fingertip to the rose in Price's lapel. He had given it to her when he had picked her up for the premiere of *Tap Me on the Shoulder,* but she had insisted he wear the token of their love.

That was the night Price Garfield had proposed for the very first time....

Hollywood, 1953

ANITA LEFT the studio limousine for the blinding world of flashbulbs outside the Los Angeles Theater.

"Miss Brooks, this way."

Her smile extending from ear to ear, she turned toward the unfamiliar voice, posed and waved as another flash went off in her face.

"Anita, is it true that you and Price have carried your on-screen romance into your personal lives?"

"Price and I are very close friends," she told the reporter.

Right behind her, Price placed an arm around her waist and pulled her along the red carpeted path cutting across the terrazzo sidewalk. Passing through the massive columned facade, they entered the lobby decorated with glittering chandeliers, monumental mirrors and a dazzling crystal fountain.

"Gosh, this is an exciting night, isn't it?"

Anita whispered, thinking that her fondest dream was about to come true.

"More exciting than you realize now," Price said.

Perceiving his nervousness, she blamed the hoopla surrounding the premiere. Price hated publicity, and the studio was promoting *Tap Me on the Shoulder* as the motion picture of the year. No expense was to be spared for the party following the screening, and everyone who was anyone in Hollywood was there to see and be seen.

This was the most important night of her life!

She went through the next few hours flying on a cloud, greeting famous and infamous stars, posing for photos, answering reporters' questions, but Price stayed in the background whenever possible. The best moment of all came after the film screening. The house lights went up and she and Price received a standing ovation.

She waved and threw kisses while Price jammed his hands into his trouser pockets and tried to smile.

The audience then retired to the basement of the theater—a ballroom where everyone could eat and drink and dance to a combo playing music from the movie. A special projector showed *Tap Me on the Shoulder* for a second time on a small screen.

"Anita, can we slip away?" Price murmured into her ear. "I have something important to ask you—"

"Slip away? Now?"

Before Price could say what was obviously on his mind, Lucille Talbot and her rawboned husband, Jim Dix, stopped to toast them with champagne.

"Hey, how does it feel to be a star?" Lucille asked.

"Wonderful," Anita answered. Price said nothing.

She could tell he was itching to get away from the gala event and the hundreds of noisy people. The knowledge spoiled her pleasure. She wanted to bask in the spotlight that had finally fallen on them with this, their fifth picture together. She'd been waiting for fame for what seemed like her entire life. Now that she and Price had obtained it together, he wanted to retreat.

"You two make a dandy couple," Jim said, "both on the screen and off."

"Especially off," Price stated.

"So when are you going to rope this little filly before she has a chance to get away?"

Price looked around nervously. "Listen, would you two mind if I got my girl in a corner all to myself for a while?"

Lucille's brows shot up. "You wanna be alone, huh? I guess we can understand that, can't we?" She aimed a melting look at her husband.

"Why, darlin', if you're not careful, you're going to find yourself thrown over my shoulder and escorted out of here, pronto."

Lucille laughed as Price pulled Anita into a recessed area away from the crowd. His face was drawn and pale and he kept clearing his throat.

"Price, is something wrong? Are you feeling well?"

"Yes. No. I—I'm not sure."

Now Anita was starting to worry. "Maybe you should sit down."

"Kneel."

"What?"

"I suppose I should kneel if I'm going to do this right," Price choked out. He got down on one knee and took her hand. "Anita, you already know how much I love you. Will you do me the honor of marrying me?"

"Marry…?"

Happiness swelled through her, and yet Anita couldn't easily agree. She had doubts about marriage. The institution hadn't worked for her mother, and they had both suffered because of the divorce. But more than that, though she did love Price with all her heart, the thought of marrying him frightened her. He was so certain of himself—most of the time, anyway—and so in command. He would run every facet of her life if she let him.

"You look shocked," Price said as he rose to his feet. "I guess you don't want to marry me then, is that it?"

"Price, you're the only man I ever want to marry," she assured him, "but this is so sudden."

"Sudden? We've known each other for almost two years. We've been in love for at least half that time. *If* you still love me."

"Of course I love you. It's just that…" Anita tried to find the words that would explain how she felt without hurting him. "I…I'm too young."

"You're eighteen. Plenty of girls get married even younger."

"Well, I'm not plenty of girls."

"No, you're not. You're a star."

He was so stiff, so hurt, Anita couldn't keep herself from wrapping her arms around his neck.

"Price, please try to understand. You're asking me to make the biggest decision of my life, because the only kind of marriage I want is one that will last until death do us part. I love you, Price." Anita was relieved when his stance softened and he lightly encircled her waist. "I'm sure you're the man for me, but I don't feel ready to make a lifetime commitment yet."

"You do love me?" he asked, sounding more positive.

"I *adore* you. All I'm asking for is some time."

Price sighed. "All right."

Anita kissed his cheek. "You're the most understanding, most wonderful man in the whole world."

Price enveloped her in an embrace and a kiss that was bittersweet for Anita. For, no matter what she told Price, no matter how much she loved and wanted to marry him in the future, an uneasiness filled her. On the outside she was gutsy and sure of herself, but inside she was haunted by a fear that she would never be able to pull out of Price's shadow.

What if she never felt ready?

Malibu, Present Day

"SCHUYLER, you can't leave. What will I do without you?"

The distinguished-looking silver-haired man raised one eyebrow. "Honestly, Justine, a woman of your age looks foolish begging."

"Then call me a fool, but don't go."

Justine threw herself against the door. Schuyler grabbed her arm and pulled her away with such force that she bumped into a pedestal, causing a sculpture to teeter and crash to the floor. Justine gasped and threw a hand up to her neck, which was adorned with sapphires the color of her eyes.

"I don't have time for your nonsense," Schuyler growled. "Xantha is waiting for me." He exited.

"Dear, sweet Xantha," Justine spit out, shoving a mass of chestnut hair from her brow. "When I get through with her, she'll be sorry she ever heard the name Schuyler Algernon Radcliffe."

The shot of Justine's spite-filled, classically beautiful face faded to black.

Gabby clapped. "To be continued."

"Always," Kit agreed as she reached over to the counter covered with brilliant blue and white Mexican tiles and snapped off the portable television. "Or so Mother hopes. She wants to keep acting as long as she can still walk and talk."

"Lana Worth is perfect for the role of Justine Hawk. Not that I think she's anything like the character in real life," Gabby added quickly.

Kit grinned. "Not a bit."

Gabby's praise pleased Kit, making him glad that he'd thought to turn on *Hawk's Roost* while they ate. The show might be overblown, but it was entertaining and had a legion of loyal fans. And he was proud of his mother. As an adult, he had an easy camaraderie with the woman who might not have had enough time for him when he was a child but had always had enough love.

"I wish you could meet Mother, but *Hawk's Roost* is on location in Monte Carlo this month."

"Monte Carlo—how exciting! I'll bet she has a lot of interesting stories to tell about working on the show," Gabby said, popping the last piece of grilled fish into her mouth.

"More than usual. Charles Brody, the man who plays Schuyler, is a practical joker. One time they had a bedroom scene to film. Mother hates those, but they go with the territory. Anyway, she was slipping discreetly between the sheets when Charles told her to look down. He'd put a huge rubber snake in the bed. Mother hates snakes, real or otherwise, so she screamed, jumped up and gave the crew something of a private show."

"She must have been horribly embarrassed."

"She grabbed the sheet and ran off the set. It took Charles a half hour of coaxing outside her dressing room to get her to come back and film the scene." Kit laughed as he remembered his mother's version of the story, which he was sure she'd embellished with her dramatics. "And then, of course, she got even a couple of days later."

Gabby grinned. "Good for her. What did she do?"

"Charles wears a hairpiece. She got some itching powder and dusted the thing. Right in the middle of a scene he started scratching his head. The director had to cut and start the scene over. After the same thing happened a few more times, he finally figured out what was going on."

"Was he angry?"

"Mom said he laughed his hairpiece off."

Gabby snickered and finished her wine. Glad he'd asked her to stay, Kit emptied the last of the Chardonnay into both glasses. She was a comfortable woman, as happy as he to eat in the cozy kitchen rather than the more formal dining area on the other side of the counter. Setting down the bottle, he stepped out to the deck and removed the last of the food from the edge of the built-in grill where he was keeping it warm.

"Would you like more of anything?" he asked, setting the platter on the edge of the table. "Fish? Another skewer of vegetables?"

"Mmm, no, nothing."

"Not even super fudge chunk ice cream?"

Gabby scrunched up her face. "Ooh, my weakness. Maybe just a small scoop…but if you can't lift me when we rehearse tomorrow, it'll be your own fault for putting temptation in my path."

"I doubt that'll be a problem," Kit said with a grin. "I'm stronger than I look."

He started to take her dish, but she put out

a staying hand. "The least I can do is help clean up."

They worked together companionably and within minutes had the kitchen in order. Gabby found the bowls and spoons while Kit took the pint of ice cream from the freezer. He wondered if she'd relaxed enough with him to talk about something that had been bothering him all day.

"What made you decide to quit Broadway?" he asked as he scooped out the ice cream.

She looked uncomfortable and raised her stubborn chin for a moment. Then she softened and, shrugging her shoulders, said, "Time. It wasn't on my side anymore."

"That can be a problem, but you don't look your age."

"So I've been told. But I was beginning to feel it. Not physically—mentally. It's difficult to keep going when you're getting nowhere."

Kit returned the carton to the freezer and slid into his seat. He appreciated how difficult it was for Gabby to share that confidence, but he couldn't stop there.

"I find it hard to believe that no one took advantage of your talent."

"There are thousands of talented hoofers looking for work in New York."

"But you have something special."

"Thanks. So do you."

They lapsed into a comfortable silence as they ate their ice cream. Maybe they had something special when they danced together, Kit thought. He'd never felt quite the same rapport with another partner...or the same aggravation. Maybe the two went hand in hand. People were bound to get on each other's nerves if they worked closely together on a day-to-day basis. Maybe working together had destroyed the romance between Price and Anita.

Not wanting to spoil his evening thinking about the past, he asked, "Ready for that swim?"

"You have a pool hidden somewhere around here? I don't think the hot tub qualifies."

"You want a pool when we have the ocean?"

"You swim in the ocean at night?"

"Sometimes. What's the matter?" he asked, lowering his voice. "Afraid of sharks?"

"Mostly the human ones," she said with a laugh.

Kit laughed, too. "Just when you thought it was safe to go back in the water… What do you say? We have an hour or so before we need to worry about the tide."

"You don't think it'll be too cold?"

"If it is, we'll just come back inside," he said.

"You have an answer for everything."

"Usually."

"Are you usually right?"

"Always."

Gabby's brows shot up. "Hmm, no overinflated ego there."

"Confidence spells success. So what'll it be?"

"You've worn me down," she said with a dramatic sigh. "Where are those swimsuits?"

"In the spare bedroom. This way."

She followed him across the living area and into a spacious guest room. He opened the closet and pulled out one of a stack of built-in drawers.

"Take your pick."

Glancing at the assortment of colors tumbled together, she said, "You must be a great host."

"I try my best." He moved away from the

closet. "You'll find several beach robes on hangers, as well."

As Kit left the room, Gabby sorted through the suits, some of which were bikinis. She held up a top and wondered if Kit had really provided it for a guest's use or if the suit belonged to a girlfriend. The thought made her drop the garment, though she didn't know why she should be uncomfortable. Of course Kit was bound to have women in his personal life. Why should she care? She was only his dance partner, she reminded herself, and a temporary one at that.

So why was she so drawn to him? Remembering the kiss she'd instigated while rehearsing, Gabby grew warm with embarrassment all over again.

She plunged her hand into the drawer and pulled out the largest piece of cloth she could find. Luckily the turquoise one-piece suit would fit. She wasted no time in trading her rehearsal clothes for it. Only after slipping into the suit did she wonder if she shouldn't have chosen more carefully. While the front was modest except for the high-cut legs, the material plunged well below her waist in back.

Gabby was thinking about looking for

something more conservative when Kit called to her from the other room.

"Hey, aren't you ready yet?"

"Just about."

Gabby grabbed a beach robe of melon terry embroidered with tropical flowers along the collar and cuffs. It would cover her well enough for the moment, and it was dark out. She fastened the front, redid her ponytail and exited the bedroom. Already waiting for her, Kit was wearing a plush deep green robe that intensified the color of the eyes that swept her length as she approached.

A bit uncomfortable under his too-careful scrutiny, she said, "Sorry if I kept you waiting."

He grinned. "I thought you were having problems with your suit straps or something."

Gabby smiled. "I've gotten into far more complicated costumes without a dresser."

Grinning, Kit picked up a couple of beach towels from a nearby chair and, with an arm around her shoulders, swept her out onto the deck. He switched on the outside lights, which illuminated not only the stairway down to the beach but the area directly in front of the house, as well. The sand glowed a soft gold against the blue-black sky. They descended the steps and quickly crossed the short expanse of beach.

"We can leave our things here," Kit said as they got to the edge of the lit sand. "Then we can see them again when we come out of the water."

They tossed the towels and robes a few yards from where breakers curled. The foaming water whispered a rhythmic sigh as it advanced and retreated. Above, the sky was clear, revealing a brilliant moon and thousands of stars. A perfect setting for romance, Gabby thought as Kit took her hand and plunged ahead. Before she could hesitate, she was enveloped by chilly water.

"Aah!" she screeched as she tried to loosen Kit's hold on her, but he quickly pulled her in deeper.

"Oh, no, you don't. You don't back out of this now."

"But the water's cold!"

"Invigorating," Kit corrected with a laugh.

"Oh, really?" With her free hand Gabby splashed him.

"Hey!"

Kit loosened his grip long enough for her to slip free. He used both hands to splash her in return. Laughing, Gabby tried to evade the torrent of water he aimed at her, but soon she was drenched, shivering and in his arms.

"You are cold. We'll have to do something about that."

Within seconds his warmth crept through her and her protest died on her lips. His touch felt so good. The romantic setting and the companionable past few hours seemed to draw them together. Above, the moon cast its sorcerer's spell.

"You know, you're very lovely, Gabby," Kit told her seriously, his face mere inches from hers.

His nearness almost took her breath away, but she attempted to joke. "Even though I'm all wet?"

"You'd be gorgeous in any circumstances."

This time she had no ready quip with which to reply. That Kit found her desirable made her toes tingle. Sharing a kiss was only natural, she realized as his lips found hers.

The warmth of their kiss contrasted sharply with the dark coldness of the water lapping around them. Her heart pounded and she wound her arms around his neck.

Then, without warning, an incoming wave threw them off balance, and they went down together, the wave carrying them toward the beach and depositing them on the sand.

Gabby laughed self-consciously, the spell broken for a moment. "Just like in the movies!"

But the intensity of Kit's gaze mesmerized her once more. "The movies," he agreed gruffly before kissing her again.

CHAPTER SEVEN

"DO YOU REALLY THINK you can convince Kit to let you wear costumes identical to my old ones?" Anita called out from the bathroom.

"I don't see why not." Gabby replaced one of her mother's originals in a zip-up dress bag. The most effective way to convince Kit of anything, she'd found, was by demonstration. "We compromised when we picked the three numbers we're going to use. And then I got him to watch the videotapes. The choreography isn't identical to Price's, but some of the movements are similar."

Gabby didn't want to tell her mother she preferred Kit's choreography to that of his father. Price's dances were sophisticated, lighthearted and charmingly romantic, but Kit's had an intensity that she personally found far more compelling.

Anita was still fussing with her hair as she glanced out through the bathroom doorway. "So you two aren't arguing anymore?"

"I didn't say that. We've gotten into a few

squabbles, but nothing serious," Gabby assured her. "I think it must be impossible to get along with a partner one hundred percent of the time."

"How well I remember."

Gabby clenched her jaw to keep from saying anything negative about Price that might put Anita into a tizzy. She hadn't gotten over her dislike of Kit's father, especially after hearing how distant Price had been to his son. How could anyone be so cold? No wonder the man had made her mother miserable.

"You are doing some of the choreography, aren't you?" Anita asked as she entered the sitting room.

Gabby tried to be evasive as she gathered her things together for rehearsal. "I make suggestions." But she could tell by the older woman's expression that she wasn't fooling anyone.

Anita crossed her arms and narrowed her eyes. "Oh-oh, that sounds familiar."

"What do you mean?"

"Price let me make suggestions, then went right ahead and did things as he wanted. Sounds as if Kit is exactly like him."

Wondering how truly alike father and son

were, Gabby shifted uneasily. She hated comparing Kit to Price, especially after their short romantic interlude on the beach the other night. Although they'd stopped before either one had gotten carried away, they had drawn closer—yet she suspected her mother was at least partially correct.

"Kit really is better at choreography than I am," Gabby said, not knowing why she was defending him. She had to go to great lengths to change his mind about the smallest detail. "But I'm contributing my share to this act, as well."

"I know you are, darling. You usually contribute more than your share. I'm just worried that Kit will use the same tactics as his father and try to overpower you with his personality." Anita seemed to withdraw for a moment of retrospection, then shook herself free of what were obviously unpleasant thoughts. "Say, shouldn't you be going?"

"Right." Kissing her mother's cheek, Gabby picked up the dress bag and her rehearsal bag and started out the door. "See you tonight."

"Oh, I'm not sure about that."

Gabby stopped in her tracks and whirled around. "You're going out again?" She was afraid all this running around would prove to be too much for her mother's health. Gabby had arrived home earlier than Anita both Wednesday and Thursday nights. "Don't you think you should rest in between social engagements?"

Anita crossed the room and picked up the purse she'd spilled onto a chair. "What's the point of sitting around here?" she asked, checking the contents of the clutch. "There's so much I want to catch up on and we only have a couple of weeks to do it all in."

"But you shouldn't overdo—"

Anita's head snapped up and her forehead pulled into a frown. "Gabrielle Brooks Lacroix! *I* am the parent, and *you* are the child. I wish you would remember that."

"But—"

"No buts. We're both adults. How would you like it if I started telling you when you could go out and what you could do and when you had to be home?"

Though she would have liked to argue that it wasn't the same thing, Gabby immediately backed down. This was supposed to be a vacation for Anita.

"All right, Mom. I guess I'm a worrywart, but it's because I love you." She threw her mother a kiss. "You and Lucille have fun."

Gabby closed the door behind her. As she jogged down the stairs, her mind was on the costume and exactly how she was going to approach Kit about duplicating it without his getting bent out of shape. A dressmaker would have less than a week to prepare her three costumes, not impossible for a pro, since she'd brought the patterns. Still, they were cutting it close, and Kit had already suggested they rent or buy ready-made costumes from a local shop.

Considering how her mother had compared Kit to Price, Gabby was determined to get her way on this one.

As if thinking about the elder Garfield had conjured him up, Price was walking in past Elsie when Gabby got to the last set of stairs. The maid poked at her thick-lensed glasses and slowly hobbled toward the kitchen. Price looked up at her, his thin face lit in a smile.

Halfway down the last steps, Gabby stopped and challenged him. "What are you doing here?"

"I was invited."

Gabby sighed with exasperation. Now why would Lucille do such a thing when she knew how much seeing Price had frazzled Anita when they'd first arrived in California?

"You'd better not upset my mother," she warned the man.

"I have no intentions of upsetting anyone," he said in the most reasonable of tones.

Gabby took a threatening step down. "You'll have to answer to me if you do."

Price merely continued smiling. "You remind me of her, you know. Pretty, full of fire."

Taken aback by the compliment, Gabby was speechless.

Unconcerned, Price rambled on in a wistful manner. "If I had married your mother, I could have had a daughter like you."

Gabby softened to his warmth until she remembered how abominably he'd treated Kit. "If I had been your daughter, you would probably have paid no more attention to me than you did to the son you do have."

A pained expression crossed Price's features. "Some people find it difficult to reach out when they're not sure of their reception," he said. "Rejection sure can be intimidating."

Could it be that he'd changed over the years? Gabby wondered. Or that the coolness between father and son had gone two ways? Then again, perhaps Price was still the selfish, demanding man who had broken her mother's heart.

"Gabby, I thought you'd left."

Anita's shocked tone made Gabby turn to see her mother coming down the stairs, her gaze shifting beyond her daughter to settle on Price.

"Maybe I shouldn't go just yet, Mom."

Anita didn't even look her way. "But Kit will be waiting for you."

"So let him wait," Gabby said. "I can call and tell him I've been held up."

"Nonsense. There's no reason for you to stay."

Gabby looked from Anita to Price, who was watching her mother with a determined gleam in the green eyes so like his son's.

"But Mom—"

"Don't 'Mom' me. Just go," Anita insisted, an edge of aggravation clipping her words. "I'll be fine."

Reluctantly Gabby gave in, but not before searing Price Garfield with a look of warning. Unfortunately the effect was spoiled by the renewed grin he unsuccessfully tried to hide from her.

Gabby flounced past the man and out of the house in a dark mood.

"I JUST DON'T UNDERSTAND why you insist on wearing exact duplicates of your mother's costumes."

"Because they're perfect both looks-wise and dance-wise!" Gabby yelled from the guest bedroom where she was undressing. "They don't get any better! I don't understand why you keep objecting."

Though she'd brought the aged costume with demonstrating it in mind, Gabby couldn't completely restrain her hostility. Price had put her back up. And she couldn't help but wonder if her mother was correct. Maybe Kit was just like Price. Maybe hoping he wasn't was a mistake.

Carefully she drew on the sequined gown that had seen better days. Still, the fragile costume was more exquisite and finely crafted than anything she'd worn in all her years on Broadway. Furthermore, it suited her perfectly.

The pale gold sequins emphasized her strawberry-blond hair. And other than being a few inches too short for her, the garment fit like a glove. The long lines of the style accentuated the length of her waist, the slenderness of her hips—or would if she could manage the zipper. Kit would have to finish the job for her.

As she walked past the mirror to the door, she noted how the sweeping skirt merely swayed gently around her legs, held in place by the weighted hemline, the secret to the costume's success.

Gabby left the bedroom to find Kit staring out to sea through the vast expanse of living room window. Was he merely watching the waves, or was he remembering their romp in the surf two nights before? They were a step farther along in their relationship than most professional partners, she thought, even though they had worked together the day before without reference to their kisses. Still, she hadn't been able to forget them.

The reminder softened Gabby's mood as she approached Kit, who looked too good in jeans and a T-shirt. His dark hair was rumpled and his feet bare. Her heart gave a little lurch when he faced her, even while his gaze critically swept over the costume.

"I'm afraid I need assistance," she admitted. "I can't do it all the way up."

"Turn around."

He gathered the edges of the dress back

with one hand and zipped with the other. His hands were so warm…

As soon as he finished, Gabby moved away and hid her discomfort in modeling the dress. Arms held out gracefully, she turned slowly before him.

"What do you think?" she asked.

"Beautiful."

Unsure whether he meant the garment or her, she said, "That's a start. But you have to see how this skirt moves when I dance. It's quite unique. Why don't you put on your shoes and I'll get the music?"

"If you insist."

Though Kit still didn't sound convinced, he wasn't as negative as he had been when she'd told him she would model the dress. Going to the stereo while he pulled on socks and shoes, Gabby cued up "Dance with Me" from *Change Partners,* the piece they'd worked on the day before.

When he was ready, she started the music and waited self-consciously as he soloed for the first thirty seconds. He played a Broadway star who wanted his lady love to change partners not only professionally, but personally, and he was down in the dumps because he hadn't yet been able to convince her he was the right man for her.

Gabby made her entrance in character and came to an abrupt halt before him. She looked around wildly and took one step in retreat. Kit grabbed her wrist and tugged so that she made a quick spin into his arms.

The weighted hem of the skirt followed her movement and snapped around them both before gracefully swinging back into place.

"See what I mean?" she said as they continued. "The skirt is fabulous, exactly what this number needs to emphasize the drama of the dance."

Rather than answering, Kit continued in silence, but Gabby noted that his focus was on the skirt. Every time they made a sharp turn, the weights forced the material to follow through and accentuate the movement.

"Hmm," Kit muttered. "Almost like a prop."

Gabby smiled. She knew she had him. "So?" she prompted with a straight face.

"You do have a point about the skirt on this particular costume...." His thoughtful gaze met her hopeful one, and he sighed in resignation. "And I guess if we have this one made up, it wouldn't hurt to go along with reproducing the other two if that will make you happy."

"Oh, it will," she assured him, wondering exactly how much her happiness meant to him.

"Then let me see if I can call in a favor from Elaine Carlisle. She used to costume my nightclub act, and my recommendation landed her her first costume drama a few years back."

Kit placed the call. Gabby was gratified when Elaine apparently agreed to help without any arm-twisting. Kit set up an appointment with her for later that afternoon.

Kit wasn't like Price after all, Gabby decided. Price would never have done a complete turnaround from his original position—at least not so agreeably.

When Kit got off the phone, he said, "One thing I insist on, though. I want the dress for the last number, "Tango Olé," to be black instead of white or pastel. Black will heighten the drama."

Gabby knew it was her turn to give in gracefully. "Black will be absolutely perfect," she said, smiling at him. She was pleased when he couldn't help but grin back at her.

AFTER SEVERAL DAYS of intensive work, Gabby was delighted by Kit's suggestion that they spend a few hours in pursuit of recreation before getting down to business on Sunday. She was to dress casually and have a light breakfast, and he would pick her up at ten.

Therefore, when she awoke to a bright, sunny morning, Gabby slipped into a deep orange sundress, French-braided her hair and spent more time than she normally would on her makeup. On her way to the kitchen she passed a ladder set up in the hallway near a wall whose plaster was crumbling. A large hole gaped near the ceiling. Obviously someone was preparing to fix the damage.

Gabby entered the kitchen to find Elsie carving up a fresh pineapple. The maid looked up from her work and peered through her thick lenses.

"In the mood for an omelet?" Elsie asked. "One of my specialties."

"Mmm, I'd love one, but my orders were to keep breakfast light."

"Croissant and coffee?"

"And maybe some of that fresh fruit."

Gabby picked up a plate to help herself, but Elsie took it from her with a cluck.

"Tsk, tsk, this is still *my* kitchen." She arranged fresh pineapple, orange wedges, strawberries and a croissant on the plate. "Here you go. Coffee's on the sideboard."

"Thanks, Elsie."

Realizing she had to be more sensitive about Elsie's feelings concerning her duties, Gabby entered the dining room. She filled her cup and was setting it down on the table when she heard a commotion in the hallway.

"I can do this myself," Chester was saying as he clumped over to the ladder, which was just within Gabby's view. He set a pan down on the attached shelf. "So stop breathing down my neck and giving me doggone instructions I didn't ask for."

Neil followed close behind and spoke over the protesting creak of the old wood as Chester rose with painful slowness. "Just because you know how to climb a ladder doesn't mean you have the first idea of how to do a good job plastering."

"You wouldn't even touch the ladder," Chester grumbled in return. "Might wrinkle your fancy duds."

Neil straightened the open throat of his short-sleeved shirt and sneered at the other man's jeans and plaid shirt.

"You could take a tip from me in the clothing department, too."

"In addition to your advice about plastering?" Chester muttered. "Sidewalk supervisors. Know-it-alls. Bah!"

Trying not to laugh, Gabby almost choked on the piece of croissant she was in the midst of swallowing. Contrary to what she'd been led to believe, not everyone in the house got along all that well.

"At least I know how to plaster correctly… if theoretically." Neil was waving a finger at the hole. "If you don't get rid of every last loose particle, the job won't be right."

"If I remove every last goldurned loose particle, there won't be no wall!" A noisy clatter emphasized Chester's outburst. "Damn it all, now look what you made me do! I dropped the trowel."

"I didn't do anything. It's your hands. You shouldn't be messing with something that's so physical in the first place, you know."

"My hands may be a little stiff, but I'm not ready for a coffin yet. Now don't give me no more lip. Just give me the trowel!"

"It's full of plaster." Neil's tone implied that Chester had lost his mind. "Even the handle is smeared with the stuff."

"Course it is—"

Gabby was about to leave the table and retrieve the tool for Chester herself when, from down the corridor, she heard footsteps and Lucille's strident voice.

"Chester, what in tarnation do you think you're doin' up on that ladder?"

The former stuntman let out a sound of exasperation. "I'm trying to make one of the repairs needed around here!"

"You know you shouldn't be climbing so much as a step stool. Get down this minute!"

"Fine!" Chester began clumping downward. "A man tries to feel useful and all he gets is instructions and flak just because he can't do what he used to!" The ladder screeched as if emphasizing his anger. "I got better things to do with my day, anyway." His shoulder knocked the wood as he stormed past it. "Let Neil finish the job."

"Sorry, Lucille," the other man said, already backing away from the teetering ladder, "these are my good clothes. I might get them dirty. I was planning to go down to the Ocean Club. Maybe I can find a wealthy woman to take me out for a good lunch."

He quickly strode away, leaving Lucille muttering after him. "Only thing worse than an old mule is an old peacock! Now look at this mess. It's worse than it was in the first place."

"Let me," Gabby said, taking a last sip of her coffee before joining Lucille in the hall. "I've had a little experience with plaster."

Eyeing the hole, which seemed even bigger than it had a few minutes ago, she only hoped the job wouldn't take too long.

"Toots, you're a peach. Well, that fixes this problem, but we gotta take care of plenty more," Lucille muttered to herself as she left Gabby alone in the hall. "Or someone does. I can't be personally responsible for everything anymore. The club's gotta succeed so we can hire the help we need around here."

Sighing, Gabby stared up at the gaping hole, a symbol of the shambles these people's lives were in. A Band-Aid couldn't fix a wound that needed major surgery, but she guessed fixing the hole would be a start. Picking up the trowel, she scraped free the plaster that was already drying and tried not to think about what would happen to the elderly people who lived in the mansion if the club didn't make it.

KIT ARRIVED exactly at ten and entered the house without knocking. "Hello! Anyone around?" he called.

"Over here. In the hall."

He followed Gabby's voice, unprepared for the sight that greeted him. Wearing a sundress, she was on a ladder putting the finishing touches to a neatly executed plaster patch.

"Decided to go into a new line of work, have you?" he asked, staring at her long, lovely legs.

"Just helping out a friend," Gabby was saying. "There. So much for that job." She set down the trowel and descended the ladder, skipping the last rung. "I can clean up this mess later on. Just give me a minute to wash my hands and I'll be ready to go."

"You'll need to wash more than your hands." Kit grinned at her while wiping a blotch of plaster off her cheek, then gave her a good once-over. "You're a mess," he said, removing another hardening blob from her bare shoulder. "And you sort of sprinkled your hair with the stuff."

Gabby sighed. "All right. Give me five minutes. I can cut the parts that are plastered if I need to."

She trudged toward the stairway, Kit close behind.

"Don't ruin your beautiful hair on my account," he told her. "I can be patient…when what I'm waiting for is worthwhile."

Gabby flashed him a smile that Kit would happily wait hours for. She took the stairs two at a time while he stared after her. Images of Gabby in his arms made him smile, too. Though they would have but an afternoon stolen from their heavy rehearsal schedule, he would savor every minute with her.

Leaving the staircase, Kit searched the downstairs rooms looking for Lucille. She would be miffed if he didn't at least make an effort to say hello. But she wasn't inside. He crossed the living room and wandered out onto the patio, his godmother's favorite resting place. Rather than Lucille, however, Kit found Jayne relaxing in a lounge chair in the shade, poring over a script.

"Good morning," he called out.

Jayne removed the half-glasses she was wearing, as if she were embarrassed at being caught in them. "I don't really need these," she said, confirming his suspicion.

"Neither does my mother, but she uses reading glasses, anyway. Don't worry," he whispered with a wink. "Your secret is safe with me."

Jayne sighed. "I'm trying to memorize lines for my audition so I won't have to use glasses."

"Audition? When you made your announcement, I had the feeling all you had to do was show up at the producer's office and the part was yours."

"You're not the only one. Unfortunately I sometimes forget my agent tends to be a bit overenthusiastic and optimistic."

"Sounds like a morale booster, though."

Jayne nodded. "And better than an agent who doesn't know that you exist. A friend of mine is saddled with a woman who wouldn't even say hello at a party unless Rose walked right up to her and reminded her she's a client."

"Time to get a new agent."

"Ugh. I've tried to tell her that for years." The blonde shook her head. "She's stuck in a rut."

"Some people like ruts. They're familiar, therefore safe."

"Even if they're bad for you," she agreed.

"What's bad for you?" Gabby asked as she appeared in the doorway, looking fresh and plaster-free, though she'd been gone an amazingly short time.

"Agents," Kit said, pleased that she'd been so quick.

"*Some* agents," Jayne amended. "Off to another hard day of rehearsal?"

"After Kit shows me some of the real Hollywood," Gabby stated. "A reward for being so dedicated."

Jayne waved them off. "Have fun, you two."

"Will do."

Kit encircled Gabby's waist and headed her back through the house toward the front door. The ladder, which was still standing in the hallway, caught his eye as they exited.

"What in the world were you doing plastering, anyway?" he asked.

"Taking over where Chester left off after Neil got on his nerves, Lucille got on his case and his hands refused to cooperate," Gabby told Kit as he helped her into his car. "Chester wants to feel useful in the worst way, but Lucille was right about his having no business on that ladder. Poor man. He could hardly get up and down the thing."

Kit thought about that and, driving away from the Silver Stallion, said, "I wonder if that medication Lucille was talking about would really improve life for Chester."

"It'll be some time before we find out."

"Unless…"

"Unless?" Gabby echoed.

"Unless I get Lucille to give me the name of Chester's doctor. Maybe I could make arrangements to buy a supply of the stuff for him."

"And then figure out a way to make Chester take it."

"Guilt?"

"That might work."

Kit felt Gabby's eyes on him. "What?"

"I was just thinking you're a pretty nice man, Christopher Garfield."

Kit rode high on Gabby's approval as he drove out of Beverly Hills and headed for Hollywood Boulevard. He wanted to show her the movie capital's origins, some of which were still viable—and visible among the fast-food places, tattoo parlors and T-shirt shops.

"It's a relief to have a few hours of breathing space," Gabby said. "What about rehearsing at Cheek to Cheek?"

"Tomorrow," Kit said. "I've been assured we can have the stage all afternoon and evening."

"Do you think four days will be enough time to work the bugs out of the routine?" she asked.

Thinking of the sweeping stage and staircase area he couldn't simulate at his beach house, Kit said, "It'll have to do. Let's keep our fingers crossed that we don't run into problems with the light grid or sound system."

He'd already met with the lighting and sound people. Technical rehearsal for the entire show would be held on Wednesday night and dress was scheduled for Thursday. As Kit began looking for a parking spot, he wondered if they weren't crazy for taking any time off whatsoever, even for a few hours. But that was ridiculous. He was developing performance jitters. What was he worried about? This was a limited engagement. A few performances and he would be back to business as usual.

For some reason the thought wasn't as appealing as it should be.

After he parked the car, he and Gabby walked hand in hand, stopping occasionally along the Walk of Fame—a pink-and-charcoal terrazzo sidewalk set with brass stars commemorating legends of the film, radio, television and recording industries. They made a quick tour of the Hollywood Museum with its exhibitions of rare costumes, props, set pieces and posters.

Things Kit had been familiar with his entire life sparkled more brightly as he saw them through Gabby's starstruck eyes. She was filled with such enthusiasm, he found it impossible to resist her positive energy. Inevitably they found themselves in front of Mann's Chinese Theater.

"I've always wanted to do this," Gabby said as she placed her feet on top of Judy Garland's smaller prints.

"Try on other people's footprints? Or have a set of your own made?"

Stepping into another set, she laughed. "C'mon, I'm not exactly a movie star, now am I?"

But he heard a wistful note when she made the denial. "You wouldn't turn down a Hollywood career, I take it."

"If one was offered to me? I wouldn't care if I was working in Hollywood instead of on Broadway, as long as I was able to perform." Then, as if having admitted something she hadn't meant to, Gabby pulled a face. "Why would *anyone* turn it down?"

"I can think of several good reasons."

"You're a strange one," she said, staring at him in her forthright manner. "Both your parents spent their entire lives in show business and you won't even fess up to being interested."

"Maybe that's because there's nothing to fess up," Kit argued.

"And maybe you never appeared in nightclubs using an alias."

Pricked by the reminder, but not wanting to delve further into his youthful misguided venture, Kit said, "I'm in the mood for brunch. Why don't we think about finding a restaurant?"

"Why don't we think about changing the subject, you mean?"

"Are you going to pick on me just because I happen to be hungry?"

"I'm picking on you because you happen to be a liar." Gabby tapped him square in the chest with an accusing finger. "You want our act to succeed just as much as I do, buddy, and not only for Lucille's sake. Don't you think it's time you admitted how much this opportunity means to you personally?"

It was time to do no such thing, Kit thought stubbornly. While he might enjoy performing, relating to an audience, having a beautiful partner who seemed to have been made to dance with him, he was using the name Garfield, performing to Price's old numbers. If they were a success, the audience would be cheering his father, not the son. How could there not be comparisons?

"Since you're not arguing with me, I must have hit a sore spot, huh?" Gabby challenged him. "Why don't you admit that you're attracted to show business?"

"Maybe because I'm not."

"And maybe you're lying. Maybe you're protecting yourself in case you couldn't make it following your heart's desire."

Kit shook his head. She was incorrigible. "With a name like Garfield," he said, "I'd probably be an overnight success."

"Maybe *that's* what you're afraid of...." To Kit's surprise, Gabby dropped the subject and skirted the forecourt of the theater, looking at one concrete slab after another. "So where do I find our parents' footprints?"

Kit pointed. "Dad's are right over there."

Gabby crossed to the slab in question, then frowned as she checked the concrete rectangles on every side of Price Garfield's. "But where are Mom's?"

"Your mother's footprints are here some-where?" If so, Kit had never noticed.

Gabby gave him an annoyed look. "Of course. She and your father were a team, re-member? They did them together after *Tap Me on the Shoulder* was such a big hit."

Kit shifted uncomfortably as the truth of what might have happened dawned on him. He hurriedly looked around, checking the slabs she didn't, hoping against hope he was wrong. But several minutes later, when they met in the middle of the forecourt, he sighed. "I'm afraid your mother's slab was removed, Gabby."

"What?"

The single word, uttered so softly, pierced his heart, but she had to know the truth. "The fate allotted to lesser legends to make room for new ones," he explained as kindly as he could. "There's limited space out here. I've heard the basement of the Chinese is literally loaded with concrete slabs of long-forgotten stars."

She stared down at his father's slab, then at him. Though her expression remained closed, her eyes filled with tears. Kit moved to touch her, to take her in his arms.

"Gabby, I'm sorry—"

"Forget it," she said softly, brushing by him before he could comfort her. "What does an old slab of concrete prove, anyway? Let's go get brunch."

CHAPTER EIGHT

THANK GOODNESS Gabby would be at the club all day and night rehearsing with Kit, Anita thought as Price ordered coffee and dessert at Hollywood Café Legends Tuesday evening. She hated sneaking around behind her own daughter's back, but after Gabby's reaction to Price's presence on Sunday, she dared not confide in the younger woman about her frustrating—and definitely ongoing—relationship with Price Garfield.

Anita stared up at the charcoal drawing of Jean Harlow hanging on the wall directly across from their table. A famous restaurant located near Paramount Studios, Hollywood Café Legends featured dozens of similar movie star portraits. She wondered if a likeness of Price was around here somewhere. Being his usual modest self, her companion wasn't likely to mention it.

Anita sighed. She knew the man inside out and couldn't forget him for a minute. She also couldn't find it in her heart to forgive him. So what was she to do?

"Marry me," Price said, as if reading her thoughts.

"What?" Shocked out of her reverie, Anita stared at the face that was as familiar to her as her own.

"Just testing." Avoiding her eyes, Price gave a nervous little laugh. "I don't want to get married again. I've proved I'm no good at it. I'm jinxed, actually." He smiled crookedly. "Things would have been different if you had married me instead of running away all those years ago."

"You chased me away."

"Now don't start telling me how overbearing I was."

"Fine. I won't."

"But you're thinking about it," he insisted correctly. "I wouldn't have been that way if I could have trusted your love."

"I told you how I felt many times."

"Whenever you weren't being escorted around town by other men."

Gritting her teeth at the familiar accusation—not to mention his jealous tone—Anita couldn't believe Price was still disgruntled over the outings the studio had set up for her so many decades ago.

"Those weren't real dates," she told him, perhaps for the hundredth time.

"Next you'll be telling me your escorts weren't real men."

"They weren't. They were actors. Mostly pretty, manufactured versions of the real thing. And what we were doing was generating valuable publicity."

"A wedding between you and me would have gotten us more publicity than you ever dreamed of."

"Don't start."

"All right," he grumbled. "It's both our faults for letting the studio interfere with our personal lives."

Their bickering was interrupted by the arrival of cake and coffee. Anita stared at the fruit-and-whipped-cream confection in front of her, thinking she'd soon have to go on a diet if Price kept taking her out to eat. She didn't have the high metabolism that seemed to have kept him thin all his life. And since she'd practically turned the dance school over to Gabby, her decrease in exercise kept her on her toes in a less satisfying way—counting calories.

Price took a bite of his dessert, then a sip of coffee. "Publicity. Sol Lowenstein always wanted control."

Anita dug at her cake in disgust. "You're going to harp about RPO? Sol is dead now, for goodness' sake."

And after the authoritative head of RPO Studios had passed away, the organization had been absorbed by one of the larger production companies.

"You fell right into Sol's hands."

Obviously Price *was* going to beat the subject into the ground. "And you didn't?"

Price glared at Anita, but she glared right back.

A big part of their problem had been the studio's jerking them around, telling them how to behave, and with whom. Sol Lowenstein had been afraid their romance might be viewed as illicit, since Anita had been so young and had had a reputation to uphold. He'd maintained that, if they wanted to continue seeing each other, there wouldn't be any problems from the studio—not to mention the press or the public—if they each agreed to go out with other people selected by the publicity department.

Price had not only despised each and every

one of those events, he'd made sure Anita had come to hate them, as well. She had always been certain they would fight afterward, sometimes on the set.

Made petulant by the memory, Anita said, "I seem to remember you dating several starlets—one of whom you eventually married."

"Now don't *you* start," Price said, the squabbling obviously getting too close for *his* comfort. Dropping his fork, he glanced around. "Where's the waiter? I want the check." He turned back to Anita. "Are you ready to leave?"

"Whenever you are."

At least they agreed on something, she thought.

He settled the bill and they left the restaurant, careful not to touch each other as they walked to the car, which they'd parked nearby on the street. Then their conversation took a friendly if impersonal turn as they rode along Hollywood's Sunset Boulevard. Remembering the good old days, Anita was put off by the sight of a flashily dressed hooker waving at the passing cars.

"I can't believe it," she said. "Living in New York is enough to make anyone aware of the seamier side of life but, for some reason,

I always kept the idealized vision I had of Hollywood."

"And this neighborhood is much better than it was ten years ago," Price told her.

Anita shook her head sadly. "Remember the ballrooms where we used to dance?" Before they'd become so famous that Price had begun avoiding public outings, she added silently, trying to sidestep another argument.

"There are still places where you can dance. Want to try one?"

Anita's heart tripped at the thought of being held in Price's arms, moving to music with him, making their own special magic. It had been so many years….

"Dance?" she whispered. "With you?"

Price sounded a little indignant when he assured her, "I haven't forgotten how."

Anita smiled. "Neither have I. So what are we waiting for?"

The Castle, a popular club, hardly resembled the elegant establishments of the past any more than its loud pounding music could be compared with the bygone era's tunes, but Anita didn't mind. And when Price presented an identification card of some sort, the young people who ran the club treated the couple with respect, even waiving the entrance fees.

Because of his fame? Anita wasn't certain. She noticed that no one paid them any mind when they joined the crowd thronging the gymnasium-like dance floor. All eyes were on the celebrities of the day. She thought a few faces looked vaguely familiar, but she couldn't identify them. The thought made her feel old…but dancing always brought back her youth.

With artificially generated fog creeping along their legs and strobe lights making their every movement look like some strange machination, she and her partner danced, their manner conservative compared to the young bodies, mostly clad in black, wildly gyrating around them. It wasn't exactly what Anita had been hoping for—Price didn't take her fully in his arms once—but she was having more fun than she'd had in years.

"Why do these kids want to look so somber?" she yelled in Price's ear, struggling to be heard above the music.

Growing tired after nearly an hour, she was also thinking about leaving. She'd worked off not only the whipped cream dessert but her irritation with her escort.

"Black is just the style." Price leaned closer to shout at Anita. "You know how it is. Remember those silly little hats you used to wear? And my double-breasted suits?"

Price moved closer again, his breath feathering Anita's ear and making goose bumps rise on her neck. "Have you had enough yet? I'm getting a little tired."

Thinking she'd give anything to be alone with him in some romantic setting, Anita nodded vigorously. Price took her hand and moved off the floor. In the lobby they picked up her wrap and headed for the door, making their way past a human river of newly arriving guests.

A young man in a black leather jacket bumped into Price, then gazed at him in surprise. "Pardon me, Gramps." His eyes swept over Anita, then returned to Price. "Isn't it a little late for you old folks to be out?"

How dare the kid speak to a legend that way! Anita narrowed her eyes, about to tell the young idiot to stuff it, only to have Price pull her close.

"Don't pay any attention to that punk," he whispered, gently guiding her away.

At least the casually dressed doorman was respectful as he sent a parking attendant after the Mercedes. "It'll only be a minute, Mr. Garfield. Have a good night."

Price nodded. "A good night to you, too."
He smiled at Anita after they'd moved to the
curb. "That young man isn't being polite because he's a fan of our movies, you know. The
Garfield Corporation owns the Castle."

"It does?"

"I showed them my corporate ID when we
came in. That's why we didn't have to pay."

"Oh, I wondered."

And in her secret heart of hearts, Anita
couldn't help being disappointed, having
thought Price, at least, would still be recognized by the younger generation. How
fleeting fame could be. Not that Price cared,
having always wanted anonymity.

While they waited for the attendant to
deliver the car, two young women strolled
by. The taller of the pair, a redhead wearing
high-heeled boots and a short skirt, turned
her head to stare.

"It *is* them," she cried.

"It is not," her companion argued. "They
can't both still be alive."

"Yes, they can and I'll prove it." The
redhead stopped and approached the older
couple. "Excuse me," she called to Anita,
then smiled hesitantly. "Um, aren't you Anita
Brooks and Price Garfield?"

Amazed, Anita simply nodded. Price remained silent at her side. The redhead came closer to peer at them, her friend following close behind.

"I knew it, I knew it! How awesome! I spotted you at the Castle. I watch all your old movies every year when they show them at New Year's."

"Really?" said Anita. She had never before imagined they might have fans this young.

"*White Tie and Tails* is my absolute favorite."

"Mine, too," Anita admitted.

The girl grinned and rummaged in her shoulder bag. "Can I have your autographs? Please? Nobody else has ever danced like you two."

"Certainly." Anita was happy to comply. Actually, if she let herself, she'd be teary-eyed. She signed the young lady's matchbook and handed it to Price. "Here." If he so much as objected, she'd kick him.

Price added his signature.

"Thanks so much," the redhead enthused, stuffing the matchbook into a zippered compartment of her purse. "Wow, if I'd recognized you sooner, Mr. Garfield, I would have asked you for a dance."

"And I would have been flattered," Price said, not sounding the least bit sarcastic.

The car arrived and he smiled at both young women before opening the door for Anita. Then he got inside and turned the car onto Vine Street.

"You really were flattered?" Anita asked before they'd gone a block. "You used to hate it when strangers wanted to dance with you."

"A man my age would be stupid not to be grateful for any woman's attention."

Anita snorted. "Woman? That redhead was a girl, barely twenty-one." She couldn't help teasing him. "I noticed the way you ogled her legs."

Price laughed. "Do I detect a bit of jealousy? You can relax. You're the only woman who holds the key to my heart. That hasn't changed in more than half a century."

Then why hadn't he had enough patience to wait until she was ready to marry him? Anita wondered for the zillionth time. Not willing to ask him, she gazed out the window at the passing lights.

On the way back to Beverly Hills Price asked her about Robert, how they'd met and what he'd been like. Uncomfortable, she made short work of the explanation and soon steered the conversation away from the man who had always felt second best when compared with Price. Instead, she told him about her children.

"Jeanne is my oldest—she and her husband are both professors at New York University. Natalie lives in New Hampshire and my son in Boston. Max is a doctor, like his father. Between them they have six children." Anita chuckled. "I'm a grandmother several times over."

"Lucky you." Price sounded envious. "I wish Kit would get married and have some children. Not that he would encourage them to hang around with their grandfather."

"Is there a problem between you two?"

"We're not exactly close."

"Why not?" Unreasonably Anita wanted to know everything about Price, even though she'd been unwilling to divulge all about her own life.

"I'm not sure. Kit resented the problems Lana and I had, our divorce. She got custody…. I just haven't seen much of my son over the years."

"You could have made an effort to see him and hash things out."

Price sighed. "I did try to talk to him when

he was younger, but he seemed to withdraw even more. And he was doubly resentful when I married again. I figured maybe he just didn't like me and never would."

"Nonsense. You gave up too easily." Anita was concerned about the real depth of sadness she heard in Price's voice. Price always seemed to give up on people too easily—including her. "Did you feel guilty about the divorce from Lana? Is that why you let Kit go without raising a fuss?"

He looked pained. "Of course I felt guilty. Who wouldn't, failing at marriage over and over?" He glanced at Anita. "Not that I ever ran around on my wives or anything like that."

"I didn't think you were the type who would."

"There always seemed to be outside conflicts, lack of communication, something. And I believe my first two wives married me purely for career advancement."

Anita nodded and swallowed. "Betty Masters."

Even now it was hard to think about the starlet, one of many whom Sol had set up with Price for publicity purposes. Anita had cried herself to sleep every night for a year after Price eloped with Betty.

"I suppose my disenchantment with marriage made it easier for me to slough off my relationship with Kit. After enough failure you kind of back away."

"But a child is different from a spouse," Anita insisted. "And you can still talk to Kit. It's never too late."

"That's what Lucille keeps telling me." Price turned the car onto a wide street with tall palm trees lining the grassy center section…and turned the conversation back in her direction. "I'm happy to see you have a good relationship with Gabrielle. You seem to be the best of friends."

Anita realized he was done discussing his son. "I'm beginning to wonder if Gabby and I are *too* close."

"How could any parent and child be too close?" he asked, sounding envious.

"I think she believes she has to take care of me." Gabby had certainly been riding herd on Anita since she'd started seeing Price. "Maybe that's why she's reluctant to marry. She was engaged two times in New York, you know, then decided to break up with the men."

"Hmm. And perhaps Kit is wary of marriage because he witnessed the mess Lana and I made of our relationship." He glanced at his watch. "But then again, we're only making suppositions. And time is flying. Let's talk about us. Instead of taking you back to Lucille's, why don't we stop by my place? It's closer and you haven't been there yet."

Anita had seen pictures of his mansion through the years, though she wasn't about to tell him so. That would be admitting her interest even when she'd been married to another man, and she would never be disloyal to Robert.

She glanced at her own watch, amazed to see it was almost 2:00 a.m. "It's late," she said.

"Not that late."

Price laid an arm across the back of the seat. "When two people love each other—"

"I never said I loved you!"

"Not in a long time." Price smiled. "But a man can tell when his girl is crazy about him."

Her pulse pounding wildly, Anita drew herself up with dignity. "Price Garfield, be the gentleman I know you are!"

But even in her indignation Anita realized

that the very thought of being held in Price's arms had stirred something inside her that she'd long thought dead. But she wouldn't—*couldn't*—let him know how much he still affected her. Not until she felt vindicated, and she didn't even know what that would entail.

"You should take advantage of the time you have," Price was saying in his most coaxing manner.

Anita shot him an annoyed look. "You're the only one trying to take advantage."

"Anita, you're impossible."

Not impossible, she thought. But she wasn't a pushover, either. Fifty-five years of estrangement could hardly be breached in a week or two.

ONLY HALF ASLEEP when her mother sneaked into the suite, Gabby raised her head from the pillow she'd plopped against the arm of the couch.

"Mom. Finally." She turned and stretched to switch the table lamp from low to bright.

Anita seemed confused and blinked in the glare. "What's the matter?"

"Nothing's the matter with me. But where have you been until—" Gabby glanced at her watch and was genuinely shocked to note the time "—two-forty-three in the morning? I've been worried."

She'd waited and waited, and had finally slipped a robe over her nightgown, then bedded herself down in the sitting room so that she could intercept her mother. She hadn't thought the hour would be this late, though.

Anita looked annoyed. "I told you I have the right to come and go as I please."

"With Price Garfield," Gabby said accusingly, sitting upright on the couch and swinging her legs to the floor. Her mother's expression told her she was dead right. "Why do you insist on seeing that jerk?"

Instead of jumping down her daughter's throat as Gabby had expected, Anita seemed to agree. "I don't know." The older woman sighed and slumped down onto a chair. "He's such an old goat—a lecherous old goat."

Gabby scowled. "He made a pass at you?"

"Not exactly a pass." Anita slipped off the satiny wrap that matched her elegant teal-colored cocktail dress and laid it nearby. "More like a suggestion."

Gabby's outrage grew. "That creep! How dare he! You have to stay away from him, Mom."

"I should." But Anita sounded far from convinced. She took off her shoes, pumps with low, narrow heels. "Whew, my feet hurt. Dancing can be painful. We went to the Castle," she explained.

"The club?" What in the world were two elderly people doing at a place like that? Gabby leaned forward to plead with her mother. "Please stay away from Price, Mom. He's a bad influence in more ways than one. If he wants to give himself a heart attack, let him, but don't risk your own health."

Now it was Anita's turn to frown. "Who says I'm risking my health?"

Gabby ran her fingers through her tousled hair. "It's almost 3:00 a.m. and…and you've been out at a club."

"So?" Anita shrugged. "I'll get up later tomorrow. And I was never in danger of dancing myself into a stupor."

Gabby was ready to grasp at anything she could think of to discourage her mother's interest. "But you admit Price isn't exactly a gentleman. He'll get you all upset like he did when we first arrived."

"Not upset enough to have a heart attack."

Annoyed her mother wouldn't make any

promises, Gabby complained, "Why won't you listen?"

Anita shook her head. "You're too protective of me, darling. You should pay more attention to your own life. I believe what I told Price is correct—you definitely are too dependent on our relationship."

Too dependent? Where had that come from? Now Gabby was hurt as well as angry.

"You discussed our private relationship with Price Garfield?"

"Only a bit. We also talked about Kit."

"Really?" Gabby said sarcastically. "I'm amazed Price was the least bit interested. He's never paid any attention to his son."

"Is that what Kit told you? Communication goes two ways, you know. It sounds like Kit can be as stubborn as his father. And, believe me, Price isn't particularly happy about the situation."

Gabby rose from the couch and folded her arms. "Well, I don't care about Price Garfield. And I don't want to be talked about behind my back. I thought you and I were close and we both liked it that way," she said, still smarting from her mother's earlier remark.

"We are close, dear," Anita said gently, "but

I don't think we should be so close that our relationship is unhealthy."

"Unhealthy?" Gabby swallowed the lump in her throat. "Am I supposed to be completely alone? You were the only parent I ever had to talk to. Dad didn't care about my goals in life. He ignored me."

Her mother frowned. "Your father loved you, Gabby. You have nothing to complain about in that respect."

"I do have a right to complain." Feelings Gabby had been holding in for years came pouring out. "Dad was always at his office or the hospital. He never had time for me, never made my dance recitals. He didn't even see me graduate from high school or college."

"Because of medical emergencies," Anita said defensively.

"There were other doctors who could have attended to his emergencies," Gabby insisted. "He was looking for an excuse to stay away. Even when I was in grade school, he came home late and didn't bother to stop by my bedroom to give me a hug before I went to sleep."

"Oh, sweetheart." Anita seemed agitated. "I know Robert loved you. He told me so."

"Then why did he act so distant?"

"You really do feel that way, don't you?"

Gabby stared at her mother. Had Anita really had a blind spot when it came to her relationship with her father? Or had she chosen to fool herself?

"When I was a little girl," she said softly, "I was afraid the problem was my own fault, but I never knew what I'd done."

Anita looked away and took a deep breath. "I guess I'll have to think about this. We can discuss it later."

At least they *would* discuss it, Gabby thought, relaxing a bit. Again she glanced at her watch. Three o'clock. "Okay, let's talk about it another time," she said, letting Anita off the hook. "I have a full day tomorrow with a final costume fitting in the morning and rehearsal the whole afternoon."

"Goodness, yes, you have to get to bed." Anita got up and embraced her. "I'm sorry if I hurt you with the dependence issue. I didn't mean to."

Gabby hugged her mother in return. "That's all right." She just wished Anita would quit reminding her of what Gabby hadn't considered a problem.

"I only want the best for you, you know." Anita stared up at her daughter intently. "I'm sure we'll always remain close, but I don't think you should make me the center of your life. You need broader horizons, perhaps marriage and children along with your career."

Career? Would she really have another chance at one? Gabby wondered.

"Love should be as important as work," Anita went on.

"I agree," Gabby said, but at the moment she was thinking only about the importance of the performance coming up. She kissed her mother's cheek. "Now let's get some sleep."

Both women retired to their own bedrooms. Despite the late hour Gabby remained awake for a while, tossing and turning and blaming Price Garfield for her restlessness. Despite her mother's disclaimers Gabby was certain the man was bad news. He had no business keeping a seventy-five-year-old woman out until all hours so that he could fill her head with nonsense.

And who was Price Garfield to say anything about parenting? Every time Gabby thought about her mother confiding in the old jerk, she saw red.

THE GARFIELD CORPORATION occupied several floors of one of the newer steel-and-glass high rises in downtown L.A. Kit was trying to catch up with his messages when, somehow having circumvented both the receptionist and his personal secretary, Gabby sailed into his office unannounced.

"Gabby?" His hand was poised in midair over the phone. But after one look at her face, he forgot about the call he'd planned to make. "What's the matter?"

Kit knew that Gabby had had a costume fitting that morning. Had something gone wrong?

"You've got to get your father under control. He's a lecherous old goat."

Kit's eyebrows shot up. "That's why you're here? He came on to you?"

Gabby looked impatient. "Of course not."

Kit let out his breath in relief. Not that he'd ever heard of his father chasing younger women.

"It's my mother he's after."

"Oh, her."

Gabby plopped down into the chair in front of the desk, crossing her long legs. Kit couldn't help taking the time to admire them in spite of his partner's obvious agitation.

"Your father and my mother stayed out until the wee hours last night," Gabby went on, leaning forward. "Tell him to leave her alone, will you? They're no good for each other."

"I fully agree. But I'm not in the habit of telling my father anything. I've already explained that we lead completely separate lives."

"You shouldn't. Maybe if Price had a half-way decent relationship with his son, someone to talk to, he wouldn't be out doing things that he shouldn't, like prancing around clubs and hitting on aging women who need their sleep."

Overlooking the too-personal comment about himself, Kit focused on the idea of Price cavorting in a club with Anita Brooks Lacroix. Unable to decide whether or not he wanted to laugh, he passed a hand in front of his mouth.

"From what Mom says, Price isn't too happy with the estrangement between the two of you," Gabby persisted.

That made Kit frown. "He talked to your mother about me?"

She nodded. "And since your father seems to be approachable, after all, you could take some responsibility and open up to him. After all, communication goes two ways."

"And obviously three and more. Pretty soon the whole town will know my business." Kit stared at her in irritation. She was going too far. "Sounds like everybody's getting into the act here. The relationship between my father and me is really none of Anita's business... or yours."

"It is when my mother and I have to suffer because of your problems."

Couldn't she understand that Price and he were totally separate entities? He was no more responsible for his father than his father was for him. "Who said my father held a gun to your mother's head and made her suffer through an evening with him?" he asked caustically. "They're both consenting adults."

"So you refuse to take a stand?"

"Why should I interfere? It isn't my place." When the intercom beeped, he responded impatiently. "Yes?"

As his secretary relayed a message about a meeting he'd had rescheduled for the following week, Kit watched Gabby drum her fingers on the arm of the chair. She certainly was in a fine snit.

She went after him as soon as he turned back to her. "I'm sure Price would listen to you—"

"Hey, if you don't want your mother going out with my father, tell her to leave *him* alone!" Kit snapped.

Gabby's blue eyes widened. "She didn't instigate this situation."

"Are you sure? Maybe Anita has been after my father from the first." Maybe she'd always wanted Price along with a career boost, Kit thought, disgruntled as he always was when he thought about a woman he didn't even know playing such an important part in his life.

"How dare you say that about my mother!"

"You declared open season on my father."

And surprisingly he was offended by the thought of an outsider's criticism. His differences with his father were one thing—he had good reason, after all.

"This discussion is going nowhere." Gabby stood up abruptly. "I'm leaving."

"That might be the best idea." Kit held himself in check so that he wouldn't say something he would regret later. "Some of us have work to do."

"You're impossible."

Getting more irritated by the moment, he grunted, "Ditto," before picking up the telephone.

"Thanks so much for your patience and understanding!" Gabby yelled as she left the office in a dramatic huff.

Kit let the receiver fall back into the cradle. He regretted not trying to make peace before the door slammed shut. He'd been enjoying Gabby's bubbly, friendly company more and more every day. He was quite fond of her. More than fond, if he was honest with himself.

But Gabby had seemed so put out—would they be able to transcend this rift? More immediately, how on earth were they going to get through the intensive rehearsal they had planned for the afternoon?

UNFORTUNATELY GABBY'S state of mind hadn't improved a whole lot by the time she met Kit at the club to practice their routines. She had tried to calm down by taking a long walk and doing a little meditation on a park bench, but she couldn't get over her disappointment that he hadn't been willing to help her deal with the problematic situation Price was causing. Furthermore, Kit hadn't seemed in the least touched when she'd told him his father regretted their estrangement.

Both Garfields obviously deserved each other.

"All right, let's try the first part again," Kit said for the umpteenth time as they worked on "Tango Olé." His eyes as hard as jade, he gazed intently at Gabby. "Whip the shawl around a little more before you throw it to the side."

"Fine."

She wondered if Kit even noticed she'd been quieter than usual. After their disagreement, she was hurt as well as angry. She'd thought they'd gotten to a certain level of camaraderie and understanding, but it seemed as if he was as expert as his father at keeping uncomfortable situations at bay.

"I think modern audiences will respond well to a more intense version of the original number," Kit went on. "We can borrow generously from real Argentinian tango."

"Uh-huh."

He glanced at her suspiciously. His voice was stiff when he said, "Take your place."

"Certainly, Mr. Tyrant," she muttered softly, drawing the long print shawl around her. For the actual performance the shawl would be glittery black.

"What did you say?"

"Nothing important."

Kit turned the music on again and approached with a brooding expression. Dressed in a black shirt and pants, his appearance was perfect for a darkly sensual dance.

Too bad Gabby wasn't able to be more appreciative.

"Turn right," Kit told her as he sidled up beside her to grasp her arm.

As if she didn't know the steps.

But she complied gracefully, gliding out of his grip, then turning to face him. As he approached a second time, she showed her character's disdain by raising her chin and turning her back. She tossed the edge of the shawl over one shoulder. He encircled her waist with his hands and lowered his mouth to her neck. She angled her head to the side, steeling herself against his warm breath.

"No. No!"

Sounding disgusted, Kit stopped and stepped back. Gabby straightened and stared at him.

"Now what's the matter?"

"We're going to have to start over…again." He turned off the music. "Your emotional intensity is just not coming across, Gabby."

"Really?" Not in the mood for his perfectionism—not to mention his further criticism—she placed her hands on her hips. "I'm feeling pretty intense right now, believe me."

"Well, the intensity isn't sensual."

"*That's* right on the mark."

Kit ignored her salvo. "Your movements can't be forced," he explained as if she were some kind of amateur. "They should be languid."

Gabby thought she was being quite reasonable when she told him, "It's a little difficult to act languid and sensual when you have to do the same thing over and over." With someone you would rather not have touch you at the moment, she added silently. "We've done this number so many times today that I'm not in the mood."

"When *will* you be in the mood?" he asked, his eyes flickering with emotion.

"Maybe never."

She would never become involved with a man who was so arrogant and demanding and cold, she assured herself. She should have known to keep her distance after what had happened to her mother.

Kit scowled. "Is that why you didn't make it on Broadway? Because you weren't professional enough to put yourself in the right mood when necessary?"

Speechless, Gabby felt her mouth drop open at the insult.

"A performer has to forget his own petty troubles," Kit intoned.

"You're pretty petty all right," she snapped, regaining the use of her tongue.

"So *I'm* the problem?" he asked.

"I'd certainly say so."

Kit was absolutely wrong about her professionalism. Gabby had never had any problems with that on the Broadway stage or in any other performance. But then she'd never before become so personally involved with a partner.

Involved? As the implications sank in, Gabby realized why she'd been so uptight lately, even when dealing with her mother.

She should never have let herself be so open.

She should never have left New York.

What was she going to do? She was in love with Price Garfield's son.

CHAPTER NINE

DESPITE THE PRESSURE of the upcoming performance, Kit had refused to relax his business responsibilities and had been spending time at the office most mornings. On Thursday, however, he only managed to squeeze in a few hours between afternoon rehearsal and dress rehearsal that evening. Susan, his efficient secretary, brought him up-to-date as quickly as possible.

"Stanton Dowling returned your call," she told him. "He's interested in discussing a merger and making you a partner in his film production company."

Always attracted to show business despite his denials, Kit had found himself considering adding such a company to the Garfield Corporation. Being the head of a production company wouldn't be the same as actually acting in the movies, he assured himself.

"Did you set a meeting date?" Kit asked.

Susan nodded. "He was eager to get going, but I told him we had to delay it for a short while. He agreed to do lunch a week from Monday." She sorted through the stack of papers in her hand and placed several invoices before him on the desk. "Oh, yes, and we've received some rather unusual bills."

His brow furrowed as he registered the name of the company. "Glitter Baby?" The store was an expensive boutique on Rodeo Drive.

"Perhaps this explains everything." Susan pointed to the name printed above the corporation address. "It says Mr. Price Garfield. Your father must have purchased some clothing and had his bills sent here."

"Must be a mistake. He's never done that before." Kit picked up an invoice to examine it more closely. "Blue-sequined gown… silver-and-black beaded gown. Silver-and-jet necklace and earrings." His brows shot up at the price of those items. And the list went on. "Why would he purchase women's glitzy evening wear?"

Appearing uncomfortable, Susan adjusted her glasses. "Does he have a girlfriend perhaps?"

Anita Brooks Lacroix—the name sprang instantly to mind. Gabby had said her mother and his father had been seeing each other. She hadn't added that Price had been furnishing Anita with a new wardrobe from one of the most exclusive stores on the Drive.

"Would you like me to call the elder Mr. Garfield and ask him about this?" Susan inquired.

"That sounds like a good idea." But before Susan left his office Kit had second thoughts. "Wait a minute. Why don't you call the boutique instead? Talk to the manager and ask her about the bills. See if you can learn the name of the woman who bought these items."

There was no use embarrassing Price. Kit's father had always been a bit touchy, but if he'd bought Gabby's mother some dresses, Kit wanted to know about it.

Thinking about the younger Brooks while Susan took care of the phone call, Kit leaned back in his chair and stared out the sixteenth-floor window at the sunny day. The rim of mountains bordering the city were a hazy violet, making the setting appear tranquil. In reality, sprawling, busy L.A. was anything but.

As was he.

Kit was still brooding about the disagreement he'd had with Gabby the morning before. If he didn't like her so much, he would have laughed in her face when she'd insisted he "make" his father leave Anita alone. What did she expect him to do—threaten Price?

Unfortunately the spat with Gabby had gone on to disrupt their afternoon rehearsal. Already edgy, Kit had gotten fed up and said things he hadn't meant. At first Gabby had sniped right back at him, but then she'd surprised him by agreeing that she'd been acting less than professional. And after that she'd behaved differently.

Kit had tried to temper his criticism accordingly, but the close rapport they'd built from daily rehearsals seemed to have changed subtly. He only wished he could put his finger on exactly how or why, so he could do something about it.

At least the glitches in "Tango Olé" had been ironed out and they'd been right on the mark during rehearsals. Barring an unforeseen catastrophe, their performance at the opening tomorrow night should be nothing short of spectacular.

He only wished he weren't bothered by the undercurrent he sensed in Gabby. His gut told him something important had been left unsaid between them....

A tap on the door interrupted his musings.

"Susan?"

The secretary entered. "The manager at Glitter Baby says an elderly lady named Lucille Talbot charged the dresses. And he apologized for his bookkeeper sending the bills to the wrong place. They were supposed to go to Mr. Price Garfield in Beverly Hills or to his office at Cheek to Cheek."

Kit couldn't hide his amazement. "My father has an office at the club?"

Susan shrugged. "Shall I send this stuff on over there?"

His suspicions growing, Kit reached for the invoices. "No, you can leave them with me."

Why had he allowed Lucille to appease him so easily when he'd questioned her about the "investment group" that owned the nostalgia club? He should have kept after her until she had given him the truth.

Now she didn't have to.

Already knowing the answers, Kit decided he would confront his father with a few uncomfortable questions, anyway.

A HALF HOUR LATER Kit set out for Hollywood. Having phoned the Garfield mansion to check on Price's whereabouts, he'd been informed that his father had gone to the nightclub. To inspect the place the day before it opened?

Hoping to catch Price red-handed, Kit left the Garfield Corporation immediately.

He wasn't in the least surprised to locate Price in the business suite on the club's second floor. Perhaps Gabby would be pleased if she knew he and his father were finally going to talk.

"Which office is yours?" Kit asked Price, gesturing toward the private rooms that opened off the central reception area.

A couple of people were busily working at the desks, taking phone reservations and making arrangements for the opening.

Price seemed surprised by his son's directness. "I don't have an office here."

"Try again." Kit handed Price the bills from Glitter Baby. "The manager of the boutique said these were supposed to be sent to you at home or at your office at the club. You own this place, don't you? You've been footing all the bills. You even loaned Lucille your chauffeur and limo." Though he hadn't recognized the driver, Kit had wondered how his godmother had suddenly gotten hold of enough cash to hire an attentive servant and a posh car for her jaunts around town.

Sighing, Price motioned Kit away from the phones and into one of the private offices. He closed the door and glanced at the invoices, though he didn't seem overly disturbed by his son's disclosure. But then he had always been a master of the cool facade.

"I don't own Cheek to Cheek completely." Price tucked the bills into his suit jacket pocket before he sat down behind a desk. A placard with his engraved name rested on its surface. "Lucille and a few other people also have percentages."

Kit perched on the edge of the opposite chair. "Very small percentages, I bet. You've duped all of us."

"Duped? That's rather strong language." Price's tone remained reasonable. "You have no reason to feel tricked or cheated. I used personal funds for this venture, not corporate monies."

"Then why weren't you honest about ownership in the first place?"

"I thought you might not agree to dance if you knew I was involved."

"You're right about that!" Kit practically exploded off the chair as he launched himself in front of his father. Fists on the desk, he said, "And *I* was right. This was all some kind of a grand scheme."

Price adjusted his expression before Kit could discern the emotion that crossed his face. "You didn't have to agree to perform," the older man pointed out.

"True." Kit straightened. "But I would have felt like a creep if I'd turned down Lucille."

"The club is going to help her get back on her feet financially, son. You should concentrate on what you're doing for her rather than worrying about my involvement."

"Lucille will really be able to make enough money to fix up her home?"

"The first couple of weeks are already fully booked. If that's any indication, I have no doubts."

Kit felt his anger deflate. Price and Lucille had been friends for years. He should have realized how much his father cared about the elderly woman.

"Don't get your back up now, Kit," Price continued. "Everyone will be depending on you tomorrow. If we can start the club out with a bang, its future will be rosy."

As always, the thought made Kit uneasy. "And what makes you think my dancing is good enough to accomplish that?" To his knowledge his father had never observed him on a dance floor.

Price avoided looking at him directly. "Anita told me you and Gabby make excellent partners."

"Oh, right, Anita." Kit was tempted to tell Price about Gabby's complaints concerning her mother, then decided to keep that information to himself. "How come you two are together all the time, anyway? I thought she was the woman who ruined your life."

Price actually looked startled. "Where did you hear that?"

"I'm not sure exactly. But I remember Mom talking about you and Anita when I was a kid."

And at that time Kit had even wondered if Anita were the underlying reason for his parents' divorce. She'd been the object of his resentment, if not hatred, for years.

"Both Anita and I made some stupid mistakes when we were young," Price said with more emotion than Kit had previously heard in his voice.

"Does that mean you no longer think she's a little chippy who used you as a stepladder for her career?" Kit asked, quoting his mother.

"For years I was so angry with her that I'm not sure what I might have said." Price gazed at his son, meeting his eyes. "I wanted to marry her. I loved...love her."

Kit was openly shocked. He sat back in his chair. "You're in love with the woman who left you all those years ago?" Why could Price show such feeling for a woman who had chosen to leave him when he couldn't do the same for his own son?

Price simply nodded. "I've always loved Anita. I thought this situation with the club might give me one last chance with her."

"That's why you backed the venture?"

"Added to my desire to help Lucille... and myself. For a long time I've felt like I had nothing left to live for." He took a deep breath, suddenly appearing worn and gray. "I have my reasons for keeping my personal investment a secret. If Anita had known, she would never have come to California... wouldn't remain here now," he added worriedly. His gaze flicked about the office, then came back to Kit. "I hope I can trust you to keep what you found out to yourself."

His father was actually asking him to keep a personal confidence. A first.

"I don't tell tales out of school," Kit said,

trying to remain divorced from his own feelings about the situation.

"I really blew it back then," Price continued. "My life would have been different if I hadn't been so stupid and proud in dealing with Anita."

Kit overlooked his once-arrogant father's acknowledgment of guilt and focused on the marriage that might have been. "Yeah, life sure would have been different if you'd tied the knot with her. I would never have been born."

Price gazed at him directly. "That's the only thing I would have regretted."

Uncomfortable, Kit didn't know what to say. His father had missed out on a lot, anyway. He returned to a safer subject. "Don't worry. I won't tell anyone that you're backing the club."

"Thanks, I appreciate that."

"And I won't mention the rest of this conversation to Lucille."

"I think that would be best. Personal relationships should always take second place when a show's in the making."

Kit fully agreed. Then he thought of Gabby. How could he ignore the charged atmosphere every time they entered the same room? He could understand how Price felt about Anita, since he himself seemed to be falling for the woman's daughter—yet another complication in the Brooks/Garfield saga.

After Kit had gone, Price sat in the office for a while, then went downstairs to take one more look at the newly completed interior of the club.

The white moldings that bordered the Romanesque arch of the stage and the smaller arch of the orchestra's alcove were trimmed in silver, making them stand out in relief against the pale gray expanse of the walls. The three tiers of tables and built-in booths for the audience were delineated by shiny tubular railings.

Standing in the entryway, Price tried to imagine how the place would look when the overhead lights were dimmed and the first show began.

The sound and lighting crews were already busy making preparations for dress rehearsal. A man nearly swung from the rafters as he adjusted a spotlight.

"That's good, Charlie," the lighting director shouted from below. "Now check the one in the middle." When the director glanced over his shoulder, he noticed Price. "Ah…

why, hello, Mr. Garfield." He smiled. "I bet you're excited about seeing your son dance tomorrow night."

Price smiled. "That I am." But he was certain Kit wouldn't be equally excited at the thought of his old man observing him. His son had even admitted he wouldn't have agreed to perform at all if he'd known Price owned the club. Price wondered if Kit knew how much that hurt.

Of course, he could hardly blame Kit for resenting him. He'd scarcely seen him since his childhood. And that was the last time Price had managed to tell his son how much he loved him. Today he had tried to work up to the subject, but he'd only made the younger man uncomfortable.

Why couldn't he say the right thing at the right time? Why did he back away at the very moment he should advance? Or worse, take the opposite, angry tack? He'd had the same problems in his relationship with Anita.

"Excuse me, Mr. Garfield," the lighting director said as he approached. "Could you step aside? We need to carry some equipment through here."

Price moved down to the dance floor level, scuffing his feet experimentally over the polished black tile surface. He gazed at the open, two-sided "flying" stairway that led up to the platform of the stage. He and Anita had danced up and down a similar set of steps in one of the dance scenes of *Tap Me on the Shoulder*. That particular set was where he and Anita had had their first big blowup….

Hollywood, 1954

HAVING FILMED a couple of solo scenes, Price hadn't seen Anita all day. When he finally found her, she was dressed in street clothes and looking over the flying staircase set on which they were to start rehearsing the next day.

"So what do you think?" he asked, coming up behind her and encircling her waist loosely with his arms.

Anita leaned back against him and giggled softly. "Gosh, I hope I won't get dizzy."

"We've danced up and down stairs before."

"But they always had walls behind them, or railings. There's nothing to hold on to here."

"You can hold on to me," Price told her as she turned to face him. He tightened his hold on her waist. He would never let her go if only she would say the word. Then he added more seriously, "Don't stare at your feet. That's the real trick."

She pushed at him playfully. "I never peek at my feet while I'm dancing. You know better than that."

He nodded. "You're a real trouper."

Anita had gotten better and better the more they'd danced together. Experienced as he was, so had he. Price drew her closer, planting a soft kiss on her cheek.

Smiling, Anita lowered her voice so that any crew members who happened to be wandering by wouldn't hear. "You're so romantic."

He smiled into her adorable, lovely face. "Speaking of romantic, where do you want to go and what time can I see you tonight? How about dinner, say about eight?"

"Tonight?" Anita sobered and drew back. "Er...I'm busy."

"Busy with what?"

"I already have plans."

He caught his breath. "A date?"

"A publicity thing." She patted his arm. "Don't worry. I'm only doing this for Sol."

But he was appalled and jealous and unable to hide his feelings. "I didn't really think you'd go through with another one of these arranged dates after the last time, Anita."

She knit her feathery brows. "You sound like you're accusing me of being unfaithful."

Well, in Price's mind, they were unofficially engaged, and she should see him exclusively no matter what the studio wanted. But Anita was always trying to placate Sol when the old tyrant got into one of his snits about something.

"Who is the man this time?" Price asked.

"Oh, one of the other RPO contract actors."

He didn't like the studied way she was trying to sound so casual. *"Who?"*

"Um, Steven James…he's had several leading roles."

"I know the parts he's had." And Price was furious. "How could you date Steven James?" he demanded. "He is so annoyingly suave…."

And at least half a head taller than he was.

Anita tried to be conciliatory as she straightened his tie. "So? You're suave, too."

"And he's handsome."

She widened her eyes fetchingly. "I like your looks better."

He didn't believe it for a moment.

"And Steven doesn't dance all that well," Anita added. "You might like to know that."

But Price felt as if a knife had been plunged into his heart. "I don't care if the man has two left feet. I just want you all to myself."

"But that's impossible in our current situation."

"Then change our situation. Tell Sol you won't do it, that we're planning to be married."

Anita was becoming agitated. Her blue eyes flashed. "Sol won't approve. And we've already discussed this. I'm not ready to tie the knot—you're being unreasonable."

"I can't object to my girl dating other men?"

"You know it won't mean anything. Why can't you trust me?"

"I'd rather have no reason for distrust," he said angrily. "You're *my* girl."

"You don't own me, Price."

"But the studio does, is that right?" Price demanded, forgetting to keep his voice low. Several crew members were watching the interchange with interest, but he didn't care. "I guess I should realize what comes first with you."

"You know I love you. You're the only one."

"So you keep telling me." He turned to

walk away. "But actions speak louder than words."

"Price! Where are you going?"

"To my dressing room."

"Come back here right now. We can't leave things like this."

He turned to gaze at her intently, noting that her firm little jaw was set. "Then call off the date and marry me—tonight. Let's elope. RPO will be flooded with enough publicity to satisfy even Sol."

She sighed and shook her head slowly. "You know I can't do that."

"Then I'll see you in rehearsal tomorrow," he said coldly, once again turning away.

"Price!"

But he kept walking, his heated reaction merely a preview of the fireworks he felt building within him.

Hollywood, Present Day

WHEN LUCILLE'S LIMOUSINE delivered her to Cheek to Cheek for dress rehearsal that evening, Gabby happened to meet Kit coming in at the same time.

"Hi."

She smiled, feeling a little thrill of excitement at the mere sight of her dance partner.

Not that she'd figured out how to handle the emotional complications their association had brought about.

"Want some help with those?" Kit asked, taking several of the heavy dress and accessory bags she was carrying. "Why didn't you have the costumes delivered to the club?"

"I wanted to show them to Mom first."

"Did she like them?"

He opened the door for her, then followed her inside, stopping to gaze at the gleaming stage and dance floor visible beyond the entryway.

"She thought they were fabulous. Your friend did a great job. I can't wait to show them off tomorrow night."

"I just hope everything goes well."

"You sound doubtful." Taking a chance that he wouldn't be offended, she joked, "Getting nervous?"

"I've been nervous from the beginning."

Gabby was surprised that Kit admitted to any sort of weakness. "I'm sure we'll be a hit. I have a good feeling about this."

He laughed. "Then I'm going to put my trust in your intuition…as well as your ability. Despite our disagreements I want you to know that you're the best partner I've ever had."

"Why thank you."

Considering his professional dancing had always been with partners, Gabby felt flattered—and a private thrill.

"And you're very professional," Kit told her. "I was out of line yesterday when I claimed otherwise."

"I knew you didn't mean it."

"But I didn't really apologize. I'm sorry."

She smiled warmly. Kit could be a real sweetheart when he tried to be. "That's okay. I probably shouldn't have jumped down your throat about your father seeing my mother."

"Considering our parents' backgrounds, I guess we'll always be haunted by them in some way or another."

Haunted? "You mean as dancers?"

"And as boyfriend and girlfriend or whatever they were."

"They were never lovers, if that's what you're hinting at."

Kit's expression was disbelieving. "That's a hard one to swallow, considering how neurotic they are over the old relationship."

"But it's true nonetheless." Gabby believed her mother, no matter what Price might have told his son. "Mom was still a kid when they became partners and only nineteen when they broke up, after all."

Kit didn't pursue the issue. "Whatever the reason, they seem to have unfinished business."

Which continued to concern Gabby. "After all these years, you'd think they'd realize it's a bit too late."

"That's up to them to decide, isn't it?" Kit asked, gazing at her assessingly.

He made her feel as if they, too, had some kind of decision to make. Remembering the personal discovery she'd made after their argument, Gabby felt a flare of nerves that had nothing to do with performing.

"I suppose so."

"Look, let's forget about Price and Anita for the next week," Kit went on. "Let's concentrate on us. I can't control my father, and I don't think you can make your mother do what you think best, either."

"Unfortunately not."

Aware that he wasn't convincing her, he finally said, "I know you feel more strongly about the situation than I, but I hope that won't come between us."

"I don't expect you to agree with me,"

Gabby said, not quite certain she was being honest. She certainly *wanted* him to agree with her. About their parents. About them. About everything. She hated fighting with Kit. With the man she loved.

"Good, because I'd hate to lose the rapport we've developed while rehearsing together," he said.

"Me, too."

Their eyes met, Kit's flickering with emotion Gabby couldn't help imagining was more than friendliness. She swallowed hard.

"I think it'll help if we always try to be honest with each other, don't you?" he asked, watching her closely.

"Openness is best," she agreed, but Gabby wasn't willing to expose her feelings yet— maybe she never would be. Taking rejection well wasn't one of her strong suits.

He paused, glancing toward the stage again. "Shall we get ready to rehearse?"

"Sure."

When Gabby reached her dressing room, she hurried inside and shut the door. Usually open and willing to take chances, she felt uncomfortable with anything less than the truth. But then again, she hadn't expected to fall for the son of her mother's old flame.

What a sticky situation!

Her business and life were in New York; Kit's in California. Even if Kit was head over heels in love with her, they didn't have much of a future together.

CHAPTER TEN

LIKE MANY PERFORMERS, Gabby always felt more confident a day or two before a performance than on the big night itself. She was so nervous before the opening on Friday that she started hyperventilating before she was even dressed. At least she knew what to do from her days on Broadway. She breathed into a paper bag to calm herself while her dresser, Maria, zipped up her white satin gown.

She knew that the jitters would only be temporary. Once she appeared in the spotlight everything would be fine. And the moment was coming up soon. Kit and Gabby were on immediately after an introductory routine by Lucille, which was coming in loud and strong over the monitor installed in Gabby's dressing room.

"You gotta be familiar with two of the greatest names in the history of dance," Lucille was saying. "Anita Brooks and Price Garfield."

"Oh, boy, we're up," Gabby muttered, pulling away from Maria.

"Break a leg, Miss Brooks," the dresser called after her.

"You're gonna think you're seeing ghosts from the past," Lucille went on.

Gabby pulled up the fluted skirts of her gown and ran from the dressing room to the wings of the small stage. Kit was already waiting there, tall and elegant in his perfectly tailored tuxedo. And he looked as cool as a cucumber, the lucky man.

"Ready?" he asked with a smile.

"I was born ready, baby," she retorted saucily, psyching herself up for the romantic dances that were to come.

"You're gorgeous."

"You're not so bad yourself."

And then came Lucille's cue. "'Mesmerizing You,' performed by Gabrielle Brooks and Kit Garfield!"

Gabby and Kit entered the stage in character. Then, descending opposite sides of the flying staircase, they met on the dance floor as the orchestra picked up the melody.

Facing the bright spots and an anonymous sea of intent faces, Gabby felt the adrenaline surge through her body. Victory swept through her even before she and Kit began to move together. This was what she had been waiting for—this sense of rightness that she had only when performing. Pretense became her reality if only for a few short moments. She stepped, turned, whirled to the music, all the time focusing on her partner and the movements of the dance.

She had never felt so alive.

On Kit's face she saw a reflection of her own all-too-real emotion. Was this part of his act, or did he care about her, too? Gabby wondered fleetingly before losing herself completely in the dance.

Graceful minutes flew by with the speed of light. Before Gabby knew it, the number was coming to a close. Kit bent her over his arm in the classic Hollywood pose. As she had in their first rehearsal, Gabby wound her arms about his neck and pulled herself up until their lips met and the music melded into a breathless silence. A single spotlight lingered on them, then dimmed to black.

Applause resounded through the club.

"Now that's real romance for ya!" Lucille cried above the noise of the enthusiastic audience.

The spots switched back to Lucille, who

sparkled in blue sequins at the microphone. Gabby and Kit exited unobtrusively. And the applause went on. Entering the stage door on the dance floor level, Gabby would have cheered if she weren't aware they had two more numbers to perform.

Kit stopped before mounting the stairs that led up to the dressing rooms and hugged her as Lucille introduced the next act. "We did great, didn't we? Just like you predicted."

"I knew my hunch would be right."

When he stooped to brush her lips with his own, she gave in to temptation and kissed him. She tried to tell him so much with that one silent embrace that Kit's eyes looked glazed when she finally pulled back.

"Whew!" He quirked his eyebrows and adjusted his bow tie.

Pleased by the reaction she'd evoked, Gabby grinned and ran her fingers through his hair.

"Now it'll have to be recombed," he complained halfheartedly.

"I just can't help myself." She leaned in toward him. "Dancing like this is just so… wonderful."

Especially since she was partnered by the incredibly sexy Kit Garfield.

His gaze intense, Kit looked as if he were about to kiss her again when Gabby's dresser appeared at the top of the stairs.

"Miss Brooks, we don't have much time to change costumes and hair."

"I'll be right there, Maria."

Kit kissed the tip of Gabby's nose before he let her go. With a last look over his shoulder, he headed for his own dressing room as Gabby started for hers.

Because she had opted for completely different looks for each number, she had a tight schedule between dances. Right now three singers doing a medley of Andrews Sisters tunes were onstage, but Gabby and Kit would soon be required to appear again.

Maria zipped and snapped her into the beautiful gold-sequined dress, then worked on her hair with a curling iron. Gabby checked the mirror and touched up her makeup. She wondered if Kit had taken her seriously. She hadn't meant to come on quite so strongly, but the heady experience of performance always opened her up emotionally.

As she made her way back to the stage, the skirts of the gold dress swayed about her legs. The costume was almost an exact duplicate of the original gown and made Gabby feel her best.

Kit's green eyes flashed admiringly as she approached. "Ready?"

"Very."

She took his hand, her clasp warm and steady, and, more than ever, Kit felt as if the two of them were right together. He didn't have the luxury of delving into the sentiment more thoroughly, since the singing trio was already exiting into the wings. He prepared himself mentally as Lucille introduced "Dance with Me."

The drama began with Kit following Gabby slowly down one side of the stairs to the opening strains of the music. A sophisticated tune with a sad, yearning undertone, the melody expressed the unrequited love of his character for hers.

At Kit's first approach he and Gabby danced side by side. She tried to escape, only to be caught before she ascended the stairs. Grasping her wrist, he swung her back into his arms. Her weighted skirts snapped around them both. They completed a few steps, dipped and whirled until she escaped again. This time Kit followed her up the stairs and danced her down the other side. The feat looked far easier than it actually was, but Kit had always looked for challenges to enhance his choreography.

When the audience went wild, applauding even as the number was in progress, Kit paused for an instant, nearly forgetting his next step. The startled look in Gabby's eyes told him she was also thrown by the unexpected reaction. But he forced himself to recover, leading his partner out onto the center of the dance floor for a waltzing movement that ended in several spins.

Again the audience clapped with enthusiasm, obviously appreciating the intricacy of the number. And Kit couldn't help but respond. Glancing over Gabby's shoulder, he picked out two ladies sitting in the lowest, closest tier and delighted them with a blinding smile. Suddenly the intoxicating immediacy of the performance made him feel as if he were dancing on air.

The number ended with them dancing first together, then separately up the flying staircase. In the last movement Gabby preceded her partner, throwing a sorrowful look over her shoulder. Kit assumed his character's dejected expression, then followed his wooing to no avail.

He actually *did* feel sad when he finally exited, knowing that his and Gabby's week at Cheek to Cheek would probably be their only chance to perform together. And he wasn't sure what he would miss more—the dancing or the most well-matched partner he'd ever had.

Kit reminded himself that the joys of professional dancing were as fleeting as fame. Furthermore, who were the audience really applauding? Kit and Gabby...or Anita and Price?

THE ORCHESTRA PLAYED dance music after the show ended, so the audience could take the floor. Wearing one of her own evening dresses, a strapless coral-colored taffeta, Gabby met Kit backstage before they joined Lucille at her personal table.

"Still think we were a hit?" Kit asked.

"You have doubts after that applause?" She touched his mouth lightly with her fingers. "You can't stop smiling, can you?"

He clasped her hand and rubbed the palm. "I had a great time."

Gabby was fairly certain that part of Kit's fun had come from the real attraction between them. That had certainly added pizzazz to their routines. "Tango Olé," the last number, had practically sizzled. Costumed in a glittery long black gown, the skirt of which had been slit to the upper thigh, Gabby had wrapped one long leg around her partner at the end of the act and had stared deeply into his eyes. If Kit's expression were any indication, he could have kissed her right there in front of the audience.

But, for the moment, the touch of his lips was gentle rather than passionate. "Shall we go see how Lucille's doing?" he asked.

Gabby kept her tone light. "Sure."

The club was packed, but its hostess had had several tables pushed together to accommodate her numerous personal guests—Jayne, Risa, Yancy, Neil, Harvey, Price and Anita and their offspring. Her cheeks flushed, Lucille looked adorable and happy in her blue-sequined, floor-length gown.

"And how about a hand for our stars!" Lucille enthused as soon as she saw the featured dancers heading in her direction.

The boarders and the elder Brooks and Garfield rose to clap, instigating another round of applause from the tables nearby. Gabby hugged her mother, then Lucille, Jayne, Yancy and Neil. She shook hands with

Harvey and leaned over to kiss Risa's cheek. Kit also hugged the women and shook hands with the men, including his father.

Gabby wasn't sure how to act toward Price, either, so she let him take the initiative, turning her cheek for his kiss when he quickly embraced her.

"You're as beautiful and talented as your mother," Price told her with a smile.

"Thanks."

Gabby tried not to frown as she noticed Anita beaming proudly at Price, then holding his hand when they sat back down.

"Here are your seats, kids, at the head of the table," Lucille told them, pulling out a chair for herself on the other side of Kit. "Order whatever you want. The drinks are on the house."

Gabby ordered wine, and while she waited for her drink to arrive, she listened to the others reminisce enthusiastically about old movie experiences. Except for Jayne. The aging glamour queen merely toyed with her margarita glass. About to ask her if something was wrong, Gabby suddenly realized someone was missing.

"Where's Chester?" she asked.

"At home," Jayne told her with a sigh. "His

arthritis took a turn for the worse. He can hardly get out of bed."

"Oh, dear," Gabby said, worried and assuming Jayne was distressed about her friend.

Kit leaned close. "I contacted Chester's doctor and made arrangements for a month's supply of that special medicine to see if it will help."

Gabby was warmed by her partner's concern. "Let's hope Chester won't be angry with you."

"I made the arrangements, but I'm only paying for a part of the medication. Lucille is taking the rest of the cost out of the club's profits. Chester doesn't have to know the details."

As a team, they had certainly done their parts to add to those profits, Gabby was happy to realize.

Everyone glanced up when the waiter delivered a bottle of champagne along with several drinks. The man placed a handful of glasses and the champagne's ice bucket in front of Price.

"Let's have a toast for Kit and Gabby," Price announced as the waiter popped the cork and poured. He stood up and raised his glass. "To my son and Anita's daughter—real chips off the old blocks."

"And fabulous dancers in their own right," Anita added quickly.

Price gazed warmly at his son. "I'm very proud of you."

Kit nodded stiffly, raising his glass to clink it with the others. Gabby was certain the "chip off the block" remark had rubbed him the wrong way.

Price turned to address his son. "Few entertainers would have dared try to pull an act like yours together in such a short time, Kit. And fewer still would have ended up with such a winner. You're not only intelligent and creative. You've also got guts."

Kit remained cool. "Too bad you didn't realize all this years ago. You could have if you'd made an effort."

Although his remarks didn't shock Gabby, she was as uncomfortable as everyone else, and for a moment there was total silence. Lucille gave Kit a dark, reproving look, then broke in with a joke as Price sat back down, his face pale.

Feeling sorry for the man despite her own problems with him, Gabby elbowed Kit.

"What's the matter with you?" she whispered. "He was being nice."

"I don't need his niceness," Kit said under his breath.

"He might need yours."

Kit frowned. "I thought you said he was a lecherous old goat."

"He's still your father." And Gabby believed in taking care of family.

"But he's years too late."

Luckily Price didn't hear. Anita was busy talking him into taking a whirl around the dance floor. When the couple first stepped into the throng of dancers already moving to the rhythms of big band music, they received some applause, but they were soon swept into the crowd. Yancy asked Lucille to dance, as well, leaving the rest of the boarders with the younger couple at the table.

"It's years too late for me, too," Harvey said mournfully, staring at the champagne left in his glass.

"What are you talking about?" Neil asked.

"Nothing important." Harvey brushed some invisible dust off the lapels of his old tuxedo and scooted his chair back. "I'm leaving."

"And where do you think you're going?" Risa inquired imperiously.

"I need to find my partner."

"Your partner?" Neil echoed as Harvey walked away from the table. "They split up almost twenty years ago. Why would he suddenly get it into his head to go looking for the guy?"

"This isn't sudden," Jayne said, her tone uneven. "Harvey's been talking about his partner a lot lately. You're so hung up on yourself that you never pay any attention."

Neil scowled, offended. "I resent that."

"But it's true."

"Well, I've got my own problems," Neil said defensively.

Gabby intervened with a positive note. "Things will work out for all of you. I'm certain of it. The club's opening success is only the beginning."

"Right," Jayne said.

But Gabby frowned. Why were the blonde's lips trembling? "What's wrong?"

"Nothing," Jayne answered curtly, then pushed back her chair and rose.

"Now where are *you* going?" Risa complained. "This is some kind of party."

"Wait." Gabby reached across the table to catch Jayne by the hand. "Are you ill?"

The older woman shook her head and burst into tears.

"Please sit down, Jayne," Kit said, obviously concerned. He rose to slide his arm around the weeping woman's shoulders and help her back into her seat. "Tell us what's bothering you."

"I don't want to ruin your opening night."

"Nothing will be ruined," Kit assured Jayne, sitting down beside her.

The blonde dabbed at her eyes and gazed from Kit to Gabby. "Well, today I...I found out I didn't get that part I told you about."

"You were turned down for the 'Jayne Hunter' type of role?" Gabby asked incredulously.

Jayne nodded. "They said the real thing was too old. I was so depressed I even thought about not coming tonight."

"Producers are vermin!" Risa stated.

"What did the idiots want? A *young* Jayne Hunter?" Neil asked kindly.

Jayne shrugged. "I guess so."

"I'll ask my mother if she can get you an audition for the new show being planned by the producers of *Hawk's Roost*," Kit suggested.

Gabby was warmed by his offer. "That sounds like a good idea."

But Jayne would have none of it. "I don't want charity."

"Come on, we all network," Neil put in.

"But my agent already tried all the soap operas," Jayne said. She counted on her fingers. "And advertising, sitcoms, television dramas—it's hopeless. I think I'm going to be losing my agent, too. The last time I worked was years ago, when I modeled some bras for a commercial."

"Do not give up yet," Risa said, emphasizing her words as though they were a speech from an old movie. "You must always have hope."

"Hope makes the world go round," Neil added. "And speaking of going round, how would you like to take a turn around the dance floor, lovely Jayne?" He winked at her. "Wouldn't a little trip along the light fantastic help you get into a better mood?"

The actress managed a shaky smile. "Maybe it would." She gazed around the table, finally focusing on Kit and Gabby. "Thanks so much for all your support. The last thing I wanted to do was ruin things on such a glorious occasion."

"You didn't," Gabby assured her, though she was saddened by Jayne's plight. She also had a few worries of her own. Tonight's performance had been a heady thrill, but she still had her unresolved feelings for Kit to deal with.

Worse, she was displeased by her mother's behavior. Anita had been glued to Price's side all night and was now dancing cheek to cheek with the old goat. Gabby had caught sight of them gliding by on the dance floor a minute ago. Romantic foolishness was understandable in a woman of her age, but Anita should know better, Gabby thought.

Her mother was too old for such nonsense.

KIT INVITED Gabby to leave with him a half hour later, even though the club's patrons were still going strong. He knew she didn't need a ride to Beverly Hills, since both Price and Lucille had cars at their disposal, but he hoped she'd want to keep him company. He felt a disproportionate satisfaction when she agreed.

"Are you tired?" Gabby asked as he drew her chair back and helped her with her wrap.

"I'm tired of this atmosphere. I'd like a little quiet."

"I can understand that. Right now a peaceful atmosphere sounds inviting."

They bid adieu to the rest of the party and left via the club's main door. On the way Kit noticed a man staring at them, his suit contrasting with the ponytail that pulled back his thinning hair. The guy looked familiar, but Kit didn't stop to place him. He and Gabby exited the club and were soon on the road.

"We really *were* great tonight," Kit told her as he relaxed behind the wheel.

"I know. We should be ecstatic."

Gabby didn't sound depressed, exactly, but she wasn't her usual vibrant self. "Did Jayne's news get to you that much?" he asked.

"Not exactly."

Usually not so compelled to be in tune with other people's attitudes, he wanted to know how Gabby felt. "What, then? Did the tension between me and my father put a damper on your spirits?"

She shook her head. "I'm not in a bad mood at all, to tell you the truth. I'm merely tired and a bit thoughtful."

"Still, I suppose I shouldn't have said what I did."

Gabby nodded. "I'm sure you hurt Price's feelings."

Kit clenched his jaw as he turned onto a crosstown freeway. He did feel guilty about rejecting his father. He'd done that twice recently. In his awkward way Price had been trying to communicate for once. Changing a lifetime of negative patterns wasn't the easiest thing in the world for either of them, however.

"The 'chip off the old block' remark probably annoyed you," Gabby commented as if she knew exactly what he'd been thinking.

"You could tell, huh?"

"You must have been very resentful from way back. Was Price really so cold to you when you were a child?"

"I always thought so. But there were other factors to take into account," Kit admitted. "My parents argued a lot the last year they were together—that affected me. And then I'm not exaggerating when I say that I hardly saw my father after the divorce." He tapped the steering wheel. "He certainly never encouraged me to learn dancing or choreography. Or anything, actually." As if he'd been afraid to interfere in his own son's life, Kit mused.

"I know what it's like to have an absentee father."

"So you said before. But I noticed you were quick enough to stick up for mine when you got the chance."

"I felt sorry for him."

Kit smiled. "You have a warm heart." It was easy to confide in Gabby. He glanced at her sideways. "Of course, you also have beautiful legs, a gorgeous figure, a lovely face..."

"But no mind to speak of," she teased.

"Come on, I was going to mention your intelligence next."

She laughed. "I have a compliment for you, too."

"Only one?"

"But it's very important." She turned toward him in a rustle of taffeta, placing a slim arm across the seat. "Ever since I've gotten to know you, I've sensed an undercurrent of rivalry toward your father."

"We aren't rivals," Kit stated immediately, wondering how the comment was working up to a compliment. "We don't even work in the same fields...usually."

"Only because *you* don't want to. It's obvious that you were born to be a dancer."

He relaxed a little. "You can utilize the same talents in many different areas."

"Don't get defensive," Gabby cut in. "What's so bad about being a dancer? And if you're worried you'll be eclipsed by Price Garfield's fame, think again. In some ways your styles are similar. But he never created such sensuality with his choreography."

Kit had to smile. "Are you sure that's not your own personal interpretation?"

Gabby laughed. "No, I think it's more than that."

Gabby turned in her seat so that she was facing forward again. She glanced out the window. "Hey, aren't we going to Beverly Hills?"

Kit gazed up at the signs over the freeway. The Pacific Coast Highway was coming up. He was on automatic pilot, his destination home.

"Oops. We seem to have passed our exits. I didn't do it on purpose. Really," he assured Gabby, giving her a sidelong glance. "But since we're headed in that direction, anyway, how about dropping by my beach house for a nightcap?"

Her tone was noncommittal when she

said, "I already had a glass of wine and some champagne."

"Your glass was half-empty, and you couldn't have had much champagne. A bottle of bubbly only goes so far with a party of ten. I just happen to have a chilled imported bottle of my own waiting in the refrigerator."

"Mmm, well, all right, if you put it that way."

Kit smiled. They could share a bottle of champagne and a late-night snack, and maybe have another late-night swim. He wasn't ready to say good-night to his lovely dance partner yet.

They arrived at the Malibu North Cove complex a little after midnight and began rehashing their evening's performance. Gabby soon regained the breathless enthusiasm that was one of the things that drew Kit to her.

"They absolutely loved us, didn't they?" she gushed as he unlocked the door of his house. "And did you see the way some of those women were staring at you?"

Kit laughed and switched on a light, allowing her to enter before him. "If you're referring to the two gray-haired ladies in the front row, I worked them a little—made eye contact and smiled directly at them."

"You sly dog." Not that she hadn't worked the audience herself once she'd realized the dancing was going over well.

"What can I do? I'm an inveterate flirt."

She turned to him with a smile of her own. "Are you?"

Rather than answering, Kit merely gave her an enigmatic look. Taking off his tuxedo jacket, he led the way across the central open room to the kitchen where he turned on another light. He removed the bottle of champagne from the refrigerator.

Making herself comfortable leaning against the counter, Gabby pursued the point. "You must have had plenty of female admirers through the years," she said. "It's a wonder you aren't married by now."

"My parents' divorce made me careful," he admitted, switching on the radio that was sitting on the tiled counter and tuning in to a jazz station.

"I can understand how what happened to your parents would affect you," Gabby said. "My grandmother was divorced when it wasn't that common. Mom always claimed that affected her attitude toward marriage, too."

Kit rinsed out a couple of fluted glasses,

then popped the cork on the champagne. Gabby watched as the golden wine fizzed and bubbled when he poured out generous servings. He handed Gabby a glass and lifted his own for a toast.

"To us."

"To us," she repeated. "The best dance team in the country!"

"How about the western hemisphere?" He smiled, his straight teeth flashing against his tan, the effect augmented by the brilliant white of his pleated shirt and satin bow tie. "Those Argentinians ought to take note. We do a mean tango."

We do, Gabby thought, downing her whole glass of champagne in one gulp. The bubbles tickled all the way to her stomach and warmed her cheeks.

Needing a bit of air, Gabby wandered into the adjoining dining area, halting before the partially open sliding doors that led out to the deck. Below, on the beach, whitecaps glowed in the moonlight, giving the dark setting an ethereal beauty.

Kit followed with the champagne and stopped behind her.

"Let me." His warm voice flowed through her as he refilled her glass.

"Thanks," she said, watching his reflection in the sliding door.

"Are you hungry? Would you like some cheese?" he asked. "Some healthy Californian multigrain chips?"

They both laughed, Gabby liking the way Kit's eyes were warmed by his smile. He reached over and slid the deck door all the way open, inviting the sounds and smell of the ocean inside.

"Can I ask you something?" Gabby said.

"Of course," he replied.

"Did you ever want fame?" she asked.

"I've never wanted to be a movie star."

"Not even in your daydreams?"

"When I was younger, I did," he finally conceded, then looked as if he were sorry he'd made the admission.

Kit returned to the kitchen, where he set down the bottle and his glass, then removed his tie and loosened the top buttons of his shirt.

"But if you want," he murmured, taking her in his arms, "we can pretend we're in a movie now."

Gabby's "Why not?" was breathless.

They danced around the huge expanse of floor still bare of its area rug as it had been during their rehearsals. Anchoring one hand at the small of Gabby's back, Kit let the other arm dangle and brush against her.

His expression was intense, his gaze hypnotic. As always when she danced, Gabby was drawn deep into another world.

Kit pulled Gabby closer and stroked her hair.

"I knew we'd be good together."

"Perfect partners in every way," she agreed.

"More than that. Deeper—"

"Ssh."

Gabby kissed Kit to stop him from bringing up anything too serious. If he did, she'd have to admit she loved him and worry about whether he loved her, too. And what good would that do, considering they'd part in little more than a week as soon as the job at Cheek to Cheek was over?

At least they could have tonight, Gabby told herself, determined to savor whatever happiness was offered her as they danced together in the beach house, lost in their own private movie.

CHAPTER ELEVEN

THE NEXT MORNING, Gabby arrived at Kit's place to find a youngish man with glasses and a ponytail lounging against the kitchen counter, talking to Kit. She looked at her watch, assuming she must be early for the brunch date Kit had insisted on when she'd said she needed to go back to the mansion and sleep. It had been a beautiful night with Kit—she'd hardly been able to tear herself away.

"My backers are committed," the man was saying to Kit. "This project's going to fly."

"And you're making the final decisions on casting, hmm?"

Casting? The word immediately caught Gabby's attention. She moved closer to get a better look at the man Kit was talking to.

He, in turn, spotted her. "Ah, if it isn't Gabrielle Brooks Lacroix."

He knew her?

"Great. I'll get a chance to talk to Gabrielle, too." He stepped forward to shake her hand.

"Hi, I'm Luke Sheffield. I saw your show last night. You were really incredible."

"I'm glad you enjoyed the performance."

"Ever had any acting experience?"

She gave Kit a questioning look, but his expression remained impassive. "A little, on Broadway."

"Excellent. I bet you had some singing lessons, too."

Gabby nodded. "I can carry a tune. What are you leading up to, anyway?"

Luke laughed. "I appreciate directness." He glanced at Kit. "As I was telling your partner here, I'm an independent producer and I'm making a movie about a dance team in the thirties. After catching your act at Cheek to Cheek last night, I thought you two would be perfect. You're a bit older than the characters as I envisioned them, but I've decided a few years aren't that important."

Paying no attention to the remark about age—coming from someone who must be all of twenty-eight—Gabby focused on the good part.

"You're producing a movie? And you want us to act in it?" In major roles if she had heard correctly.

"You'll dance, act, sing."

Gabby felt like singing right now. "Why that's wonderful!" she enthused, bouncing over to her partner to grasp his hand. "Isn't it, Kit?"

He smiled and gave her hand a squeeze, though he didn't seem excited. "I'm flattered."

"Once you read the script, you'll love it," Luke told them.

"I'm sure we will," Gabby agreed.

Unless the movie was a real loser, she already knew what her answer would be. This was the sort of chance she'd only dreamed of when she'd agreed to come to L.A.

Luke pushed at his glasses. "And we'll have to set up contracts and hash over money matters and such. My people will negotiate with your people." He opened the leather bag he was carrying and tried to balance it on his knee. "I've got two scripts in here somewhere."

Gabby suddenly realized they were all standing around. Surely Kit wouldn't mind if she were hospitable.

"Why don't you have a seat at the table, Luke, where you'll be more comfortable?" She wanted to hear every detail of his proposal. "Would you like some coffee?"

"Thanks, but I have to be going." Finally locating the scripts, the young producer handed thick binders to Gabby and Kit, who immediately set his down on the counter. Then Luke reached into the pocket of his leather jacket and pulled out his card. "Call me after you look over the material."

"We certainly will," Gabby promised.

"Real nice to meet you." Luke shook both their hands. "I hope things will work out between us. This movie should be a winner."

"Nice to meet you, too," Kit told the other man as he showed him to the door.

Gabby was busily leafing through her copy of the script when he rejoined her. "The movie's called *Tango*—isn't that appropriate?"

"Sounds like a good title for a dance movie." He took hold of her shoulders and moved her into the kitchen. "Want some coffee?"

She grinned. "Sure. Are we eating here? Wait, don't tell me—you cook?"

"Of course. Eggs and bacon?" he asked. He took the script from her hands and laid it on the counter beside his. Then he enfolded her in his arms. "I haven't so much as gotten a good-morning kiss yet."

She kissed him but became uncomfortable

quickly. Kissing in the cold, clear light of morning was far too real. She already knew she would suffer emotionally when they had to part; she didn't want her heart to be completely and utterly broken.

A little voice whispered, *But what if we don't have to part?*

She was relieved when he finally raised his head to gaze at her.

"You look gorgeous."

"Thank you," she said, leaning back to put a few inches between them. Then she brought up the subject she really wanted to discuss. "Isn't it fabulous that we've been offered movie roles? Aren't you excited?"

He had to realize making the movie would keep them together much longer than they originally thought, she rationalized. Perhaps she'd even find a way to stay in California permanently. Near Kit.

"I'm not terribly excited, no." He let go of Gabby and turned to the counter to switch on the coffee maker.

She was concerned by his negative remark. "Does Luke Sheffield have a bad reputation? Do you know something I don't?"

Kit shrugged. "He's legit. But it really doesn't matter. I'm not interested."

"Not interested? This could be our big chance."

"Maybe, maybe not. One movie doesn't assure anyone a career in Hollywood. I don't want to hurt your feelings, but you sound a little naive."

"I'm not naive," she said testily. "I've worked on Broadway."

"Working in the movies can easily start and end with one role."

"One leading role is more than I've ever been offered. Besides, you have to take risks if you want to get somewhere." And they had the opportunity of getting somewhere together, she thought. "Why on earth wouldn't you want to try this?"

"I'm no actor or singer. And despite this act we're doing together, I'm no longer a professional dancer."

"You could be if you admitted the truth to yourself," Gabby insisted. "You would never have agreed to dance and to take so much time out from your business if you hadn't *wanted* to do it." Thinking about his other objection, she added, "Your father wasn't strong in the acting or singing departments, either, but his dancing made up for it."

Kit's hand froze as he set the coffee can on the shelf. "My father?"

Oh-oh, now she'd waved the red flag.

"My job is running the Garfield Corporation," he stated firmly.

Gabby wanted to tear her hair out. Because of some stupid competition phobia he had about his father, Kit was going to let a career opportunity slip right through his fingers, not to mention rip it out of hers at the same time. Furthermore, he was eliminating the possibility of working together and seeing each other in the future. Surely he knew she'd have to go back to New York when their stint at the club was through. She felt as if she were in the throes of a nightmare.

Unwilling to be so easily dissuaded, she made one last try. "But when I first got here this morning, I heard you and Luke talking, and you sounded interested."

"I was only asking questions because I've been considering expanding the corporation by adding a film production company."

"And wouldn't acting in a movie be good experience for you as an owner?" she pointed out.

"Not particularly. It isn't the same thing." He poured them both a mug of coffee, handed her one and turned to the refrigerator. "Did you say you wanted orange juice? Fresh or frozen?"

"Neither at the moment. I've changed my mind." She didn't even feel like drinking the coffee. She clung to the cup numbly. "You won't even consider making the movie?"

He shook his head. "Don't you think I could have tried my fortune with the movies a long time ago if that's what I wanted? With my mother's connections?"

"And your father's." Neither of which option Gabby had. "That's the problem, isn't it? Last night you admitted you dreamed about being a star when you were younger. But you couldn't stand being compared to Price, so you even danced under an alias. And you've made it perfectly clear that you set out to succeed in an area he didn't care about."

"Look," Kit said tightly, "if you want to take the role in Sheffield's production, go ahead."

"Luke won't want me solo. He wants a dance team."

"He didn't say that. You could get another partner."

Gabby was hurt by the very suggestion. "I

could never find another who was as good as you."

"Oh, come now." He slid his arm around her shoulders, but she moved away.

"In my opinion, you're being stubborn and selfish."

His eyes hardened. "Because I won't do what you want?"

"Because you're lying to yourself. You're passing up a chance in a million and forcing me to pass on it, too."

Now he really looked angry. "What's going on here, anyway?"

"I'm reacting to your unreasonableness."

She couldn't believe that he would turn down a done deal. No one could dance the way he did and not love it. He just wasn't making sense.

Kit went on. "What's important to you? How can you ignore what's happened between us, how we feel about each other?"

Thinking that Kit might be trying to tell her he cared, Gabby softened for a moment. But then she took a mental step back and wondered if he expected her to give up her life in New York and hang around L.A. just to be near him. Fat chance.

"We never made any declarations," she said coolly.

"You're being pretty self-centered here, Gabby."

"*I'm* self-centered? Because I don't see things *your* way?" She banged the mug down on the table and picked up her copy of the script. "I'm leaving."

"Wait." He stepped in her path as she tried to escape. "You don't have time to go back to Lucille's."

"I have plenty of time." She clutched the script to her chest tightly. "It's nine-thirty in the morning. We won't be performing until eight this evening."

"But we need to do a cleanup rehearsal this afternoon. We were out of sync a couple of times last night."

"Nobody even noticed. Besides, what do you care? You're not a professional dancer!" She flounced past him, heading for the bathroom. "I'm not going to rehearse today. And I'm not going to be driven mad by your perfectionism." Or his selfishness. "You can practice by yourself."

"Gabby!"

But she slammed the bathroom door and locked it, taking a deep breath. Sunlight filtered through the skylight, glimmering off the fronds of the huge fern hanging underneath. The atmosphere was meant to be tranquil. She felt anything but. And now she was going to have to find a taxi to take her back to Beverly Hills, or phone Lucille and ask her to send the car back. Embarrassing.

Meanwhile, Kit continued cooking the brunch he had planned for them. The activity made him feel only a little less frustrated and angry, but he was resolved to remain calm. Gabby was behaving irrationally enough for both of them. Having gotten it into her head that she wanted a movie role, she was obviously willing to sacrifice everything else for it, including a relationship with him.

Shades of Anita Brooks and Price Garfield!

Was there a curse on their parents that had filtered down to them? Kit realized he'd shown very poor judgment by getting involved with Anita's daughter in the first place. Perhaps she was the ambitious sort of woman who would stop at nothing to reach the top. Maybe she'd even thought she could make some connections through him and was now disappointed.

Appalled at the very thought, Kit wondered

if she might have been pretending to have feelings for him to further her goals.

The sound of the bathroom door opening got his attention, and he found Gabby gazing around as if searching for something.

"What are you looking for?"

"I want the number for a taxi."

One look at her angry if open and appealing face made him reject the worst of his paranoid suspicions. Canny at sizing people up, he surely would have known if she were a blatant, callous user. And she had a heart—she'd certainly gone out of her way to be kind to Lucille and her boarders. So what was wrong with him that he was ready to jump to such a ridiculous conclusion?

"You won't need to call a taxi," he told her gruffly. "I'll drive you to Beverly Hills."

She put her hands on her hips. "You mean you aren't going to try to lock me up here and make me rehearse?"

"If you're adamant about not going over the dances again, then we'll have to forgo them."

"I guess when you work with a partner, the individuals don't always get to do what they want."

Meaning *he* wouldn't agree to act in the movie. Lord, the woman could be irritating.

Keeping his tongue in check, Kit simply asked, "Are you ready to go?"

"Are you sure you wouldn't prefer I take a taxi?"

Obviously she didn't want to spend more time with him than necessary. "It would cost a fortune, and it would take forever. If I take you, you'll be more rested."

She grimaced and muttered, "I should have known you'd have your own reasons."

They left a few minutes later. Quiet and pensive, Gabby leaned toward the window on the passenger side of the car as if to put as much distance as possible between them. Kit only hoped her attitude would improve before their performance that night.

HAPPY THAT SHE WOULD be able to avoid Lucille's sharp eyes, Gabby used her key and sneaked up the mansion's staircase undetected. When she reached the suite she was sharing with her mother, however, she opened the door and found Anita sitting in a chair and riffling through a magazine.

Her mother peered at Gabby over her reading glasses. "You're back already?"

Gabby didn't want the older woman to know the extent of her involvement with Kit, especially since she herself was so disapproving of Anita's relationship with Kit's father. The last thing she wanted to do was admit all that had happened between them.

She thought fast. "Our brunch plans changed, that's all."

Anita frowned. "Are you all right? You look upset."

"I'm fine. I promise." Without thinking, she threw the script onto an end table.

Anita stared at the binder. "What's that?"

Discouraged, Gabby hadn't even considered telling her mother about the offer. "It's a script for a movie called *Tango.*" Again she felt resentment toward Kit. "We were approached by an independent producer who wants to cast us in the leads."

"A movie? And you've been offered a leading role?" Anita immediately approached to hug her daughter tightly. "How wonderful!" Then the older woman held Gabby at arm's length. Her expression was proud. "This is the break we've been hoping for! I knew something would happen if we came to California. Wait, you're not smiling."

"Kit isn't interested."

"What is his problem?" the older woman asked, her tone incredulous.

"He doesn't want to act or sing. And he doesn't consider dancing at Cheek to Cheek a professional engagement."

"My heavens, he's content to waste his talent? Even his father says Kit is fantastic."

"I know. But Kit could care less what anyone thinks, especially his father."

Anita shook her head. "That was apparent last night. Everyone could tell Price was trying to reach out to his son. And Kit would have none of it. That young man's got an attitude."

Gabby fully agreed. "He's willful, arrogant and pigheaded. He wouldn't even read the script. I got so disgusted that we ended up having a fight."

"Poor baby."

"He said I was self-centered." When her mother quirked her eyebrows, Gabby went on to explain. "He thinks it's selfish of me to want him to take a movie role so I can have one, too. I told Kit *he* was being selfish by refusing."

She wasn't going to explain her more complex motives for wanting to capitalize on the opportunity. She couldn't tell Anita that she loved Kit and that making a movie would give them more of a long-term chance to build a relationship.

"It sounds like you're asking him to have all his teeth pulled out rather than star in a movie."

"Doesn't it?"

"Oh, dear, this is terribly upsetting." Picking up the script, Anita glanced at it.

Gabby watched her, feeling a bit guilty for giving her mother a hard time rather than a shoulder to lean on when Anita had been complaining about Price the other night. But surely that was different. Anita was only trying to come to terms with her old feelings—to rid herself of them, Gabby told herself—while she was trying to come to terms with new, acceptable ones.

Gabby stretched out on the bed, fluffing up a couple of pillows behind her. Anita relaxed on the ornate chaise longue that sat in front of the bedroom window. Reading glasses perched on her nose, the older woman thumbed through the first few pages of the script.

"I'd have to read this more thoroughly to give you my opinion," Anita said. "But it certainly sets the mood. It looks promising.

"You mean it *would* be promising. I'm not

even sure I'll read it at all. I might feel too bad about the missed opportunity."

"Can't you convince Kit to change his mind?"

"I don't want to try. He's adamant about his disliking show business."

"He's a chip off the old block in more ways than one." Anita shook her head. "Price used to claim he hated the business, too."

"But he worked in it, anyway."

"He said that was only because he didn't have another way to earn a decent living." Anita took off her reading glasses. "He did love creating dance routines, though, if not performing them. Once he got started in professional choreography, he would have had a difficult time giving it all up."

"Kit's just as talented," Gabby maintained. "I don't see how he can work in a corporation day in and day out."

"Such a waste."

"But try to tell him that. He's impossible."

"Don't forget that he's only known about the script for a few hours," Anita pointed out. "Perhaps you should give him some time to think about it. He didn't want to work at Cheek to Cheek at first, either. Lucille says he used the excuse of helping her to avoid facing his own desires. He may be tempted yet."

Gabby smiled. "You really believe that, don't you?"

"I've had more experience dealing with Garfield men than you, darling. Price is as stubborn as a mule. In the old days I knew I had to remain cool and logical so that we wouldn't argue when I was trying to get him to change his mind about something." She paused. "Not that I always had the patience to do so. I sometimes lost my temper and didn't give a fig."

"You're only human."

"Nevertheless, if *I* were dealing with Kit in this situation, I'd try to curb my own anger and resentment so that I could appeal to him both logically and emotionally."

"How's that?"

Gabby was seriously interested. Her mother could be quite clever. Dare she let a shred of hope creep into her heart?

Anita went on. "As I've already mentioned, give Kit some time. Read over the script, and when he's reasonable again, point out its money-making potential."

"He already has enough money."

"Then tell him it has artistic depth—the

kind that demands a truly wonderful dancer/
choreographer. Suggest that 'art' will suffer
because of his refusal to be in the movie."

Gabby chuckled.

"But that's really true, dear," Anita insisted. "Be sincere with Kit. Tell him how
much it means to you to be able to dance
professionally. Perhaps he doesn't get the
same thrill from dancing—though I find that
highly unlikely—but tell him there's nothing you would rather do and that you long
to share your grand passion with the largest
audience possible. Movies are seen by more
people than musicals or plays, you know."

Gabby wasn't sure Kit would go for that,
but it might be worth a try. "And by people
of all generations. Audiences are still thrilled
by your old dance movies."

Anita smiled. "Yes, I ran into a young fan
the other night. She watches Price and me
every New Year's, and she actually wanted
our autographs."

"How nice."

Gabby remembered the absence of Anita's
footprints in front of Mann's Chinese Theater
and wondered how long it would be before
her mother found out.

"I guess I forgot to tell you about the autographs," Anita went on. "But we were discussing my difficulties with Price at the time."

Again Gabby felt guilty. "And I'm sorry I wasn't as supportive as I should have been. I guess I did more lecturing than listening."

"You were merely stating your opinion. I've been thinking about what you said about your father. Do you remember when you began to feel he was distant?"

"I don't know. Maybe I was nine or ten."

"Hmm, I wondered. About that time Robert and I had a big disagreement about something that must have been bothering him for years. He demanded that I throw out all of my Hollywood memorabilia."

"Your dresses and publicity photos?" Gabby knew how her mother loved the stuff.

"And the old films, too. I refused."

"But why would he insist you do that?"

"He knew I'd always loved Price Garfield."

Gabby almost dared not ask. "More than Dad?"

"I loved your father dearly," Anita insisted. "He had nothing to fear. If Price had divorced every one of his wives and come to me on his knees, I would never have left Robert for him."

"Then Dad was wrong."

"For the most part." This time Anita spoke more slowly, "There's a special bond between dance partners like Price and me. I couldn't help missing that interchange, and your father...well, he couldn't provide it." The older woman's eyes filled with tears. "I guess Robert was correct in a way, though I would have died rather than admit it to him when he was alive."

Somehow, deep inside, Gabby wasn't surprised. She slid out of bed and went to her mother's side. "Oh, Mom," she murmured, placing an arm around Anita's shoulders.

"You know how it is when you love something so much. I missed acting and moviemaking and Los Angeles. Broadway was never the same." Anita wiped her eyes. "I don't know how much all that played a part in the rift between me and your father. It probably wasn't just Price."

"I understand."

Gabby thought of her own heartbreak when she gave up all hopes of dancing professionally. What if she had had a husband who wanted her to throw out all her old programs and costumes? But then, of course, a rival like Price Garfield wouldn't be a factor. She guessed she could understand her father's resentment, too.

"I never thought Robert would let our problem come between him and one of our children," Anita continued.

Gabby gazed at her intently. "Are you saying he did, though? You wouldn't admit it the other night."

"I didn't want to admit it to myself. But now I wonder." The older woman's voice was sad. "When you were nine, you suddenly shot up, and you were doing especially well in your dancing lessons. You were always a star at class recitals as well as the little shows you put on at home. Robert mentioned more than once how much you resembled me physically, too."

Gabby swallowed and Anita patted her hand. Her father had remained distant from his own child because her looks and talent reminded him of his wife? The explanation made her sad. Her father had in a way rejected the devotion each of them could have given him.

"Robert did love you, darling," Anita said softly. "I'm certain of that. But he simply couldn't stand the idea of being second with me, even though I reassured him he was number one over and over." Anita sighed. "He wouldn't believe me. And he expanded his practice, kept himself busy. Too busy to attend dance recitals."

Both women were silent for a moment, then Gabby spoke up. "I guess I understand now, though I can't help resenting Dad for his behavior."

"Then blame me, as well—it's probably as much my fault as his."

"Because you loved California and movies?"

"Because I foolishly ran away from it. And, more important, because I—" Anita stopped in midsentence. "Never mind. The past is the past." Again she grew teary. "I'm so sorry my problems caused you pain, sweetheart."

"Please don't blame yourself." Gabby embraced her mother. "And I'm not in pain, especially now that we've talked this out."

Indeed, Gabby felt as if part of the burden of her father's rejection had been lifted from her heart. But she was more certain than ever that her mother had always loved Price Garfield, whether or not she would admit it. At least that impossible love must have mellowed by now.

A woman her mother's age shouldn't be torn by the throes of passion.

CHAPTER TWELVE

"I TOLD YOU we needed a cleanup rehearsal," Kit groused as he and Gabby stood in the wings, waiting to go out for their third and last dance Saturday night.

"It wouldn't have helped." Gabby gave an exaggerated sigh. "And I didn't make a mistake. Anyone can slip, and I caught myself. No one noticed."

On edge, he couldn't help but be annoyed that she didn't seem to be unsettled, as well. He had hoped she would have softened toward him by now. Unless, of course, she didn't have any feelings for him.

"Everyone had to notice your little slip," he insisted. "There was a definite pause, and you wobbled when you danced up the steps."

She scowled. "Maybe for a microsecond."

"Trivialize precision if you want!" Kit said, not caring that his mood was becoming blacker by the moment. "It makes the difference between a good and a great performance."

Gabby set her jaw. "The audience applauded long and loud, Kit. We were great! Now why don't you relax already and shut up."

"Shut up?" Now he was downright angry. "Is that the way to talk to your partner?"

"It is if my partner is trying to give me a hard time. That's what this drill is about." She crossed her arms over her chest and stared at him defiantly. "You're being obnoxious."

"If you think I have nothing better to do than give you a hard time, you're egotistical."

"And you're cold and arrogant."

"Oh? And am I supposed to feel warm toward you after you walked out on me this morning?"

Every time Kit took Gabby in his arms, he was reminded that she'd left him without a backward glance. He'd thought they had something special together, but he must have overestimated their mutual attraction. That thought made him feel foolish.

"At the moment I don't care how you feel," she insisted.

As if he hadn't guessed. "Did you ever care?"

"I won't even bother answering that."

Things were quickly getting out of hand,

but Kit wasn't in the mood to back off. When the stage manager cued them, he couldn't stop himself from making one last sarcastic remark.

"Ready? Here's hoping you make it through this one without stumbling."

"Stuff it up your nose, Garfield," Gabby snapped.

The fiery music of "Tango Olé" intruded on their argument, and they glided out into the heat of the spotlights and slithered down the steps to the dance floor below. Kit approached Gabby and she turned her back on cue, flipping her glittery black shawl over her shoulder with such force that the fringe struck him in the face.

He grimaced but didn't miss a step. As choreographed, he clasped Gabby's arm before lowering his lips to her throat. She winced as she pulled away, making him realize he'd grasped her too tightly. Not that he'd meant to. Their real-life emotions were spilling over into the dance, threatening to ruin the routine. Still, he couldn't curb his hostility at the click of her heels.

They glared at each other as the number progressed, Gabby whirling her shawl around her in a frenzy. For a moment Kit wondered if she were going to toss the garment directly in his face, but when she threw it to the side, the shawl missed him by several inches. Grasping her arm again, he spun her fiercely from left to right, then back into his embrace. Lips slightly parted, she lifted her chin and stared down her small nose with a frigid blue gaze that was in direct contrast with her sensual expression.

The air around them seemed to crackle.

At least the character of the Latin dance seemed to fit their moods, Kit thought.

Circling each other like adversaries, their hostility was definitely a reflection of grand passion. But was it all manufactured? he wondered. Or did Gabby feel as he did? Even in the midst of their quarrel, he'd wanted to take her in his arms. And that feeling was growing.

In the final movement Kit held Gabby's waist as she wrapped her leg around him and flung back her head. The lights dimmed and Kit breathed a sigh of relief when she freed him and moved away. They'd executed "Tango Olé" flawlessly.

They left the stage to thunderous applause.

Once backstage, Gabby turned to him accusingly. "You hurt my arm."

"You flipped your shawl in my face," he returned.

"That was an accident."

"So was my grip. I didn't mean to hurt you. If so, I could have dropped you on one of the lifts."

"And ruin the dance entirely? I don't think you'd go that far, Mr. Perfect."

As if he would purposely hurt her!

She tossed her head and started off for her dressing room, Kit on her heels.

One of the stagehands gazed at them admiringly as they passed. "Wow, you two were something else. That was the best tango I've ever seen."

They both slowed down.

"You really think so?" Kit asked.

The stagehand nodded. "You two were smoking!"

"Smoking is a fairly accurate description," Gabby said.

"Steaming is also a good word," Kit added, unable to hold back a grin.

"Steamy?" the stagehand said.

"No, *steaming*," Gabby put in, actually chuckling before she turned away.

And Kit swore he heard her laugh aloud before she closed the door of her dressing room. Irritating as she might be, at least she had a sense of humor. Maybe she would come around, admit she was wrong, beg his forgiveness.

And maybe pigs could fly, a little voice added.

Shaking his head, wondering what in the world he'd gotten himself into by allowing himself to become personally involved with Gabby, Kit stalked to his own dressing room.

Maybe they were both too stubborn ever to work out a relationship.

GABBY'S HIGH SPIRITS were only temporary. They plunged to a new low as Maria helped her remove the tango costume. The dresser hung the garment and, after being assured she wouldn't be needed further, left the room.

Gabby removed her stage makeup and changed into her own bright lavender crepe evening dress. The last dance had been spectacular, and the stagehand's remarks had been funny, but the petty fight she'd had with Kit had been deplorable. How could they have sunk to such a level? She hated feeling hurt and angry whenever she so much as looked at him.

At least he cared enough to feel hurt, as well.

He'd been offended this morning when he thought she seemed more interested in career matters than their relationship. He was crazy to think she had no feelings for him; even though she fought it, she realized she loved him more than ever. But no matter which way she looked at it, their situation was complicated and problematic.

Gabby sat in front of the dressing room mirror to apply fresh mascara and eyeliner. She assumed Lucille wanted her to join the hostess's personal party out front again. Would she be expected to sit beside her partner? Probably. She and Kit would have to put on a good face for the others. At the thought of the discomfort they would both experience, she sighed in frustration.

Ready a few minutes later, Gabby strolled slowly past Kit's dressing room, noting the sliver of light beneath the closed door. Dance music drifted from the stage area, and she wished for nothing more than to be in Kit's arms, where she belonged. She decided to face him right that moment and talk things out. So much for the patience her mother had suggested. She knocked loudly.

"Come in."

Kit's neutral tone rather surprised her. She opened the door to find him leaning back in his chair, his feet propped on the dressing table. His head was thrown back as though he, too, were reliving the night, wishing they were still dancing together. When he saw her, his expression changed subtly, but he was quick to recover.

She stepped inside and shut the door behind her. "I hated feeling angry with you."

"Does that mean you aren't anymore?" he asked coolly.

"Now I'm just hurt."

She hated wearing her heart on her sleeve, too, but she couldn't let bad feelings continue to build between them.

"And you want to talk about it?"

"If you're willing."

He gazed at her intently. "I'd like to see things between us cleared up."

"We were both using the dance as a metaphor for other issues."

"Obviously."

She felt relieved that he seemed so calm; perhaps he'd already had enough time to cool down. Now it was up to her to straighten things out between them. But how to start?

"Have a seat," he suggested, taking his feet off the table.

"I'm sorry I lost my temper with you," she began. "But I think I should explain where I was coming from this morning." Gabby paused. This was harder than she'd expected, and he wasn't giving her any encouragement. He was staring at her with that enigmatic expression that he seemed to have perfected. "You may have a career to go back to when this engagement is over—a job that satisfies you. I don't."

"I thought you ran a dance school."

"That's right. But I'm not exactly thrilled with the idea of teaching classes for the rest of my life," she told him in a low voice. "And I've never confessed that to anyone other than myself, so don't spread it around, all right?"

"Who would I tell?"

"Your father, my mother. I don't want to hurt her."

"Your secret's safe."

"It's not that I don't enjoy working with students, exactly. But I need a better avenue for my creativity. Perhaps I'd feel differently if I'd ever reached the top of my profession. As it was, my heart was broken when I retired from Broadway." She paused, gazing at her feet. "I'm ashamed to admit it, but that's the truth."

Kit couldn't help but feel touched by her vulnerability. "You're not a failure, Gabby. Luck and timing are also very important in show business success. And you're very talented. If you try, I'm sure you can dream up plenty of other ways to exercise your skills."

"I don't know whether I could love anything as much as dancing."

He remained sympathetic. Although he hated to admit it, he himself had fond memories of his club performance days, and he was going to miss performing even more after the stint at Cheek to Cheek.

"I was so hopeful when Luke Sheffield approached us about the movie this morning," Gabby went on. "At least I would have several more months of dancing and the possibility of making further connections."

The movie again. "I understand, but—"

"Do you really?" she cut in swiftly. She leaned forward. "You seem to have overlooked another advantage working on a movie together would offer us. I'd be staying in California for a while instead of returning to New York." When he remained silent, she went on. "We could be together personally…if that matters to you."

"It matters to me. But I don't see that this movie is the only way we can continue our relationship. Or that it promises a career to come."

"What else do you suggest?"

"Airline tickets aren't so expensive between New York and L.A. We could still see each other."

She didn't appear happy with that solution. "Three or four times a year at the most. No, I wouldn't go for that."

No? The thought of never seeing her again hit him even harder than he would have expected.

"Why wouldn't traveling back and forth work?" he asked, hoping to persuade her. "Maybe you're not used to long-distance relationships." He stood up and approached her. "I've done it. I grew up with it. My mother was on location when she met my father and most of the time during their marriage."

"Which ended in divorce."

True. Kit had also broken up with the girl-friend he'd traveled to see after only two trips. And his feelings for Gabby ran much deeper than they had for any other woman. His gaze swept over her, the sheen of her red-gold hair, the ivory perfection of her shoulders and arms above the beaded bodice of the silky lavender dress, the sincere clarity of her aqua-blue eyes when she looked up at him. His heart tripped, making him feel young and silly.

"A bicoastal relationship may be trendy, but I guess I want our relationship to be a bit more old-fashioned and fulfilling," she admitted. "Why can't you at least take a look at the script?"

"One script, one movie can't be the solution," he insisted logically.

"Say 'might not be.' That's less negative."

"If that's what you want."

"And furthermore, you could be wrong. This movie could be a start in the right direction, Kit. We would be working together for months. Who knows what might happen after that, what we could make happen?" Her expression hinted at a multitude of hopes. "I don't expect one movie to make me a big star. I only want the chance to dance professionally as long as possible...*with you*."

"Our dancing *has* been an incredible experience," he agreed.

Sensual, dynamic, inspiring. The perfection of their partnership had added another dimension to their relationship...had made a difference in his life, he had to admit.

"Won't you please read the script?" Gabby asked again.

Kit was trying to imagine how he would get along without her if she returned to New York.

"You'll enjoy doing more performing and choreography," she continued. "You love dancing. You couldn't be so good at it otherwise."

He sighed. He couldn't hide his most secret desires from her.

"So will you or won't you?" she persisted.

"All right." Despite all his rationalization about not wanting to make a movie, he had to give in or lose her. "I'll read the thing. I suppose committing an hour and a half of my time couldn't hurt."

"Wonderful!" She rose to face him, her soft lips curving into a beautiful smile.

"But I'm not promising anything."

"The fact that you're willing to be open-minded is enough for me right now."

But what about later? Kit wondered. What would happen if he decided he wasn't interested in making the movie? Incredibly the thought frightened him.

"Thank you so much, Kit," she murmured, moving nearer to kiss him.

Her lips were feather-soft. Overwhelmed by Gabby's closeness, inhaling her light perfumed scent, he felt the love that had begun on the dance floor flowing through him. Over the wall speaker a love tune drifted in from the club. How appropriate.

Kit slid his hands along the warm smoothness of Gabby's arms. "I guess that bicoastal thing isn't really all that appealing when you get down to it," he told her gruffly. "I don't want you to leave California before we have a chance to explore the possibilities."

"Good, because I don't want to go."

Dangling herself in connection with a movie deal could smack of emotional blackmail, Kit realized. But what were the alternatives? He wasn't exactly ready to suggest she move in with him or get married, and he could understand her reluctance to become involved in a long-distance relationship. For that matter, he was reluctant, too, when he really thought about it. He wanted her in his arms as often as possible.

"I don't even want you to leave this dressing room," he murmured, pulling her against him.

"So make me stay."

He acquiesced, leaning in to kiss her.

"I don't know what will happen tomorrow, or even next week, but I'll take advantage of what you're willing to give right now," she said.

He pulled her to him tightly, as if holding her would keep her from leaving him. He kissed her delicately, sweetly.

"I love you, Gabby," he said softly, the words slipping out before he knew he was going to say them.

"I love you, too, Kit."

He kissed her, wondering why the magnitude of their declarations didn't have the power to frighten him. Instead, it seemed so natural.

And if they both cared so much, surely they could work out their future together.

AFTER THE SHOW, Price and Anita waited almost an hour at Lucille's table for Kit and Gabby.

"I wonder what's taking them so long," Anita fretted.

"I'll go see," Price offered.

He slipped backstage to see what was going on. He wasn't prepared for the murmured voices and low laughs coming from Kit's dressing room. But then he shouldn't be so surprised, Price told himself as he hurried away, a bit embarrassed. Both he and Lucille had noticed the looks that passed between Kit and Gabby and had discussed the amount of time they spent together above and beyond rehearsal.

If Anita hadn't realized the kids had a thing for each other by now, she must be going blind. Price didn't intend to tell her, however. He wasn't sure how she would handle the information and decided to avoid discussing their children's possible relationship altogether.

"So what's the delay?" Anita asked immediately when he returned to the table.

Price thought fast as he sat down. "They were tired and decided to leave."

"Too tired to stick around for even fifteen minutes?"

He shrugged nonchalantly. "Apparently. You know they've been rehearsing every spare moment."

Anita looked disapproving. "Gabby *has* been extremely exhausted by the rehearsals."

Exactly how upset would Anita be if she knew there was a second generation romance going on? Selfishly he hoped the additional complication wouldn't harm his own pursuit of the woman he loved. They finally seemed to be hitting it off without the constant bickering that had been such a hurdle only a week ago.

He scooted his chair closer to Anita's and took a sip of wine. At the moment he had his girl all to himself. Some of Lucille's other guests were dancing and the rest, including several of the boarders, were clustered at the other end of the table, gossiping among themselves.

He slid an arm across the back of Anita's chair.

She leaned away. "So what do we do?"

He frowned in annoyance. "Do about what?"

"Kit and Gabby. They're burning the candle at both ends."

"They're adults, Anita, and they're obviously having a good time. I don't think we should do anything."

"But…they're always together," Anita explained, hesitating a little, as if she wanted to choose her words carefully. "And they're both single. It might be very easy for them to become interested in each other."

Aha. Maybe she wasn't so blind, after all.

He gave her a nonchalant shrug. "I guess we'll have to let nature take its course."

Anita frowned. "I don't know if Kit would be good for Gabby."

Price couldn't help bristling. "And what's the matter with my son? He's successful and good-looking and a fine human being."

"But he must be a fairly confirmed bachelor by this age."

"Maybe he hasn't run into the right girl yet."

"Is he kind and considerate?"

"More than that, he's big-hearted—ask Lucille how good he's been to her over the years. And he's got straight-shooting values, as well," Price insisted.

"Considering the fact that you spend no time together, how would you know?"

"I've kept track of him from the time he was in grade school." He shifted uncomfortably at the admission.

Anita's expression was curious. "Even though you didn't keep up a real relationship?"

"I've always had someone keep an eye on Kit for me. Even now. Several old associates work within the Garfield Corporation. My son is hardworking, honest, sharp—"

"All right, all right," she interrupted, laughing. "He's a wonderful choice for my daughter to date. I wasn't trying to malign your family honor."

Price glanced down at the club's crowded dance floor, wondering if he should ask Anita to dance or to get her out of there. He didn't want Kit and Gabby to show suddenly and expose his lie. When Anita leaned back in her chair and yawned, he was relieved.

"You're tired," he said.

"A little. We've had a lot of late nights."

"Since Gabby and Kit aren't going to join us, why don't I take you home?" Still, he would have liked to hold her while they danced.

"Sounds sensible."

Saying good-night to Lucille and the others, they left the club. Soon they were driving along the quiet streets of Beverly Hills, passing by sprawling houses.

"I suppose I couldn't talk you into stopping by my place for a short while?" Price asked.

Anita had to admit she was curious about seeing the interior of his mansion…. "Maybe for half an hour."

"We'll leave whenever you say."

Anita didn't see the harm; they'd been getting along so well lately. And she felt particularly warm toward Price for the way he'd stuck up for his son earlier. He obviously loved Kit, whether or not he was able to communicate his feelings. If only he could open up more, be more sure of himself. But then he'd always had that problem with insecurity.

A few blocks later Price turned the car into a winding drive that led to a wrought-iron gate, which he opened with a remote-control. Beyond lay wide-landscaped lawns and Price's beautiful mansion with an attached four-car garage. The house was even more imposing than it had appeared in photographs, though it wasn't as fanciful or huge as Lucille's.

Price led her inside and showed her through the first floor before taking her up the stairs. Anita wasn't sure how she'd feel if he made a risqué suggestion again. It had been so long since they'd really kissed. So far he'd only nuzzled her lightly while dancing. Her pulse racing at the thought, she had to admit she wouldn't object if he kissed her.

"And here's the screening room," Price was

saying as he switched on the light in yet another room.

"Lovely."

Anita glanced about, admiring the thick gray wall-to-wall carpeting and the deeper gray velvet sectional sofa that took up a large part of the room. The sofa faced a massive black lacquer storage unit that lined an entire wall. In contrast with the low-key traditional or antique furnishings throughout the rest of the house, the ambience of this room was quite modern.

"But where's the screen?" Anita asked.

Price slid back one of the storage unit's larger panels. Behind it was a four-by-five-foot projection screen.

"And I suppose you have all of your old movies?"

"Of course. And I have a special shelf for the ones we made together. Want to see one?"

Anita laughed. "An entire movie? Not tonight."

"Are you sure? I've got a great setup in here."

"Thanks, but I'll pass."

The nostalgia would get to her at the moment, she was certain. And that was silly, considering the man who'd affected her so deeply all these years was standing right beside her. To put herself in a more comfortable frame of mind, however, she continued to inspect the storage unit, noting it had several rows of drawers.

"You must have lots of films," she commented.

"Uh-huh, and even more memorabilia of other sorts."

"Including your old tuxedo?"

"And a few of the feathers from that infernal dress in *White Tie and Tails.*"

Anita laughed. "You must be joking."

"Not at all. Somebody picked them up off the floor during filming, saved them and gave them to me a few months after you left for New York." He slid open one of the larger drawers, rummaging between a stack of photograph albums and scrapbooks. Finally he drew out a tightly sealed plastic bag and handed it to her. "Here you go."

The white feathers were yellow now but still intact. Anita drew a shaky breath and forced herself to smile. If she didn't smile, she would cry.

"You sneezed up a storm when I wore these."

"And you laughed because you knew I was allergic."

"I didn't mean any serious harm."

"Even if you did, I forgive you." He gazed at her intently, his green eyes asking her to remember the past they'd shared.

How could she ever forget it?

Uncomfortable, Anita swallowed the lump in her throat and picked up a blue album that was lying on top of the pile in the drawer. She leafed through it quickly, recognizing dozens of old photographs of herself and Price, including stills from their movies.

He came closer, gazing over her shoulder. His breath feathered her neck, making her shiver.

"So what's in the other albums?" she asked.

"A little of this and a little of that."

She put down the blue album and picked up a red one that was full of newspaper clippings, playbills and programs. *Her* playbills and programs and reviews, Anita suddenly realized, recognizing the titles of the ill-starred musicals in which she'd performed.

"How did you get this stuff?" she asked him. "Did you come to New York?" Had he been sitting in the audience while she sang and danced unaware that he was watching?

He didn't answer directly. "It's not hard to get anything you want if you have enough connections."

Touched by Price's nostalgic side, Anita wasn't sure what to say. He'd kept up his interest in her even when they were apart. Of course, there had also been his wives….

"Do you have an album of Lana Worth's movies somewhere around here, as well?" And Betty Masters's? Anita wondered, curious if not willing to look them over.

"I don't have them anymore."

Good. At least she didn't have to share drawer space with those other women, Anita thought. Flipping to the back of the red album, she found a more recent program.

"This is one of the productions Gabby had a part in," she noted in surprise. "How sweet."

"Well, had things turned out differently, I could have been her father."

"Yes," Anita agreed simply.

"Not that I don't also take pride in Kit." Price reached around her to withdraw yet another album. "I obtained copies of his high school and college yearbooks and then I collected these clippings when Kit was competing professionally in ballroom." He opened the album and pointed to a page proudly.

"First in the Modern and Latin division. The kid was always damn good with his feet."

And his father had been a distant sentimentalist. "Too bad you couldn't have told Kit how you felt years ago."

Price nodded. "At least I'm going to tell him now."

"Even though he snipes at you?" Anita had felt terrible when Price's feelings had been hurt the night before.

"I won't give up or walk away. It may take some time to get through to Kit, but I know he's a decent man at heart. I'm going to take your advice about it never being too late. My son has always been important to me. It's time he knew it."

"Oh, Price."

She touched his hand, smiling at him warmly. Beneath his cool exterior Price had always been caring, though he'd sometimes had difficulty expressing that caring openly... or without being demanding and controlling. But he was trying to change; he *had* changed if he was willing to try to develop a relationship with his son. Suddenly the obstacles of the past seemed to dissolve, and Anita felt closer to Price than she ever had before.

"Kit could have been *your* son, you know,"

he pointed out. His voice was sad, his expression faraway, as if gazing back at the years of separation. "What really happened? How could we have been so stupid?"

Tears filled Anita's eyes. She couldn't stop them if she tried. "I don't know."

Price took a deep, uneven breath. "Don't cry, Nita. We're together right now at least."

"But it's been so long. And you were watching over me...us...all this time."

"I've never stopped loving you." Price kissed her cheek and sat her down on the couch. Then he wrapped his arms around her. "I only hope you never forgot me."

"Never," she said simply.

"We're a couple of old fools, aren't we?"

Anita nodded and blew her nose in a tissue. "But I guess you're never too old to make a fool of yourself."

And she was probably about to take another step in that same direction as she leaned over to press her lips against those of the man she loved. Price gathered her closer, deepening the kiss. She wound her arms about his neck, her heart pounding. She'd been innocent back when they'd worked together, but now she knew what loving really meant, and she wanted to experience every facet of the emotion with Price Garfield.

   At last.

CHAPTER THIRTEEN

"ISN'T THE PACIFIC beautiful?" Anita asked breathlessly, holding hands with Price as they sat side by side on canvas beach chairs the next afternoon. "I always thought the Atlantic looked cold and gray by comparison."

Her escort smiled. "You're a true California girl."

"Maybe, but nobody's going to get me into a bikini."

"You're no fun."

Anita punched his arm playfully.

"What's this about fun?" Lucille rasped from where she was stretched out on a portable chaise.

"Price was saying I'm no fun because I opted not to wear a bikini to Jayne's beach party," Anita explained.

"I'm just happy you could come," Jayne said as she stirred coals on a portable grill. "It's nothing fancy, but I want to celebrate. I could hardly believe it when my agent called this morning and told me I got a part, small though it may be."

Actually, Jayne would be playing a dead body in the movie for which she'd read for the 'Jayne Hunter' role. Anita knew the few moments on-screen couldn't make up for the woman's larger disappointment, but for the moment Jayne was happy.

"I don't know if anyone will recognize me stretched out on the floor of an elevator," she was saying. "But at least I'll be paid scale for a week's worth of work. I'm not proud. Making some money is good news to me."

"You would have heard the good news yesterday if Elsie had remembered to give you the message," Neil pointed out. "That woman's memory is getting as bad as her hearing and eyesight."

"Don't give poor old Elsie a hard time," Lucille said sharply. "She tries her best. She didn't even wanna come along today because she was feeling poorly and figured she should cook and clean up."

Finished arranging hot dogs and hamburgers on the grill, Jayne pushed back a lock of hair. "I told her she didn't have to work."

"But she'd feel terrible if she couldn't," Lucille said.

"We all have to adjust to our physical limitations as we grow older," Risa commented. Decked out in a long caftan and a wide hat to protect her delicate skin, the elderly actress leaned back in her beach chair and brushed some sand off her skirt.

"Speaking of limitations, how's Chester?" Anita asked.

"He says the new medicine's making him feel better," Lucille said, "but I think it's too soon to tell. It's gonna take a while."

"He got out of bed and walked around this morning," Yancy added.

Anita nodded. "That sounds promising."

"Yeah, now if we only knew where Harvey disappeared to on Friday night, the household would be in pretty good shape," Lucille said.

"Harvey's been gone two nights now?" Anita asked, immediately concerned. Gabby had told her that the comedian left the club to look for his partner, but she hadn't realized he'd been gone all this time.

"Should we drive around and search for him?" Price inquired.

"Nah, I already did that and didn't see hide nor hair of the old coot," Lucille told them. "I don't think we should worry quite yet. Harvey disappeared a coupla years back, then turned up again a few days later."

Anita shook her head. If it wasn't one thing, it was inevitably another at Lucille's house. At least she always seemed capable of dealing with the stress. But then Anita wondered if the constant problems made Lucille feel more alive somehow.

Jayne's brows were furrowed as she turned the burgers. "I only hope Harvey hasn't been mugged or something. Elderly people are often seen as targets by thieves and gangs."

Risa sniffed and raised her aristocratic nose. "Hmph. The elderly in this society receive little respect from anyone. If you're over sixty-five, you might as well be dead."

"That's an exaggeration," Anita objected.

"But not by much," Yancy insisted. "We live in a throwaway, youth-worshipping society. If something's old and wrinkled, you toss it. Elders aren't respected for their wisdom the way they are in Pueblo Indian tribes or China."

"These days you don't have to be sixty-five to be thrown away," Jayne put in with a grimace. "You can be out of style at forty-five."

"Or even thirty-five," Risa said. "Perhaps

we should all become militant and join the—
what is the name of that organization?"

"The Gray Panthers," Yancy said with a
grin. "I can see it now—we'll have the one
and only chapter in Beverly Hills. That'll get
the neighbors up in arms. We'll march and
carry signs, train ourselves in kung fu and
karate."

Neil laughed. "But Risa will want a lace
collar for her uniform."

The conversation turned to more pleasant
topics as Jayne dished out the food—hot dogs,
hamburgers, potato salad, baked beans, fruit,
celebratory sparkling wine and soft drinks.

After they'd eaten, Price and Anita took
a stroll down the beach. It was a beautiful
Sunday, but this particular stretch of Santa
Monica oceanfront was deserted, since it was
privately owned. Luckily Lucille still had
connections and had called an old acquain-
tance who'd been willing to let them have
a party on her property. The only people in
sight were a couple of surfers fighting with
the waves in the distance.

"So what's next?" Price asked after he and
Anita had walked hand in hand for a while,
listening to the crash of incoming breakers.
"Where do we go from here? That conversa-

tion about aging made me think about how little time we have left."

Anita squeezed his hand reassuringly. "Don't let it get you down. We can't worry about tomorrow. We have to enjoy today."

"But we can still make a few plans. I think we should get married."

Anita's heart skipped a beat. She could hardly believe she was nervous at the mention of marriage to Price after all these years. Instead of agreeing with him, she commented, "I thought you didn't want to get married again. You said you were jinxed."

He nodded. "Because I didn't hook up with the right woman in the first place. But surely it'll be different with you and me. We love each other and always have." He stopped and turned toward her. "We can fly to Las Vegas this very night and visit a wedding chapel."

Hadn't he noticed that she hadn't given him an answer? "One of those tacky little places?"

He seemed disappointed. "Would you rather have a fancier wedding?"

"At the very least I would want to inform my children before making a major change in my life." *If* she agreed to marry him.

"Hmm. You might have a problem with Gabby. I don't think she likes me very much.

We'd do better to elope and take care of details afterward."

Anita said nothing, thinking about Gabby as she stared down at her gritty, sand-covered feet. Her daughter had been sleeping when they left Lucille's house, obviously having come in late again the night before. But Gabby wasn't the real problem here. Anita herself was reluctant to make plans right away, probably because of the difficulties she'd always had with Price. Even though she loved the man, she couldn't help being afraid.

"You can have a bag packed and we can leave right after the show at the club," Price continued enthusiastically. "If you want, we could even stay over a night or two in Vegas to celebrate. The Wynn is supposed to be the height of luxury—"

"Hold on," Anita interrupted. "You're making plans before I've agreed to anything."

"You don't want to go to Las Vegas?"

"I might not even want to get married, at least not tonight. I need some time to think."

Price's mouth formed a straight line. "I can't believe this—you sound the same as you did in 1954."

"As do you. You're still assuming things

and making plans." Anita fumed. He always had to have control.

He sighed. "How long do I have to wait for an answer?"

"A few days." He looked so downcast that she felt guilty about not agreeing directly. "I love you, Price, and I'm fairly certain I want to marry you. Just give me some time to get used to the idea."

"All right." Tucking her arm inside of his, he started walking again. "I only hope you won't let Gabby talk you out of this. But if she tries, why don't you suggest she move to California, as well? There might be certain attractions for her out here already."

"You mean work?"

"Or romance," Price said smugly. "Gabby and Kit have been seeing each other, you know."

"I realized a bond was forming, but I wasn't sure how serious it was. Do you know more than I?"

He cleared his throat. "Enough to think they might be quite serious."

"Good heavens! This situation is getting more and more complicated."

"More complicated than I ever expected when I set it up."

Anita focused on his last words. "When you did what?"

To his credit Price looked embarrassed. Then he confessed, "I suppose I might as well get it out in the open. It's going to come out someday, anyway. I own the largest percentage of Cheek to Cheek. I suggested that Lucille contact you in New York so that Gabby and Kit could dance together. I figured you'd come along if Lucille encouraged you and we'd have another chance to get together."

She pulled away from him. "You *arranged* everything?"

He appeared worried. "Please don't get upset. I didn't know how else we could come in contact."

"You didn't have to be devious or so distrustful. You can write—why didn't you send a letter?"

"I thought you'd throw it away."

"Then you could have hopped on a plane!" Anita said, her anger rising.

"I was afraid you would refuse to see me." He tried to convince her. "Look, everything's working out. We made up, Lucille has a money-making venture and Kit and Gabby are doing what they do best. What's the harm?"

Anita couldn't believe the man's gall. "I thought you had changed, but you're as manipulative and high-handed as you ever were!"

She turned and flounced away.

"Anita!" Price followed swiftly, his feet spraying sand. "Come on, we belong together. You admitted that last night. Who cares how that came to be?"

"I care," she stated, seething now. "You know I hate being controlled and manipulated."

"There's no way I could ever control you."

"But you'll keep trying!"

Out of breath, he paused, obviously slowed by his age.

Having the advantage of a few less years and the greater stamina of anger, Anita kept marching.

"Anita!" he shouted. "Don't do this to me again!"

"Get lost!"

He could go home and paste some more photos in his albums, a place where paper people and their lives could easily be controlled. In his son's case, perhaps Price had always felt that was safer, anyway.

"Anita!"

Price's voice grew fainter as she hurried on. He didn't run to catch her, and when she turned a few minutes later, he'd disappeared.

Not knowing whether she felt relieved or disappointed, Anita wept and stared out to sea. The breakers rolling in brought back the memory of a grandiose party she'd attended with Price, the last social occasion they'd shared before he'd married and she'd fled for New York.

Odd, but the gathering had even been near this very area, at a great house that no longer existed except for its servants quarters, now the Sand and Sea Club.

She and Price had argued on the beach....

Santa Monica, 1954

"I CAN'T BELIEVE you'd be so underhanded!" Anita accused Price angrily, placing her hands on her black-satin-clad hips. "And I don't know how you thought you'd get away with it."

"There's no harm done," Price insisted. "I told Scotty it was only a joke. He's just as happy with his new date, and you're with me."

"Only long enough to tell you off!"

"Anita," Price said placatingly, taking her elbow to lead her toward the beach and away from the crowd milling around the beautiful seaside house. "You don't want to make a scene."

She shook him off but kept walking. "I'll make a scene if I want to!" She stopped and faced him defiantly. "We're going to have it out right here and now!"

"Whatever you say."

"You really have some nerve! You're the one who gets his own way no matter what, and I'm tired of it."

He gazed at her longingly, his expression sad. "No, I haven't gotten my way at all or we'd be married."

"Don't start with that!"

Anita was furious. Price had finally gone too far. Jealous over her publicity date for the eight-hundred-guest party, he'd had someone call Scott Murphy to tell him Anita was ill, then had had Anita phoned and informed that Scotty had broken his leg.

Offering himself as her escort instead—though he'd admitted he would have preferred having dinner with her alone—Price had been "kind" enough to take her to the event. She'd thought she would sink right through the floor when they encountered a perfectly healthy Scotty, date in tow, and the ruse had been disclosed.

Anita stomped off along the beach again, her evening sandals already full of sand. Price matched her determined pace while, behind them, music from a live orchestra drifted from the mansion and mingled with the tinkling sounds of the full-size carousel between the servants' quarters and the tennis courts.

Tonight glittering movie moguls and stars rubbed elbows with the wealthy elite of Los Angeles, drinking cocktails and champagne, dancing and splashing in the estate's swimming pools, one of which was spanned by a Venetian marble footbridge. But Anita no longer felt like enjoying the spectacle.

When they'd put some distance between themselves and the party, Price finally halted, assumed a patient expression and turned toward his companion, obviously waiting for her to unleash her ire. But the walk had cooled Anita off a little, making her think about how deep and complex the problems between Price and herself really were.

The infuriating man would have to cease trying to control her—or else.

"I won't be manipulated again," she began.

"I won't ever marry you if you don't stop pulling stunts like this." She took a deep breath. "Maybe part of the problem is that we only make movies together. My agent thinks I should try one solo."

His eyebrows shot up. "What?"

She had long feared that her popularity rested on dancing with Price, and she was considering taking her agent's suggestion.

"We don't have to star in the same movies. We're two different people."

"Who love each other..."

She could tell he was extremely upset, but she refused to become completely conciliatory. "We can still see each other while we work on our own projects. And I didn't say I wouldn't perform with you once in a while."

He shook his head adamantly. "That's not okay with me."

"Then it'll have to not be okay."

"Don't I have anything to say about this?"

Feeling a bit guilty, she explained, "I would've talked it out with you at a better time if you hadn't made me so angry tonight."

"There would never be a good time for this sort of news." He gazed down the beach, then at her, his expression cold. "But I see what you're getting at—you've used me."

"Used you?"

Price leaned toward her, his eyes piercing. "You've established your career and you think you don't need me anymore. You've been stringing me along with this love-and-marriage business, haven't you?"

Taken aback, she bit her lip. "No." Though the emotion had seared her heart, she'd always loved Price.

He didn't believe her. "No wonder you keep saying you want to wait. But how long would that be? Two movies? Two years? Never? You're as ambitious as the rest of the starlets in Hollywood."

Now Anita was hurt as well as angry. Price had never before gotten ugly with her. She pushed him and he stumbled backward. "If anyone's used anybody, it's you. You wouldn't be a star if it weren't for our dancing." Tears burned her eyes, but she wasn't about to let them fall. "And…and you forced your style on me…ruined my individuality!"

Her accusations seemed to incense Price even more. "You never had any intention of marrying me and you've been lying through your teeth about being in love with me."

Unable to stand it any longer, Anita backed away, her thoughts jumbled, her emotions painful. "If that's what you really believe, why don't you go and find someone else to marry, Price? Some starlet with half a brain... to make up for the missing half of yours!"

She turned and sprinted down the beach, finally pausing to take off her heels when she almost stumbled and fell. As she neared the mansion, a tipsy couple playing in the waves in full evening dress glanced at her, but Anita was crying too hard to pay any attention. When she approached a cabana at the edge of the sand, she went inside to try to pull herself together.

Sometime later, she emerged, having dried her tears and blown her nose. It was all over between Price and her. Thank goodness he hadn't insisted on driving tonight. She would find her chauffeur and go home on her own. On the way to the gate of the estate, she noticed a large knot of people gathered around the wooden platform near the carousel. Music blasted from the orchestra and the crowd was clapping.

Curious in spite of her terrible mood, Anita came closer to peek. A couple danced across the boards, the man's movements smooth and practiced and graceful—Price! And he was twirling Betty Masters into his arms, then waltzing her in circles as they put on a private show, a first for Price Garfield.

The crowd applauded again. Anita felt an icy chill creep up her spine, then settle somewhere in the vicinity of her heart. Betty Masters, a peroxide platinum blond starlet, had been one of Price's annoying publicity dates. He'd told Anita that Betty was forward and capricious and a bit short on culture. Had he changed his mind about her?

Surely he wouldn't be stupid enough to marry a girl like that.

Would he?

Telling herself she couldn't care less, Anita turned her back on the public display. She and Price had wrapped up their most recent movie, *Maxine,* a week ago, and their partnership was over.

She told herself she would be far better off without him. She also told herself she *wasn't* being torn apart.

She cried all the way home, anyway.

She and Price Garfield were through.

Beverly Hills, Present Day

GABBY HAD ONLY BEEN awake for an hour or so and was drinking a cup of coffee as she dressed when she heard Lucille and the other members of the household arrive downstairs. Curious about where they'd been, Gabby quickly pulled on a short-sleeved sweater and jeans, then went out on the landing to call to the group. As she looked down, however, her mother came huffing up the stairs.

"Are you okay?"

Anita seemed breathless. Her nose was pink from the sun and her hair was wind-blown. "I'm exhausted from running up and down the beach…and I'm also disgusted," she told her daughter.

Gabby had heard that tone in her mother's voice often enough to know what it meant. "Oh, great. Must be Price again."

"I'm afraid so." Anita headed for the suite and collapsed on the couch. "But don't bother telling me he's bad for me or anything like that. I went into the situation with my eyes open. It's my own fault."

Gabby kept her mouth shut, despite her annoyance with Price. Now she felt too uncomfortable to share her good news about Kit's agreeing to look at the script, and she certainly couldn't intimate the depth of their blossoming relationship. Her mother might think her disloyal.

"Price Garfield is impossible," Anita stated. "He hasn't changed at all."

"It's too late for anyone or anything to change, isn't it?" Gabby ventured.

"Probably. I must be crazy to have dreamed there might be a chance for us."

"What kind of a chance were you considering? Friendship?" Gabby tried to keep the disapproval from her voice when she added, "Dating?"

"Last night I actually thought about marriage."

Not having expected that answer in a million years, Gabby was momentarily speechless. "You…you…thought about marrying that old goat?" she finally managed.

"Only in passing."

Now Gabby was really worried. She paced in front of her mother as she said, "Price wasn't able to make five other marriages work. We have to get you back to New York before he convinces you to do something foolish."

And Gabby herself would have to accompany her mother, she realized with a sinking heart. A movie in California was out of the question if Anita was this embroiled and upset. And she had no business even considering a relationship with Kit....

Suddenly depressed, Gabby noticed Anita staring at her assessingly.

"We?" her mother echoed. "Don't worry about coming back to New York right away, dear, even if I decide to leave a few days early. Just concentrate on yourself and that movie. Has Kit agreed to read the script yet?"

Now Gabby had to discuss the matter whether she wanted to or not. "He's reading it, but he probably won't agree to do the project."

"Don't be so negative. And congratulations on bringing him this far this fast. You must have used some brilliant diplomacy."

Gabby shrugged. "I merely tried to reason with him. He's a nice man when he's relaxed."

"You really like him, don't you?"

Anita's tone put Gabby on guard. Was there a hidden meaning in her mother's question? Did she know more than she let on? She and Kit hadn't been very discreet, spending so much time together. Still, her mother didn't know anything for certain.

"I like Kit most of the time," Gabby said truthfully. And also loved and occasionally hated him.

"You two make a dynamic pair."

Gabby agreed. "We play off each other well on the dance floor." But that was all she was willing to say.

"You and Kit seem to get along off the dance floor, as well," Anita observed.

Gabby tried to remain evasive. "Pretty much."

"Hmm." Obviously realizing her daughter wasn't going to say more about her partner, Anita finally changed the subject. "Well, I don't want this problem between Price and me ruining your career opportunity. If you can talk Kit into making *Tango,* stay in California and do it. Remember what I said from the beginning—a Garfield owes a Brooks a career."

"But you and I...we'd be living thousands of miles apart," Gabby pointed out. Her mother was in her seventies and needed someone to keep an eye on her. Her older sisters and brother didn't seem to understand that.

"You'd only be in California for a while."

Maybe, thought Gabby, wondering what would happen if she did stay. Would she be able to leave Kit afterward?

Anita sighed. "I really have made you too

dependent on me. Working at something that excites you is very important."

The dependence issue again. Gabby frowned. "But loving someone special is also important," she said, meaning her love for her mother. "If you have to choose, what's it to be, work or love?"

Anita didn't reply for a moment, merely looked thoughtful. And when she finally spoke, her words surprised Gabby.

"I'm not sure. I guess you'd have to weigh a decision as important as that—"

"Gabby!"

The yell from the stairwell startled both women.

Lucille shouted again. "Kit is here to pick you up!"

Gabby rose quickly and ran out into the hallway, peering over the railing. "Tell him I'll be down in a minute!" When she came back to the suite, she explained to her mother, "We're supposed to go to Malibu to do some last-minute rehearsing." She didn't add that it was also to enjoy each other's company.

"I see."

Gabby had gotten so involved with the conversation with Anita that she'd forgotten Kit was on his way. She sat down on the couch and took her mother's hand. "I can stay here with you instead if you want. I know you're still upset."

Anita sat up straighter. "I'm not upset. Please go."

"Are you sure?"

Gabby herself had mixed feelings about spending any more time than necessary with Kit now. One way or another her heart would be broken, but surely it would be easier if she didn't let their relationship develop further.

"I'm absolutely certain." Anita squeezed her daughter's hand and rose. "I'm going to take a nice long bath and lie down for a while."

Reluctantly deciding to go, Gabby entered her bedroom. She grabbed the dress she planned to wear after the show. Taking that and the small carryall in which she usually packed her shoes and other essentials, she hurried downstairs, expecting Kit to be waiting impatiently. She was surprised to see that his attention was riveted on an unexpected visitor.

Lucille and everyone else were gathered around Harvey and the thin, grubby, elderly stranger in the hallway.

"Dave needs some decent food and a place

to sleep," Harvey was explaining. "I found him wandering around near Watts this morning. I've been searching the streets for him night and day since I left the club Friday."

"I didn't want you to see me in this condition, Harv," Dave muttered in a deep, gruff voice.

Harvey patted him on the back. "Hey, don't be embarrassed. We've all been down and out."

Neil gave the stranger a thorough once-over. "I hate to say this," the fastidious man said, "but you could also stand a flea bath, Dave."

The man gazed at the floor as if he wanted to sink through the tile. "It's those damn flophouses…and the boxes I sleep in when I can't afford anything better."

"Forget about the bath right now," Lucille told Dave. "You look like you could use some grub. Elsie will fill that stomach in no time."

Gabby met Kit's gaze as she approached. He leaned over to whisper in her ear, "That's Harvey's ex-partner."

The years hadn't been kind to the man. From his appearance, he was not only in need of cleaning up, but he was also probably suffering from malnutrition.

"Come on, Davey-boy." Harvey motioned for Dave to follow him. "Let's go eat."

Kit and Gabby headed in the other direction.

As soon as they were outside the house, Gabby remarked, "The poor man."

"Another candidate for Lucille's unofficial retirement home."

"Can she take in another?" Dave obviously had very little money and might be a burden at the moment.

"She *will* take him in—you can bet on it."

As Kit helped her into the car, Gabby thought about her worries concerning her mother. At least Anita wasn't impoverished and living on the street. Not that Gabby wouldn't do her best to take care of her, no matter what she had to sacrifice.

"DON'T YOU WANT a cleanup rehearsal?" Gabby asked Kit, moving from the open door of the beach house out onto the deck. "I thought that's what we were supposed to be doing."

"Rehearsing's not at the top of my list today." Kit frowned, annoyed that she kept flitting about instead of settling down, preferably in his arms. "And I didn't think it would be of paramount importance to you, either. Are you nervous about something?"

"I have a lot on my mind."

Perhaps because she was considering the ramifications of the feelings they'd declared for each other. Kit himself had lain awake for hours trying to decide what to do. He'd finally come to some conclusions, however.

He made himself comfortable on one of the deck's built-in benches and patted the space beside him. "Come on over here next to me. I want to talk to you."

"I'm fine where I am." Though her shoulders seemed tense, she smiled.

"Please, Gabby."

Finally she gave way. He took her hand and pulled her onto the bench, then slid an arm around her.

"Now tell me what's the matter," he demanded softly, cradling her chin so that she would look at him. "You're as tight as a bowstring. You haven't changed your mind about being in love with me, have you?"

"No."

"Well, neither have I. Now we have to decide what we're going to do about it."

When he released her face, she glanced away, gazing out at the sea. He had the distinct feeling the subject was making her even more uneasy. But their situation had to be resolved sometime. She didn't say anything, so he figured it was up to him to start.

"First off, you want to stay in California," Kit began. "Right?"

Gabby didn't reply for a second. "Have you read the script of *Tango?*"

"I haven't had time."

"But that has something to do with my remaining in California." A tiny line formed between her eyes. "You couldn't even read the beginning. I stayed up last night until I got through the whole thing. It's really good."

But the script wasn't uppermost in Kit's mind. "You don't need the movie as an excuse to stay in California. We could get married."

Gabby parted her lips and stared at him in amazement—not the reaction Kit had hoped for. Then she swallowed hard and whispered, "M-married? You're proposing?"

"We love each other and have something special going for us. So why not get married?"

"How romantic," she murmured, sounding more put off than pleased.

"Gabby, I've just about turned myself inside out dealing with the idea of marriage. I didn't exactly have a role model in that department. It's a scary proposition," he admitted. "And it's a bit bizarre, my hooking up with Anita Brooks's daughter."

She glared at him. "Yes, and we've known each other for such a short time," she added, sounding thoroughly insulted.

Kit tried soothing her. "But I decided to listen to my gut-level feelings, Gabby. I really love you. Marriage seems right."

"But it's so serious," she said, frowning. "I don't want a Hollywood marriage that lasts a few years—"

"Neither do I," he put in swiftly. "I've seen them up close. If you really feel uncomfortable just going out and doing it, though, we could be engaged for a while."

"That's still a very serious step to take." Gabby rose and paced toward the railing of the deck, where she turned to face him. "And I need to work. If we don't do the movie... I'll have to go back to New York and run the school."

"Why? You can start another school of your own out here—or work for the Garfield Dance Studios."

She shook her head. "I told you teaching wasn't my favorite activity."

"Wait a minute." Kit wasn't sure he liked what he was hearing. "I'm getting confused. First you say you have to run your mother's dance school, but when I suggest you do the same for me, you say you don't like teaching. Maybe you're not sure what you want to do." He realized she was trying to hide a stricken expression. Maybe she *was* just confused. "You can take your time as far as I'm concerned," he assured her. "I won't let you starve."

"I'm not worried I'll starve."

"Then what's the problem?"

"Everything's so complicated, now," she whispered more to herself than to him. She was clutching the railing so tightly that her knuckles were white. "Dancing is part of my heart and soul, Kit. I'd like to have the chance to make it in my profession, but you don't seem to be able to understand that."

"I do understand—"

"Then why are you depriving me of the opportunity of a lifetime? You proved you can take time off from the corporation if you want. Let others shoulder the responsibility for a while. You'll always have the option of going back to the business. It's not as if you'll *have* to star in movies forever. How can you ask me to make a personal commitment when you refuse to make a professional commitment that would mean so much to me?"

Suddenly Kit saw the light. "Wait a minute. You're telling me I have to make this stupid movie or you won't consider my proposal?" Angry, he stood up to face her. "That's some kind of love you claim to feel for me."

"What about you? Why won't you help me out? And how can I marry you when you won't admit performing is important to you, too? You're not honest with yourself, so how can you be honest with me?"

"Come off it, Gabby. You're trying to blackmail me into doing what you want." Kit had never been so hurt or disappointed in his life. "Well, forget it."

"Blackmail?" Her eyes widened. "Perhaps I should leave."

"Go ahead. You seem to be good at running away. Your mother probably set the example for you, taking off for New York the way she did. Not that it did her any good."

Gabby's face turned white. "Don't you dare bring up my mother! Price ruined her career! A Garfield owes us something for that. I wouldn't have come to Hollywood at all if I'd thought otherwise."

Now Kit was getting the big picture, and it wasn't pretty. In pain, he wanted to lash out.

"I don't owe you anything," he snapped. "Your mother *used* my father to climb as far as she got." Despite Price's claims to the contrary. The old man was probably so besotted now, he'd forgotten what happened. "Looks like your mother taught you how to do some fancy using, too."

Gabby sucked in her breath. "You're just as cruel and heartless and cold as your father!"

At the moment Kit indeed felt frozen. When Gabby flounced by, he didn't try to stop her. But he had to have the last word.

"I assume this means you're rejecting my proposal," he gibed sarcastically.

She whirled around in the doorway. "You assume right. I think you need someone much more amenable. Why don't you follow your father's footsteps and find yourself a nice little empty-headed tart?"

"Maybe I will."

"And make sure she can dance," Gabby added. "I'm leaving for New York first thing in the morning. You'll have to find another partner to dance with you at the club this coming week."

"What?" That she was leaving him—and

Lucille—in the lurch made him see red. "You're being ridiculous!"

"And so are you, Kit!" she raged before stalking away. She grabbed the dress and the bag she'd left in the living room and slammed out the front door.

Kit smashed his fist against the side of the house, hardly registering the pain. What a mess! The club would be closed on Monday and Tuesday, so he had two days to find a new partner, teach her the choreography and get her costumed. Not that any other woman could partner him the way Gabby had.

Meanwhile, he also had to pull himself back together after taking such a big emotional risk.

That was the most difficult thing he had ever had to do in his life.

CHAPTER FOURTEEN

INSTEAD OF ATTEMPTING to return to Lucille's, Gabby called a taxi from a pay phone, waited almost an hour for the vehicle to arrive, then had the driver deliver her to Cheek to Cheek. She didn't want her mother or anyone else to see the tearstains on her face and ask questions. The situation was bad enough without upsetting the others.

Forget Kit Garfield, anyway!

Forget Price!

Gabby wished she'd never come to California.

After letting go with a few tension-relieving screams in her dressing room closet—an old trick an acting coach had once taught her—Gabby stretched out on the chaise longue and tried to relax.

Fat chance.

Before she knew it she was weeping openly again. When she finally managed to get herself under control, she felt completely wrung out. And her eyes were certain to be puffy and red, her nose bulbous. She would have to do some wizardly makeup job on herself to look halfway presentable. At least she'd arrived early and would have plenty of time to spend on the task.

A brisk knock on the locked door made her jump. Was the dresser also early?

"Gabby? Gabby, are you in there?"

She rose at the sound of her mother's voice. "Mom?"

"Let me in, sweetheart." Anita knocked again.

Gabby quickly wiped her eyes with a tissue and blew her nose. She unlocked the door and opened it a crack. "What are you doing here?"

Anita didn't answer. She took one look at her daughter's face and exclaimed, "You've been crying! I knew it. I knew something was wrong."

"Knew it how? Are you psychic?" Gabby asked, giving in and opening the door fully.

Anita rushed in, her rose-colored evening gown sweeping the floor. "Something awful has happened, hasn't it?" She clucked over her daughter like a protective hen. "I had the most terrible feeling when I phoned Kit and found out you had left."

"Why did you need to find me now?" she asked anxiously. "You knew we'd see each other after the show."

Anita indicated the shopping bag in her hand. "Your bedroom door was open, and when I glanced in, I noticed your street shoes and your makeup kit."

Gabby suddenly realized she hadn't finished packing the carryall in her hurry to leave the house. No wonder the bag had felt so light.

"I scooped everything up and tried to phone you to tell you I was bringing your things to the club. I really got worried when Kit said he had no idea where you'd gone."

Gabby's jaw jutted at the mention of the man's name. "And probably sounded like he didn't care, either."

"You two have had a fight, haven't you?"

"A big one."

"Oh, dear."

Gabby shut and locked the door. "The clash was inevitable."

"But you were doing so well."

"Until I made the mistake of getting personally involved."

"Oh, dear," Anita murmured again.

"But I could have made an even bigger

mistake if I'd let myself," Gabby admitted. "I'm glad I found out what Kit was really like before it was too late. He wanted me to marry him."

"Oh, dear!" Anita looked as if she was ready to faint.

Concerned, Gabby led her mother over to the chair and made her sit. Now why had she told Anita that?

"Calm down, Mom. We don't have to stay here. I called the airport, and there are plenty of available seats on planes taking off for New York tonight. We can pack and head for the airport right after the show."

"But you have another week of performances," Anita pointed out, obviously stunned. "Lucille is counting on you."

Gabby had already considered the problem of Lucille and her needy boarders. She felt guilty as all get-out, but she hadn't asked for the responsibility that her mother's old friend had heaped on her shoulders. Now she felt the weight more than ever. What if she walked and the club failed because of her? What would happen to Lucille then? And to Chester and the rest of them? Oh, what a mess!

"So what am I supposed to do?" Eyes stinging, Gabby felt like crying again. "I simply can't stand being around Kit with things as they are. I'll be doing well to make it through tonight without breaking. He can find another partner," she said, as much for her own benefit as for her mother's. "He knows plenty of people in show business."

Anita shook her head sharply as if she was trying to clear it. "This is all my fault."

"Why are you always blaming yourself?" Gabby asked. "You didn't ask me to get involved with your old dancing partner's son. You wanted me to take this job because you thought it might give me another chance at success. Risks sometimes fail."

"What about that movie?"

"Kit didn't even bother to read the script. He was too afraid that I'd be *using* him to further my career. He's as much of a jerk as Price."

"I don't understand. On one hand, Kit loves you enough to marry you. On the other, he distrusts you and thinks you'd try to use him."

"Well, he didn't accuse me of attempting to use him until after I backed away from his proposal."

"You said no?"

"I didn't give him an answer. Personally I

thought it came too soon. We've only known each other a few weeks."

"Did you tell him that?"

"Of course. And he knows that making a movie would allow us to spend more time together." Gabby plopped down on the edge of the chaise. "The least Kit could do is agree to give the movie deal half a chance."

The older woman was silent for a moment. Then she sighed. "Things are finally becoming clearer. Kit wants a relationship and you want to make a movie."

"It's not that cut-and-dried." Gabby swallowed. "I love Kit, Mom, and I told him so, but I'm not going to give up everything for him."

"But you want him to give up his business for your career."

"It's not the same thing! The situation is so unfair. Kit loves performing, but he simply won't work in show business because he has this hang-up about competing with his father."

Anita smoothed her skirts, appearing thoughtful. "I'm sure this competitive thing has something to do with Kit's resentment of Price."

"But that's not my problem."

"No, but in a way it's probably mine." Before Gabby could question her about that odd statement, Anita inquired, "You're sure you love Kit? It's not just an infatuation?"

"I only wish. There's a special bond between us—I could feel it from the first. We complement each other perfectly. I've never known another man who was as stimulating and challenging."

Anita was nodding as if she understood. "He's there to catch you when you come out of a turn or a lift. He feels the same rhythm you do. Intelligent, as well as a bit argumentative. Which can be very exciting. And then there's all that warmth and caring hidden beneath his cool exterior just ready to be probed." Anita smiled wistfully.

"I wasn't aware you knew Kit so well," Gabby said.

"I was talking about Price, not his son." The older woman gazed thoughtfully at her daughter. "But let's get back to you. What are you going to do about Kit?"

"I don't know. When we go back to New York, I'll have to get over him."

"But you won't."

"Yes, I will. Out of sight, out of mind, as they say."

"You're wrong."

Gabby flinched as if she'd been struck.

"I'm only warning you because I love you, darling." Anita leaned forward, reaching across the space between them to take hold of her daughter's hand. "Don't let history repeat itself. I made the mistake of thinking I would get over Price Garfield when I left for New York, and I never did."

Gabby refused to believe she was in for the same brand of heartbreak she'd recognized in her mother all these years. "Then you should have forced yourself to get over it. You two are poison together."

"Wrong again. Price and I created a poisonous atmosphere because we listened to our fears instead of our hearts."

"There you go blaming yourself again—"

"It *is* my fault," Anita cut in. "I ran away instead of trying to deal with the situation like an adult. I gave up on the special man I loved as well as the work that excited me. I was afraid Price would overshadow or dominate me, and I was afraid I'd never make it in the movies alone."

"You were still very young when you left."

"I was very sophisticated for my age,

Gabby. I hadn't exactly led a sheltered life, and I'd been working for several years."

"But Price *did* try to dominate you. I remember your stories."

"I taught you well, didn't I?" Anita said softly. "Price was so dominating because of his own fear. He thought he had to control me to keep me in his life. We both would have benefited if we'd controlled our tempers and tried to work things out. Instead, we jumped off the deep end—I ran away to New York to prove I could become a star without him, while he married someone else to prove he could love without me. We both failed."

"But there's also luck involved in trying to make it in show business," Gabby reminded her mother.

"But since I didn't follow my heart's true desires, that made my failures seem even worse." Anita's gaze was sharp. "People fool themselves, thinking they'll avoid pain by setting goals that are second best. You might as well reach for the highest and win or lose for real. Nothing else really matters."

"That's beautifully put, Mom, and very wise."

"You helped me reach those conclusions. I kept thinking about what one should do if faced with the problem of choosing between work and love. The decision should never be made lightly, but I believe you have to listen to your heart rather than your fear. By allowing myself to be guided by my fear, I didn't try for my first choice in either love or work...may Robert forgive me," Anita whispered, a teardrop running down her cheek.

"Oh, Mom."

When Gabby started to rise, intending to embrace her mother, Anita motioned for her to stay seated.

"Don't encourage me. I don't want to get maudlin," the older woman insisted. "I've done enough regretting through the years. I'm going to focus on the good parts of both the past and the present. And enjoy the time I have left with Price."

"Price? I thought you wanted nothing more to do with him."

"That was fear speaking again. I called him after you left this afternoon and he came by to talk things out. We're finally going to do what we should have done more than fifty years ago—have a full-scale whirlwind romance—and marriage. We're eloping, flying to Las Vegas after the show tonight."

"Mom!" Gabby was appalled.

"Please be happy for me," Anita pleaded.

Gabby wished she could. "You're going to be hurt."

"Then I'll be hurt while trying to reach my highest goal. I love Price madly."

"But you're in your seventies. Don't you think a romance at that age is a little…unrealistic?"

Anita gave her an appalled glare. "Gabrielle Brooks Lacroix, how can you say such a thing? There are no age limits to love. How can you be so prejudiced?"

"I'm not prejudiced." But despite her denial Gabby squirmed under her mother's intense gaze.

Then Anita quirked her brows. "Or is it something else that's bothering you?"

"This news is so sudden. Marriage is so drastic."

"And you're feeling bereft?"

Gabby swallowed the lump in her throat. "I thought we'd always have each other, I guess…."

"Of course you'll always have me, sweetheart." Anita clasped her daughter's hand again. "We'll see each other no matter what you decide to do. You're my daughter, and I'll never stop loving you. I would be thrilled if you moved to California. And, if you start another school, I'll happily advise you. But you don't have to live in the same building or watch over me."

"But I want to protect you."

"You aren't protecting me by keeping me away from the man I love. And you shouldn't let me interfere with your personal life, either. Does your sense of responsibility to me have anything to do with the problems you're having with Kit?"

"He doesn't particularly like you," Gabby mumbled, uncomfortable with that truth.

"I'm sure he heard plenty of horror stories from his father. I told you an equal number about Price."

"They were only stories?"

"Exaggerations." Anita went on, "How could you have even considered marrying Kit if you thought you had to go back to New York to take care of me?"

"That was a problem," Gabby admitted.

"One you shouldn't have had to face. I really think if you weren't so dependent on me, you wouldn't have broken off your two engagements."

With a sigh of exasperation Gabby insisted, "I just feel close to you."

"We've become too close if that stops us from seizing our hearts' desires. And I'm afraid I fostered that dependence." She held up a hand when Gabby tried to interrupt. "I didn't have the career I wanted. I ran away from the love of my life. You were young and fresh and resembled me. I put aside my goals and tried to live them out through you instead."

"But I always wanted to be a dancer," Gabby objected, though she was beginning to see her mother's point. "If dancing was wrong for me, I wouldn't have gotten as far as I did."

"I'm not saying you don't have your own natural talent, but I focused on it and on you. I always wanted you to confide every single one of your hopes and doubts and secrets. You told me more than you told your friends."

The reality of the situation sinking in at last, Gabby asked, "What did that hurt?"

"You've as much as admitted you wouldn't marry a man you love because you feel you have to take care of me."

Gabby knew it was time she faced the truth: she had been using her feelings for her mother to prevent her from forging new bonds with someone else. It had been her special brand of self-protection, because she had always known in her heart that her parents hadn't really been happy together.

"And now that I think of it," Anita went on, "our bond might have had some influence on your father. You and I talked about nothing but dance and ambition and the future. Perhaps Robert felt left out."

Anita's eyes filled with tears. Gabby felt a bit misty herself. Now she wouldn't have her mother…and she wouldn't have Kit, either. Why had she been so stupid? She'd handled her relationship all wrong, had wrecked it with preconceived notions and with mistaken selflessness where her mother was concerned.

Noises from outside the dressing room told her the stage crew had arrived and was setting up.

"Don't let my painful mistakes cause you pain, as well," Anita urged her daughter. "Kit's suffered because of Price's divorces. A child's ideal of love and marriage usually comes from their parents'."

Gabby nodded. "I never thought you or Dad were happy."

"In truth, Robert and I were happier than many couples and we loved our children. I was very thankful for what I had." She wiped her eyes with a tissue. "It's just that I've come to an old crossroads now and I'm going to turn in the direction I wanted to go in the first place."

"You're marrying Price," Gabby said, surprised that she didn't feel bitter.

"Price drove me here and is waiting outside. I hope you don't mind that we're eloping. I thought about notifying your sisters and brother first, but I decided I didn't want to wait." Anita rose and smoothed her long skirts. "I'll call them tomorrow."

Someone tapped on the door.

"Just a minute," Gabby called.

"You need to get ready," Anita said. She smiled tremulously. "Price and I are leaving right after the show. Please give me your blessing, Gabby. It will mean a lot to me."

"You've got my blessing and more." Gabby took hold of her mother's shoulders and held her at arm's length. "And you look beautiful."

At seventy-five Anita was a few pounds heavier than she'd like but had managed to keep her curves. And time hadn't dimmed the lovely face haloed by naturally wavy white hair. At the moment Gabby could swear her mother looked even younger than usual. Perhaps love and excitement had added the extra sparkle.

"I hope you'll be happier than you've ever been in your life, Mom," Gabby said, pulling her mother close for a hug.

"Thank you."

Anita hugged her daughter in return and kissed Gabby on the cheek. Both women were teary-eyed when they broke apart.

"I don't know what to tell you about Kit," Anita said, turning toward the door. "All I can suggest is that you listen to your heart."

Maria was waiting in the hallway outside and hurried in as Anita left. Glancing at her watch, Gabby realized they had a lot of work to do with makeup, hair and dressing. She wouldn't have time to digest all the revelations her mother's heart-to-heart had brought about.

But one thing was certain: she wasn't going to give up on Kit just yet.

KIT THOUGHT he looked like death warmed over as he stared at himself in the dressing room mirror. His eyes seemed to burn in his face above the pristine white of his collar and tie. He'd had to put an ice pack on his bruised hand to get the swelling down, and there were skinned areas across the knuckles. He was only thankful he hadn't tried kicking his house.

When the door opened behind him, Kit glared at the visitor, a little surprised but no less annoyed to see his father.

Price shut the door and approached. "I guess you're in a fine mood."

"I've had a crummy day."

"Uh-huh. Want to tell me about it?"

"You've got to be kidding."

"Actually…no, I'm not."

Price sat down on the chaise longue, arranging the tails of his old but well-preserved tuxedo. Kit thought the suit gave his father the same dapper appearance he'd had in his movies.

"We've been needing to talk for the past thirty-some years," Price said seriously.

Kit couldn't keep the irony from his tone. "Maybe, but twenty minutes before a show begins isn't exactly a good time to play catch-up."

"But it's time enough to make a new beginning. I *have* to talk to you now, Kit. Anita just told me what happened this afternoon between you and Gabby. If you really love her, don't let her go."

Kit was startled. "What Gabby and I are to each other is none of your business."

"You're wrong. I feel as though I've stepped back in time. Anita and I started this whole mess with our hot tempers and misunderstandings. She'd tell me I was destroying her individual style or some such and I'd counterclaim that she was using me."

"She didn't?"

"We were both full of raspberries. If I had been more levelheaded, had tried to reason with Anita instead of trying to possess her, we would have married and I'd be a different man...and a much better father. I've neglected you badly, haven't I?"

Taken aback by his father's honesty, Kit admitted, "I could have used more attention."

"And I never once told you I loved you."

Kit's jaw tightened. "Not that I remember."

"Well, I do."

Was he supposed to say he loved his father in return? Kit wondered.

But Price went on. "I don't expect an immediate response. I want to earn the words from you one of these days. We have to get to know each other, see each other more often. Are you willing?"

The older man actually looked vulnerable,

and unable to remain untouched by his gesture, Kit agreed. "We could get together for lunch or dinner...."

"Or merely to talk."

"You might not like everything I have to say."

"I can take whatever you dish out. And if it's criticism, I probably deserve it. The only excuse I can offer is that I became pretty warped and distrustful after several failed marriages."

"Divorce isn't a good experience for anyone who's involved," Kit conceded.

"And I wasn't the best at communication and understanding in the first place. I was always afraid the people I loved wouldn't love me in return, so I'd either try to keep them at arm's length or else exert some sort of control over them." Price grinned wryly. "Anita was very angry when she found out I'd tricked her into coming to L.A. with her daughter."

"But she forgave you?"

"Yes, thank God. Anita's a wonderful woman at heart...and so's her daughter. Give Gabby another chance."

So far he'd respected everything Price had said, but Kit wasn't so certain he was right about Gabby. "She said some pretty terrible things."

"And you didn't? The girl probably inherited her mother's temper along with her heart. I can tell you a lot about Brooks women. Reason with them. Fight for them. I'm not letting Anita go again. We need to make the most of the time we have left."

Focusing on the mention of time, Kit suddenly wondered if his father were ill. "Have you got a heart problem or something?" he asked worriedly.

Price laughed. "I'm just getting old. No one lives forever, you know."

And Kit owed it to himself to try to gain whatever he could from a father/son relationship while it was available, he realized, contemplating Price's mortality. He watched him rise to go.

"After the show, Anita and I are flying to Vegas to get married," the older man announced. "But I'll be back in a couple of days to keep those lunch or dinner dates we talked about."

"Good." Kit followed Price to the door. "Congratulations on your marriage."

"Does that mean you're giving me your blessing?"

"You might need it," Kit said lightly.

Price turned, smiling. "I'm giving you my blessing as well, for whatever you decide to do."

"I appreciate that."

When his father kept standing there, looking more and more uncomfortable, Kit decided he would have to be the one to take the initiative. He embraced Price, who hugged him tightly in return and slapped him on the back.

As Kit released him, Price avoided his eyes and cleared his throat. "Break a leg, kid."

"Thanks…Dad."

The stage manager was already waving at Kit as Price walked away, indicating that the main act should be going on in five minutes. Kit stared into the mirror one last time and smoothed his hair, wondering what to do about Gabby. No matter how angry he'd been with her earlier, he decided, he would take his father's advice about dealing with a Brooks woman. Reason with them, fight for them…don't let them go.

He thought about what it would be like to take Gabby in his arms for the first dance. He was looking forward to it—to his partner and to the dance itself. He'd denied his deepest desires for so long. He had refused to follow in his father's footsteps because he'd felt rejected by Price. Instead of emulating the man he had always loved, he'd made it a point to be different. And in doing so he'd only hurt himself.

He'd gone through life denying himself everything he had ever wanted. His father. His dancing. Even the woman he loved. And all because of his pride. It was time he learned how to change.

But Gabby would have to do some changing as well.

Thinking about convincing Gabby of that made sweat bead on Kit's brow, but he was determined to get through to her. Even though he had no idea of what he'd say when the show was over, they were going to talk if he had to carry her into his dressing room to do so.

The thought put a smile on his face as he hurried to make his cue.

GABBY WAS a little late for the first number, but no one seemed to mind. Lucille improvised a joke to fill in the empty minutes and got the audience laughing. Kit said nothing and performed sublimely. Gabby imagined that his eyes were full of emotion. Her own feelings were touched by the combination of the music, her partner and his romantic intensity. Whether she liked it or not, she became "mesmerized" by Kit all over again and nearly wept when they kissed at the end of the number.

The applause had never seemed so enthusiastic.

Afterward, uncomfortable and fearing she'd spill her guts at the slightest provocation, she fled to her dressing room to change for the second number. When she came back to the wings, however, Kit was already standing there, watching the "Andrews Sisters" trio finish their act out front. Gabby halted, intending to back away.

Kit turned. "Don't go," he said softly.

"Why not?" Her heart pounded, and she wondered what he had in mind.

"I'm sorry I made those crummy remarks about your mother. I don't even know her that well."

Gabby nodded, tempted to say that he'd have the chance to do so soon, but she held her tongue. Kit probably didn't know about the elopement.

"I'm also sorry I insulted you," Kit went on. "In my heart I know better."

Gabby smiled, her lips trembling slightly. She felt unaccountably shy. "Apology accepted. I didn't mean the nasty things I said, either. And I'm not about to let Lucille down, so I won't leave town until this engagement is over. You won't have to find a new partner."

"I'm glad. I could never replace you."

What did he mean by that? As a partner or as a woman? When he continued gazing steadily at her, she glanced away, pretending to straighten the sequined folds of her gold skirts.

"We always seem to be apologizing to each other, don't we?" Kit noted.

"Perhaps that's because we're both volatile personalities."

"And because we've been playing out our parents' tragic love affair."

Gabby swallowed. "We've been haunted." She focused on the words "have been." The old Brooks/Garfield feud, she suddenly realized, was coming to an end.

Kit offered her his arm when the trio's last song ended. But she let go of him and descended the flying staircase in front of her partner. The yearning "Dance with Me" number suited Gabby's mood perfectly. She parted with Kit, then reached for him again and again, fearing she'd lose the greatest love of her life. He reached for her in turn, his expression sad but hopeful.

When she left him finally, fleeing up the steps at the end of the act, she turned to glance sorrowfully over her shoulder...and felt compelled to improvise.

Instead of allowing him to follow separately, she paused and held out her hand for his grasp. He took it immediately, his clasp warm, and they climbed the rest of the steps together. As the spots faded, the crowd cheered.

In the wings the stage manager kept them from rushing to their rooms. "Lucille wants to talk to you," he whispered as the elderly woman announced the next act.

A moment later, glittering in black and silver, Lucille joined them. "The two of you are getting better every night." She hugged them both. "I can't thank you enough for what ya've been doing for me and everybody else."

"It's our pleasure," Kit said, meaning it.

He slid an arm around Gabby's waist, wishing he could kiss her. The gesture she'd just made had touched his heart, and he was tempted to read a deeper meaning into it.

His attention was recalled to Lucille when she said, "You're probably gonna get some wild applause after the last number like you did the last couple of nights. How about doing an encore?"

"We didn't prepare a fourth number," Kit said.

"So improvise! You kids are so good together, you could do it in your sleep."

Blushing, Gabby suggested, "How about 'Dance of Love'?" She glanced at Kit. "What do you think?"

"Sure," he agreed. "We can do a couple of turns around the floor. We were meant to dance together."

"I'll tell the orchestra." Lucille smiled. "Too bad we can't announce Anita and Price's marriage. They always promised me I could be a bridesmaid, and now they're gonna elope."

"Maybe we should have a nice reception for them when they come back," Kit suggested. When Gabby gave him a surprised look, he said, "My father told me."

"A reception sounds great," Lucille said. "We'll have it at my place. Isn't it a stitch those two old fools are finally gonna tie the knot?"

"A real stitch," Kit said with a laugh. Not about to let Lucille foot the bill, he said, "I'll help with the reception."

"So will I," Gabby offered.

"You two are somethin' else." Lucille sobered. "Seriously, you're so damn good together, you nearly make my hair stand on end. I just wish we could keep you longer, even if it was only for weekends. Think about it. And you're not your parents' ghosts either—I only say that in my monologue because this is a nostalgia club. You're originals."

"Thank you," Gabby said sincerely. "I need to hear that." She addressed Kit, "And I'm sure you appreciate it, too."

For once he didn't feel prickly about the topic. He shrugged. "I'm flattered we're being compared to legends like Anita Brooks and Price Garfield."

Gabby's eyes widened in surprise. Then the stage manager got their attention. Exchanging one last hug with Lucille, Kit headed for his dressing room and Gabby for hers. They changed in record time and met back in the wings a few minutes before they had to go on.

Gabby took Kit by complete surprise when she softly said, "I'm interested in that serious relationship if the invitation is still open. How about my being your girl to start? Give me some time to get used to the idea of something more permanent."

Kit's heart soared. He wouldn't have to kidnap her to talk to her after all. "Whatever you want." Now that he had her, he didn't intend to let the woman he loved walk out of his life.

"And I'll take care of my professional goals on my own if you're not interested in dance as a career."

"Don't give up your dreams," Kit told her.

She smiled. "I don't intend to, but maybe I can alter them somewhat."

"Maybe you won't have to right away," Kit told her. "There's Lucille's offer, which sounds good to me…and then, I finally read the script. I love it."

"You read it?" Her eyes glittered. "When?"

"Today, while I was sitting around with an ice pack on my hand. I punched the house when you left," he explained, feeling a flush of embarrassment rise along his neck. "And you're not going to do a great project like that with someone else. You deserve the perfect partner—me."

Gabby laughed. "Someone modest. But what about your business?"

"I can find someone to take over for me temporarily. That way I can find out for certain what I really want to do with the rest of my life. For the first time I'm allowing myself a real choice. Since I intend to buy into a production company, maybe I can make a deal to work on both sides of the camera. How does coproducer sound?"

"Like a great title," Gabby said with a big grin.

Then they had no more time to talk with words. They were on and had to express their feelings in dance with hundreds of people looking on. They executed "Tango Olé" with as much joy as passion. Gabby was going to stay in California and be his girl, and Kit felt as if he were on top of the world.

When the number ended, and the spots faded, Gabby whispered, "I love you, Kit."

"I love you, too."

Rather than leaving the stage in character, as Kit had choreographed, he lowered his head to kiss her, paying little attention to the resounding applause. The spots came back up, and they were still embracing. Someone threw a long-stemmed red rose onto the floor. Another bounced off Gabby, and she laughed, breaking away from Kit to pick up the flowers.

Gabby flashed Kit a look and held out her free hand, which he took immediately. This was the happiest night of her life!

Lucille was at the microphone. "Since we figured you might like an encore, Kit and Gabby have agreed to do 'Dance of Love' from *White Tie and Tails.*"

Gabby quickly tucked the roses into her costume so that her hands were free when Kit took her into his arms. She gazed deeply into his eyes as they moved around the floor. Kit knew the routine by heart, just as she did. Rather than improvising, they were honoring their parents.

She blinked hard not to cry.

When the music paused, she turned away. Kit grasped her wrist and pulled her back to him. Their lips locked, they moved slowly to the rhythm of the sophisticated dance of love. Again she tried to escape, but he imprisoned her and moved her across the floor with sensuous, flowing steps.

When Kit grabbed Gabby by the waist

and lifted her above him, she felt a swell of emotion. He let her down slowly, holding her body against him as the music climbed. But instead of continuing, he kissed her. Gabby lost herself in the embrace until the cheering began. She glanced up, thinking the approval was for them until she realized they were in the dark beyond the spotlights.

The audience was standing now, practically shouting its approval at the scene in the middle of the floor. Price and Anita were dancing together as if they had always been doing so.

"After all these years…" she whispered.

Kit whirled Gabby around the stage until they joined their parents. She freed one of the roses from her costume and handed it to her mother. Beaming, Anita accepted it, and the audience roared its approval.

Then, his lips nestled in her hair, Kit murmured, "They're finally together as they were meant to be all along. Let's learn from their mistakes."

Tears of happiness rolled down Gabby's cheeks. Despite her fears, something told her that when she and Kit were old and gray, they, too, would still be dancing cheek to cheek.

* * * * *